MW01225233

1

Also by David Funk

On the Banks of the Irtysh River

The Last Train to Leningrad

A Novel

Based on a true story

---

by

David Funk

Acknowledgements

This novel could not have been written except for the invaluable help of those who were willing to tell their stories and those who were willing to read and edit mine. Thanks to my father, Abraham Funk, who piqued my interest by speaking of his Russian experiences when I was a child and then waited for me to begin asking questions about his childhood when I was an adult. Thanks also to Dad's sister, Aunt Annie Funk, who spent hours at her diningroom table reminiscing while I took notes and patiently answered my questions during many impromptu phone calls. The roundtable with cousins Ingrid Chow, Alice Yewell, and Judy Armstrong also provided family memories to include in the narrative. Thanks to my story editor, Angela Funk, my copy editors, Paul Funk and Cheryl Funk, and to Dr. John B. Toews whose expert knowledge of the period ensured the historical accuracy of the novel. Thanks also to the many people who asked about the progress of the writing, who encouraged me, and kindly said they could hardly wait for the book to be finished. Finally, I am so grateful for the support and encouragement of my lovely wife, Shirl, who has been a 'writer's widow' for far too many uncounted hours over the past couple of years.

For Abe

History is nothing more
than the thin thread of what is remembered
stretched over the ocean
of what has been forgotten.

Milan Kundera
—The Joke

Contents

Part 1

Lyubimovka

When comes my moment to untether?
'it's time!' and freedom hears my hail.

Pushkin
—Eugene Onegin

Chapter 1

May 1911

Springtime in St. Petersburg is a time of rebirth for its winter-weary residents. After months of subzero weather they happily doff their fur hats and coats and bask in the warming temperatures as they promenade along the city's walkways and canals where the last vestiges of the ice upon which they had skated and frolicked float leisurely away.

Franz Funk had never before walked the cobbled streets of St Petersburg. The splendors of this city built on a swamp by the Tsar, Peter the Great, were beyond anything he could ever have imagined. He marveled at the canals, the bridges, the paved roads and sidewalks, and gaped at the massive buildings of stone with their gilded columns, ornate cornices, and tall glass windows beyond counting.

As he walked, Franz shivered from the chill of a sudden breeze. He wished he had not left his worsted wool overcoat in his hotel room. Looking about him, he realized amidst the chiseled beauty of the royal city he felt vaguely ill at ease. He longed for the smell of fresh grass and apple blossoms, for some delicate greenery to break up the rigid opulence that met his eyes wherever he looked. He was a man of the land, a farmer, and was used to studying the seasons and the plants of the earth. His skills, honed since he first became a landowner at the age of fourteen, were in coaxing seed grains to grow tall and full, and nurturing trees that bore fruit in an abundance that had, over the years, made him a modestly wealthy man. Nothing in his life had prepared him for these affluent urban sights that overwhelmed and took captive his senses.

Since he had a few hours to idle away before his appointment at the General Administration of Land Use and Agriculture building on Saint Isaac's Square, Franz decided he would visit the fabled Winter Palace. For a time he walked along the Neva River, looking at the many ships and boats tied to the piers and at the grand buildings along the waterfront. After asking for directions from several passers-by, he finally found his way to Nevsky Prospekt. His mood became solemn as he walked by the Alexander Gardens and, though he knew he would see none, he looked for blood on the paving stones.

Franz remembered accounts he had read of the protests, six years earlier, when thousands of workers with their wives and children had marched with patriotic fervor along the road singing the hymns of their faith and "God Save the Tsar." They hoped to convince their ruler by their peaceful presence to accept their petition for better working conditions, hours, and pay; they could no longer tolerate the abuses of their autocratic bosses. The crowds were met by a wall of infantry that shot volley after volley into the their ranks, and Cossacks on horseback who charged them with saber and lance. Hundreds died and in horrified response, protests spread throughout the country. The revolt had been cruelly suppressed, but the disillusionment with the Tsar's rule and the anger at his cruelty lived on. The desire for and the fear of revolution now dominated conversations in the drawing rooms of Russian society.

After Franz crossed the great square fronting the palace of the Tsar he continued walking until he came to the path that led back to the bank of the Neva River. He passed the Small Hermitage and saw beside it the doors to the Hermitage Museum. He craned his neck backward in an effort to see the top of the five meter high Atlantes supporting the stone portico and thought if he looked long enough he might see sweat form on the brows of the human figures that strained to hold up the stone roof above the entryway.

Paying the small entrance fee, Franz slowly wandered the Museum's halls and corridors, gazing at masterpiece after masterpiece. He was seeing a history of European art displayed before his eyes. Franz knew nothing about art, but the beautiful works drew him ever inward. Coming into a large room, he noticed a crowd of people standing quietly at its center. Sensing the reverence permeating the air, he moved courteously through the onlookers. Some had tears in their eyes, others' lips were moving in silent prayer. He brushed against a woman and reached out his hand to her arm in awkward apology for his intrusion. Finally, Franz stood before the painting.

The light on the canvas was focused on an emotional tableau. Indeed, the light seemed to emanate from the figure at its center. Franz knew immediately he was looking at a depiction of his Lord, crucified, dead, and now to be buried. Nicodemus grasps Jesus about his hips as another man holds Jesus' arm from above—standing on a ladder, braced by the cross itself—to help make safe the Christ's descent. Mary, the mother of Jesus stands below, supported by bystanders as she faints at the pain of her loss. Mary Magdalene gently spreads a shroud on the ground to receive the pale, limp corpse. Standing amongst the worshippers, Franz momentarily perceived movement in the painting—the crowd on Rembrandt's canvas has somehow expanded outward—and all in the hall are drawn in.

Looking at the artist's vision of his Lord's suffering, Franz was profoundly moved. He remembered again the violence that had occurred only a few years ago on the streets around the Winter Palace, and aware of the misery in which Russia's millions continued to exist, he thought, "And yet my God, here you are in Christ reconciling the world to yourself. What great love!"

Franz Funk was a man of deep faith.

When he arrived at Saint Isaac's Square, Franz was ushered into the office of a bureaucrat of the third grade. Even as he took his seat before the man's desk, Franz noticed the monocle pinched between his right cheek and eyebrow. A gold chain about the man's neck promised rescue, should the glass fall from its precarious position. Franz also noticed the last crumbs of a lunch captured in his beard. He wondered vaguely what other morsels might be found if one was to dig about within the thick tangles of chin hair hanging down to the man's chest. The man was dressed well enough, in a double-breasted wool suit and cravat, but his unruly facial hair put the lie to his attempted elegance.

The bureaucrat introduced himself as Mr. Yeshevsky. Yeshevsky was a serious servant of the Tsar, and had attained his rank through many years—seven for each grade—of diligent service. Getting right to the point, he said, "Mr. Funk, from your correspondence I received in—let me see," he shuffled through a sheaf of papers, found the one he was looking for, quickly perused it and continued, "ah, yes, it came to our office in February—I see you would like to purchase a piece of property somewhere in western Siberia."

"Yes," said Franz. "I had hoped to benefit from the land give-away the Tsar instituted there a few years ago, but I'm afraid I have waited too long. I am told all of the good arable land has been dispersed."

"I know nothing about what is or isn't available in that regard," murmured the bureaucrat while stroking his beard. "You would have to make your inquiries at the office in Omsk." With both hands he patted his chest and found a pipe in a breast pocket. "Be that as it may, I happen to be aware of a property that may be to your satisfaction."

Franz nodded eagerly.

Yeshevsky took a nail from his desk drawer and began to dig about in the bowl of his pipe. He tapped the pipe on the edge of his wastebasket. A snowfall of ash was released and fell slowly down.

"But first, let me ask you about yourself. I do not dispose of the Tsar's lands to anyone who happens to have the money to purchase them. May I have your identity card, please?"

Franz was ready for the request. He placed his identity card on the desk.

Yeshevsky took it in his delicate hands.

"Franz Peter Funk," he read. He was silent as he contemplated the rest of the card's details and frowned as he came to the line indicating Franz's ethnicity. "German, are you?"

"Yes, German Mennonite," Franz replied.

"You are a Mennonite. Yes, I've heard of your people."

Yeshevsky had been in the department for many years and had met other Mennonites looking to acquire larger pieces of land. Often they came for information. Occasionally, as in this case, he could offer a piece of unwanted property that had come into the government's possession. The Mennonites he had met had seemed to him to be a canny, hard-working people.

Yeshevsky's curiosity had led him to learn Catherine the Great had taken possession of Crimea and south Ukraine through a treaty ending the Russo-Turkish war in 1774. The problem was, aside from the nomadic tribes living there, the region was largely uninhabited. To solidify Russia's dominion over the region and to make use of its fertile soil, the Tsarina needed settlers to farm the land. With the reputation of being skilled and resourceful farmers, the Mennonites of Prussia were offered a golden handshake giving them large tracts of free land and guaranteeing their religious and cultural traditions for generations to come. Of great importance to the Mennonites was the promise of exemption from service in Russia's armed forces, for they firmly believed in the Bible's injunction to love their enemy and their neighbor as themselves. The condition that they promise not to proselytize their Russian neighbors was of no concern; after two centuries of persecution and marginalization, they were happy to be allowed to live and let live.

Franz Funk said, "Members of my family have been citizens of Russia since the late 1700s. Our ancestors emigrated from Lithuania, in 1789. They had lived in Prussia before that. They came at the invitation of the Tsarina, Catherine, settled in the south, and together with other families established a colony, Chortitza. We have lived there ever since. I was born there, in Neu Kronsweide.

Yeshevsky looked disapprovingly at Franz. He did not think much of a man who refused the opportunity to fight for his country. He stuffed some tobacco in his pipe, tamped it, and then, losing interest, set the pipe on his desk.

"You're a pacifist," Yeshevsky said in an accusing tone.

"Yes, but we still love Russia and serve where we are welcome. I spent three years in a forestry camp by the Sea of Azov. It is an agreement we have with the government which allows us the alternative service." Before he could stop the words, Franz added bitterly, "My wife and child died within days of each other while I was at the camp. The administration refused me permission to attend their funerals."

"We all must make sacrifices for the Tsar," Yeshevsky said, though what sacrifice he had made he could not remember. Somehow he had managed to escape military service, though this did not affect his disapproval of others who avoided it as well; and over his years as a civil servant, with no wife or children to look after, he had managed to feather his solitary nest quite comfortably. The thought cheered him. Looking again at Franz's identity card he said, "Yes, well, it says here you are married."

"A few years after my first wife died, I married Anna Penner. She had nine children from her first marriage to Jacob Willms. He died tragically."

Jacob Willms had been in his yard with a neighbor who had

brought a piece of equipment on a wagon pulled by a team of horses. The load was heavy, and as it was being unloaded the wagon's rear axle broke and the equipment tumbled onto the ground. The chaos of the accident spooked the horses. They thundered around the yard and, their way blocked by a barn, charged back to where Jacob and his neighbor danced from side to side, waving their arms in a futile effort to stop the runaways. The frightened horses were beyond obeying any command. The neighbor managed to jump out of the way; Jacob Willms was not as fast. In the intervening years after her husband's death and before her marriage to Franz Funk, Anna fed her family by sewing and altering clothing for the people of her village, and through the gifts of their kindness. Anna was nine years older than Franz.

"We have added three children of our own," Franz commented. "You can understand, with so many children, we need a sizeable property—good farmable land."

"Yes, well, let me tell you what I have to offer. There is available for purchase an estate of two hundred acres, lying two kilometers north of Isylkul on the Trans-Siberian Railway line. It is about 200 kilometers, give or take a few, west of Omsk." Yeshevsky smiled. "It has recently come into our possession and the Tsar has no interest in keeping it." He nodded, and sitting up straighter, pointed his index finger at the ceiling as if he were about to make a profound statement. "As a man for whom loving your neighbor seems to be of utmost importance, you may be interested to know the previous owner gave the estate the name, Lyubimovka."

Franz Funk knew Lyubimovka meant, "Village of Love."

Lyubimovka had been given its grand, hopeful name by, Prince Dmitry Alexandrovich Khilkov, for whom the pursuit and practice of Christian love had ended very badly.

Prince Dmitry Alexandrovich was a dreamer and an activist. Seeing the abject poverty of his peasant countrymen, the young prince grew disenchanted with his country's tsarist monarchy and his own privileged, noble heritage. He became a follower of Count Leo Tolstoy, whose estate at Yasnaya Polyana he visited often and from whom he learned the simple pacifist Christian principle of loving your neighbor as yourself, and the equally simple but, in a country ruled by the firm grasp of a divine-right monarchy, vastly more dangerous principle of anarchism which rejected all forms of formal government.

Prince Dmitry sought to put his convictions into action on his estate two and a half kilometers north of Isylkul, a small town in southwest Siberia that for decades had provided an overnight rest stop for travelers on the great Trakt, or Post, Road connecting European Russia with the Far East. Isylkul boasted a new stationhouse on the recently completed Trans-Siberian Railway the Tsar had had built to encourage the resettlement of peasants from overcrowded European Russia to the vast, empty spaces of Siberia. As an overlooked property of his family's fortune, the land had lain forgotten and neglected since it was bestowed on his grandfather through the munificent gratitude of Tsar Alexander I as a reward for his heroic exploits during the Great Patriotic War of 1812. When Prince Dmitry remembered the estate he had inherited, the irony that he was intending to use land given for bravery in battle for the establishment of a place of peace and love was not lost on him. It would be a fitting use of the Tsar's gift, and it would be an ideal place in which to create his own modest utopia.

The prince gathered together a small group of peasant families with whom he, his wife, Elena, and their children could live and work as equals in peace and harmony. He called their meager, hopeful community Lyubimovka, Village of Love, because above all things, love was to rule all their thoughts and actions.

The tiny society lived together in happy, communal poverty. They built primitive wattle and daub-walled, thatch-roofed houses in which to dwell and tirelessly farmed the land. A forest of pine and fir, as well as small-leafed trees like birch, aspen and larch covered part of the estate, so the community had plenty of wood for building and heating their homes. Working side-by-side, nobleman and peasants guided their horse-drawn plows across the virgin steppe and sowed the upturned, rich soil with wheat for their bread and barley for their animals. They planted an orchard of hardy fruit trees and large gardens of vegetables for their table.

Not content to merely create his own Tolstoyan colony, Prince Dmitry wrote and distributed tracts deploring the miserable conditions in which Russia's peasants lived. He called for the redistribution of land-ownership among the peasants who worked the land and whose livelihood depended upon it.

It did not take long for the prince's revolutionary activities to be noticed by the Okhrana, the Tsar's Secret Police. His shocking naivety and burning idealism led to his downfall. After the failed revolution of 1905 in which his part was the writing of revolutionary pamphlets encouraging the hopeless display of defiance, Prince Dmitry was arrested and exiled from his beloved family and his country. All of his properties were forfeit to the Tsar.

Of course, Yeshevsky did not mention any of the details relating to the seizure of Lyubimovka and the fate of its previous owner. Instead he said, "Naturally, you must understand, I have not seen the property. But I am assured it is excellent farmland, rich soil and flat as my desktop. Part of the land is forested." He paused. "And there is a small village," he added as an afterthought.

Franz's heart leaped at the opportunity. Arable land, close to the railway, houses included; it was perfect. And the estate's name, Lyubimovka, pulled at his romantic nature.

There was no question of negotiating a price. The bureaucrat made it clear this was a 'take it or leave it' offer. Franz agreed to the terms and a deal was struck.

In the spring of the following year, Franz Funk and his wife, Anna, moved to their new home in Siberia. Seven of Anna's children by her previous marriage were firmly established in their own lives, so they chose to remain in south Russia. Franz and Anna took with them their three young adult children: Peter, Johan and Sara. Anna's children George and Cornelius Willms and their wives Helena and Rose followed them soon after.

Chapter 2

September 1928

Purchasing Lyubimovka was a dream realized for Franz and Anna Funk and their children. Life in Lyubimovka was initially everything they had desired and hoped for. They worked hard and diligently, and became known throughout the region for their innovative methods for growing fruit trees in the harsh Siberian climate of hot summers and frigid winters. Peter, Johan and Sara married and raised families with loving care in the traditions of their faith. The land rewarded their labor with rich crops of fruits and grain; the cattle and pigs they husbanded were welcomed at the local bazaar where they sold quickly and profitably. The family prospered.

Five years passed peaceably. In their isolated village, with only the occasional rumor of the unrest fomenting in the wider world, the Funks had little warning of the events that would upend their tiny community as surely as if they had been struck by an earthquake of the highest magnitude.

Dreams are the children of hope and desire. They motivate; they inspire; they are guiding lights. Unfortunately, the paths of life are narrow and the dreams of one are often in conflict with the dreams of another. One dreams of a land covered in rich forest; another dreams of homes built of sturdy wood. One dreams of a country in which he has the freedom to chose his own destiny; another dreams of a land in which the many are made to serve the needs of the few. And who is to know why one succeeds while the other fails, as surely they must?

In the autumn of 1917, the Bolshevik dreams of Vladimir Ilyich Lenin were realized when his forces seized power in St Petersburg in a revolution that had been long in the making. In the years following, his communist policies increasingly regulated and limited the ability of Russia's farmers to earn their living. One morning the Funk family woke to the realization the land they owned had been taken from them without compensation. The local soviet allocated thirteen acres to each household. The rest of the estate now belonged to the collective people of Russia as represented by the state. Caught in the communist web, it seemed to the Funks, they were trapped in a world in which the present was filled with unexpected, insurmountable difficulties, and where they could do little to better their future.

Johan Funk drew in a long slow breath, savoring the dusty scent of cut grain carried to him on the warm breeze. As he released the air from his lungs, Johan listened to the distant clacking of the old binder working on his wheat field. It was cutting a neat swath and tying the golden stalks into fat bundles before dropping them one after the other in a long ragged line upon the ground. Three boys ran behind, piling the sheaves into stooks to dry. The rows of stooks reminded Johan of an encampment of teepees on the prairie. He had seen a picture of one—he thought it was of a Blackfoot village, if he remembered correctly—in a magazine his cousin Peter Enns had sent from Canada. The shouts and laughter of the boys frolicking while they worked mingled with the noisy percussion of the machine being pulled by a troika of sweating horses. The horses' heads dipped and rose rhythmically in time with the effort of each step across the field. The tall grain hid their thick legs and heavy hooves.

Johan was standing upon a broken, yellow carpet created by the fallen leaves of a lone, aged birch that grew on the verge of his wheat field. He was a man of average height and build. Lean and agile, he was exceptionally strong for his size. When competing in friendly wrestling matches with the other men of his village, as they were wont to do on an idle Sunday afternoon, he had yet to be thrown to the ground. Johan wore a pencil thin duster of a mustache beneath his small, straight nose. His chin was clean-shaven. When wearing his fine bowler hat and tailored wool suit to church services on Sunday mornings, he cut the figure of a fine country gentleman. Johan's wide-brimmed straw hat sat firmly above his pale forehead to shade his slate-blue eyes. His face had lost the self-assurance it had once displayed, but there remained a look of determination in his gaze.

Johan heaved a sigh and, shifting his feet, leaned with his left shoulder against the tree's rugged silvery trunk. He ignored the pricks of its gnarly bark through his thin grey cotton shirt, the sleeves of which were rolled up on his tanned, muscular arms. Johan enjoyed watching his sons as they worked. Their carefree attitude lifted his spirits. Somehow, they were able to find joy, even when there was little reason for it.

As Johan watched the horses plow their way through the golden field of wheat, he knew appearances were misleading. The grain was tall, but the ears were thin and malformed. Blight had overtaken the wheat after a cold, wet spring growing season. There would be plenty of straw to burn to heat his home, but little bread to eat. It would not be their first hungry winter. They had survived others. He knew they could get through another.

"Hopefully, there will be enough grain with which to pay the new government taxes and requisitions," Johan thought. "The question is, how much will the soviet demand this time?" The soviet was the local committee that oversaw the production of all the farms in the area around Isylkul. Under pressure from Moscow, they were increasingly making demands that were impossible for anyone to meet. "Perhaps Peter will be able to talk some sense into them."

Peter was Johan's older brother. He had only recently been elected to the soviet in Isylkul. Not at all happy about his nomination, but realizing refusing to serve might mean more trouble for the family, Peter had told his brother he was hoping, perhaps, he could contribute positively to the work of the committee by bringing his farmer's wisdom to balance the blatant incompetence of its other members.

Johan looked resentfully at fields the family had once owned, now lying unused in the distance. Since they had been seized by the government, his family had been forbidden to set foot upon them. Like all the farmers in the region, Johan was confused by Moscow's senseless policies and alarmed by the open animosity they met any time they had dealings with the communists.

"People would laugh at the communists' incomprehensible laws and demands, if experience hadn't already taught them the Bolsheviks are ruthless in the pursuit of their goals. It's clear Stalin is determined to destroy every family farm in Russia. Moreover, they seem determined to destroy the farmers themselves!" Johan thought nervously. A chill of apprehension ran through him.

Johan had heard of farmers being required to deliver more grain to the government depots than they had actually harvested. To pay their grain taxes, they had been forced to buy grain on the black market. Some, who could not pay, had been evicted from their farms—put out onto the street with little more than the clothes on their backs! Families with small children! It was unthinkable! Just the other day he had heard about the Penners, a hardworking couple with three toddlers being forced from their home. Armed men had appeared on their yard and given them an hour to pack. "But why?" Hugo Penner had asked. "Unpaid taxes," they were told. "Where will we go?" they had asked. "Not our problem," one man had replied. "The street is large; there is lots of room there for the likes of you," another had said. At gunpoint they had been marched onto the road. Their house had been boarded up. "You will all be arrested if it is discovered you have returned here," was the parting threat. It was only the kindness of neighbors who fed them and gave them a place to sleep that was allowing the family to survive.

Johan's thoughts kept racing. "The communists want more and more grain to feed the workers in their cities. If they left us alone, we could produce all they need and more. Yet we are constantly being harassed and the prices we are paid continually shrink. Not only that, but more often than not, the grain we deliver sits in piles beside the railway track and is left to rot!" Johan could not understand the communist mind. Nor could he grasp the corruption and inefficiencies that were the hallmarks of everything they did.

Spitting out the stalk of Russian wild-rye grass on which he had been chewing, Johan reached into the pocket of his trousers. He pulled out the freshly laundered and pressed linen handkerchief he had taken that morning from the bureau in his bedroom. Removing the hat from his head, he wiped his pale sweaty brow. He noticed a hole in the peak of his hat where he always grasped it; the straw was breaking down.

"I'll have to look for another hat at the bazaar next time I'm in town," Johan thought absent-mindedly.

Johan looked at his handkerchief before returning it to his pocket and winced when he saw the filthy brown smear coloring its surface.

"Elizabeth is not going to be happy that I have soiled the

handkerchief so quickly," he thought with a guilty smile. His wife had a quick temper and was quick to complain. "But then," he reasoned, "while she grouses about the amount of laundry needing to be done, what with three boys getting filthy working in the barn and on the fields and little Katrina who loves to play in the dirt, it is not she but Larushka who does the washing."

Shortly after his family's move to Siberia, Johan had returned to Friedensfeld, in the Ukraine, to marry Elizabeth Friesen. They had been childhood friends in the small community, growing up in the same church and attending the same school. He had never loved another and knew he never would. The day she agreed to their marriage had been the happiest of his young life. Elizabeth, with her wavy brown hair the color of well-baked wheat bread, her hazel eyes, soft chin and pouty lips, dressed in her wedding finery, had been the most beautiful bride he could have imagined.

Now, at the age of 37, having given birth to five children—all of whom were still living, thanks be to God—Elizabeth could not manage without her domestic help. Certainly, at almost ten years of age, Maria was a big help around the house. Indeed, all the children were expected to do chores once they were judged to be ready for the responsibility, usually around the age of seven. Franz had just turned fifteen. Abe was twelve, and Wilhelm, eleven. The boys all had their assigned jobs in the barn and on the fields. They already did the work of grown men. The girls helped in the house, learning all they needed to know in order to keep a clean, orderly home. When they grew up, the children would be fully prepared to accept the roles dictated for them by the adult world. Even so, Elizabeth could not be without the extra pair of grown-up hands to help keep her house up to the standard she demanded.

Larushka, as everyone called her—her real name was Larissa—was the petite Russian who helped Elizabeth Funk with all of the household duties. Elizabeth was often ill. Johan's wife had a constitution he liked to think of as being 'delicate.' Too much stress typically sent her straight to bed with a migraine, although in a crisis she could take control and be a commanding personality. At any rate, there was no question Elizabeth should have a servant. It was the expectation of every well-to-do Mennonite matron to have hired help. And Johan was only too happy to provide a helper for her. It made life for everyone in the family much more pleasant.

"No, Elizabeth has little reason to complain," Johan concluded.

With this thought Johan sought to comfort himself, but knew he would probably feel the sting of his wife's tongue nonetheless. He rued that he had dirtied the handkerchief and chastised himself for his thoughtlessness. Better to have used the tail of his shirt.

Across the field Johan could see Pavel Dmitrienko, Larissa's husband, flick the reins to encourage the team of three horses pulling the binder as he guided them through a sharp turn. Pavel and Larissa had moved into an abandoned house on the outskirts of the estate a year or two before the revolution and had worked for the Funk family ever since. Pavel was the only one of Johan's hired men who had remained with him after the troubles of 1923. Though the arrangement was frowned upon at best and considered counter-revolutionary at worst, it seemed the local police until now were simply turning a blind eye.

Johan thought about how amicable his family's relationship with Pavel and Larissa had been over the years. Both families had prospered while enjoying a friendship that had slowly grown out of the fertile soil of their mutual respect. He knew theirs was not typical of the relationship that existed between many German Mennonite farmers and their hired Russian workers. Johan was grateful for the example his father had set. Franz Funk had always paid his workers fair wages and on workdays regularly invited them to join him for their mid-day meal in the parlor of his home. Johan gladly did the same.

A warm breeze stirred the leaves above him. Johan enjoyed the air caressing his face. The racket of the binder was softer now, coming from the far end of the field. A bird sang nearby.

As his thoughts drifted idly, Johan wondered at the fact that the Mennonite community to which he belonged still considered itself German and not Russian. His family had lived in Russia for more than a century and yet they still clung to the language and traditions of the Prussian lowlands from whence they'd come.

"How many years has it been?" Johan pondered. "Almost one hundred and fifty? This piece of Russia, this ground on which I'm standing, this earth with its black soil that, when tilled and cared for, grows whatever a wise farmer plants, it feels like home. It is home. It is where I belong, where my family and I have flourished, where our children were born, where we walk, work, pray, and worship our God with our fellow Mennonite believers. Yet we consider ourselves no more Russian today than on the day our forefathers first arrived."

As a persecuted religious minority the Mennonites had jumped at the chance for a fresh start in a land where their rights of religious freedom, language, and education were promised in perpetuity. Until the depredations of the Communists, they had been among Russia's most successful farmers. But they had separated themselves from the Russian population. More than the obvious physical separation that existed between their prosperous colonies and the impoverished Russian villages, there was a cultural and religious divide between the two groups that went far beyond the tidy farmhouses marked by white picket fences and neat, tree-lined roads leading into the steppe toward the dilapidated collections of thatched izbas—the hovels of the Russian peasants shared by cows, goats and people alike. Almost a century and a half had passed and his people still wore different clothing from their Russian neighbors. They still spoke a different language, ate different food, sang different songs, refused to send their young men to serve in their country's armed forces, and worshipped in different churches. Their cultural and religious ethnicity created a barrier that had never been broken.

Johan did not linger on the question of whether or not those historic choices had been a grave mistake. He was a citizen of Russia in legal terms, though he did not feel like one. Nor was he sure he was accepted as one. The personal identity papers he was required to carry with him at all times lest someone in authority ask to see them said he was German.

Johan thought of the government controls that were increasingly being imposed upon their lives. The future weighed heavily upon him. He worried for his children.

"I wonder how it will all end?" he muttered.

A fly buzzed Johan's face. He brushed it away as a memory came to mind. It had happened during the dark last days of the Great War that had ended only ten years before. With the beginning of hostilities between their two countries, Germans in Russia were considered to be pariahs and worse. They were hated and distrusted by the people among whom they lived. Once respected neighbors were looked upon with suspicion as spies and traitors.

Johan remembered the summer evening when four riders appeared in his village. The day had been hot and the air was still. He remembered that detail for the air is seldom still on the steppe. The thugs had ridden on the dirt road from Isylkul and the dust stirred by their horses' hooves hung in the air behind them like smoke from a smoldering grassfire. Sensing trouble, he sent a nearby grandchild to fetch his father and other men from the village.

Later, Johan remarked on how seemingly nonchalant the ruffians' entrance had been. Their horses were not lathered with sweat; the men were in no hurry. They rode as if each was alone, silent as stone, and they never wavered from their course. They had made straight for Isaac Dueck's house. Why Isaac, everyone in the village had wondered later? Why the house of the man who taught their children in the schoolroom in Franz and Anna's home? Was it a random choice? Was it because Isaac's home was the first in the village to be encountered on the lonely road from Isylkul? The villagers mulled the questions over later, but there were no answers.

One of the Russians, a large man with a pocked face as weathered as a riverbed, and wearing a dirty sheepskin coat and hat, brought his horse up close to the white gate in the neat picket fence surrounding Isaac's front yard. He leaned down, flipped the latch and kicked the gate open. The men rode their horses through the yard, trampling the vegetables growing there. They halted by the short staircase leading up to Isaac's porch. As one, they dismounted and climbed the stairs. The large man pounded his hairy fist on Isaac's door.

There was no immediate response so the Russian pounded again on the door, this time with more force. The door timidly opened a crack. Isaac asked what the men wanted. The violence began with no warning. Without uttering a word, the Russian roughly pushed the door open with one hand while grabbing Isaac by the neck with the other. Isaac was lifted off his feet and flung outside where he tumbled down the stairs. The thugs followed him. Isaac was a small man and stood no chance against the one, let alone the four. His cries for mercy were punctuated by thumps and thuds as the men struck and kicked him. Their cruelty was amplified by their determined silence.

Isaac's wife, Rachel, ran onto the porch screaming for the beating to end and weeping to see her husband's pain and humiliation.

26

Her two small children stood wide-eyed and silent on either side of her, twining their fingers in her apron, disbelieving what their senses were telling them.

Hearing the commotion, Johan ran toward the Dueck's house. He was quickly followed by the other men of Lyubimovka. They arrived at the scene just as the thugs had manhandled Isaac onto one of their horses. Isaac was lying across the horse's back, his legs dangling on one side, his arms and head on the other. He seemed dazed or unconscious. A gash on his forehead was dripping blood through his hair and onto the ground below. The big Russian had his felt boot in the stirrup and was hoisting himself onto the horse with Isaac.

At the gate Johan's father, Franz Funk, stepped forward. "What are you doing? Stop this!" he said firmly.

The big Russian settled himself in his saddle and jerked the reins to turn the horse's head toward where Franz stood, feet apart, hands relaxed at his sides. Johan, his brother, Peter, and Cornelius Klassen, their sister Sara's husband, stood behind Franz. Their hands grasped shovels and pitchforks.

"Get outta my way," growled the Russian.

"No," Franz said. "Let Isaac go."

"This ain't none a' yer business!" one of the men shouted.

The riverbed's eyes became dark with hatred. "The goddamned Germans killed my brother. What we're doin' here is an eye fer an eye!"

Franz thought quickly. He put his hands up in the air as a sign of appeasement.

"I am grieved you lost your brother. But comrades, you are making a grave mistake."

Franz thought by calling the ruffians 'comrades,' he might appeal to their communist sense of universal brotherhood. His tone softened as he tried to defuse the situation, but he spoke clearly and firmly. "This man is not a German! He is Dutch! We are all Dutch in this village! This village is a Dutch village! Our ancestors came from Holland!" Franz looked from one Russian to the other, trying to catch each man's eye. "We are not German! We are not German!" He kept repeating himself and his voice took on a pleading note.

There was truth to Franz's startling declaration, if one counted back four hundred years, Johan would later say, as he retold their experience that night. Their family had originally come from the Netherlands.

The Russians argued amongst themselves and looked confused. They cursed and waved their arms about, invoking the name of God and his saints and shouting at the small band standing resolute before them. Franz was adamant and, bolstered by his sons, held his ground. There was nothing the Russians could say to counter his assertion. Finally the four thugs relented. Exasperated, the big Russian dumped poor Isaac onto the ground where he lay hardly breathing. Franz Funk and his sons scrambled out of the way as the Russians kicked their horses into a gallop and fled the village. A dusty cloud followed their leaving.

Over time, Isaac recovered fully from his beating. And for the next few years, whenever questions of their heritage arose, the residents of Lyubimovka had all been of Dutch ancestry.

Johan looked upwards into the vast expanse of Siberian sky forming a towering cerulean bowl over the broad Russian steppe. The plain lay flat as his wooden kitchen table for hundreds of kilometers in every direction, its grassy surface broken by wide forests, insect-plagued marshes and thousands of shallow ponds and small lakes. The fiery white sun, crowned with a growing orange halo was low in the sky, heralding the promise of relief from the day's heat. Its course to the distant horizon dipped through an atmosphere dirty with the dust of the harvest. A smear of dark, low-lying clouds hovered ominously in the distance.

Johan glanced over to where his father sat close by on the flat top of a rotting stump—all that was left of an old birch that had been cut down years ago for firewood. Franz was also watching the harvest. His right hand rested atop the crook of the finely carved cane he employed to steady his balance. The previous winter he had carved the cane from the dried branch of an apple tree in his orchard. It seemed the arthritis in his legs was becoming worse with each passing year. Franz sat in silence. His grubby woolen visor cap was pulled tightly down on his forehead. His white beard and mustache partially hid his thin, pallid lips that were closed in a frowning grimace. His eyes, once a startling blue, had faded to a dull grey in recent months.

Johan softly sighed for he knew it was not arthritis that weighed upon his father's mind. Ever since his father's months-long imprisonment in spring, he had been a changed man. The terrifying experience had taken the sparkle from his eyes and added years to his fragile frame. He had lost weight. His face was drawn. His body was stooped. It was as if his once strong back could no longer handle the weight of living.

Thoughts of his own brush with imprisonment six years earlier intruded upon Johan's mind like dry lightning on a summer day. The experience haunted him at the most unexpected moments. He colored with embarrassment still when he allowed himself to remember his frantic flight. Had he overreacted?

"I hope the weather holds," Johan said in an attempt at conversation with his silent father. "We are late with the harvesting. One more field and we'll be done." Trying to sound reassuring, he added, "I'm sure, when all is said and done, there will be enough grain to pay our taxes and see us through the winter. "

The words sounded hollow as a stork's leg-bone. They fell to the ground unnoticed; Franz gave no indication he had heard. And it was just as well, for Johan didn't believe them even as they fled his tongue.

Looking up, Johan saw a large flock of geese winging across the sky in a series of fragmented formations. They were low enough so that he could see their orange legs and feet tucked up neatly behind the black bars marking their grey breasts. Their white heads led the way, fixed in space, steady and poker-straight despite the constant beating of their meter-wide wings. Johan had observed the migration of these geese for years now, but had never learned their name.

"What freedom!" he thought. "To be able to take to the sky and be carried on wings to faraway places. Imagine being able to go wherever you wanted with nothing to stop you but your own desire."

The migration of the geese always heralded a change in the weather. They had the uncanny ability of knowing when to leave, just before the first heavy frost or deep snowfall. The constant clamor of the geese's honking grated Johan's ears. Their cacophony suggested to him the sounds the alto section of his choir at the church in Friedensruh might make if all of the women were at the same time suffering from colds and a complete lack of rhythm. Or, of the old babushkas at the bazaar in

Isylkul scolding a group of unruly children. He chuckled at the thought.

Johan swatted his hat against his pant leg a couple of times to remove the dust that had collected upon it. "Come, Father," he said. "We should get back to the house. Mother will have tea ready for you."

Johan took a firm grip of his father's elbow and helped him to his feet. Together they turned and slowly walked down the worn path to his home in Lyubimovka.

Chapter 3

October 1923

In the dim, dusty light, Johan Funk was staring at his empty granary. The walls and floor were grey. The dust motes hanging in the air were grey. The smell of the room was grey. He wondered desperately how he was going to feed his family through the coming winter. And where would he find the seed to plant his fields come spring? Using the edge of a shovel, Johan began scraping the cracks between the floorboards. He could see kernels were trapped there. To help loosen them, he began tapping on the floor, hitting it again and again, each time with increasing urgency. He must rescue as many grains as he could. His arm twitched in time with the motion.

The sudden involuntary movement of his arm woke Johan. A feeling of relief washed over him as he realized what he had been experiencing was a bad dream.

But the tapping sound continued.

Johan opened his eyes in the darkness and looked to find the source of the annoying sound. He got out of bed, careful not to wake Elizabeth who snored softly beside him under the goose-down comforter she had made. He parted the curtains of the bedroom window and peered out into the night.

Standing there, his moon-shadowed face a hands-breadth from the glass pane was Arkady Vargunin, one of Johan's hired men. His fist was raised, knuckles ready to begin another round of urgent rapping. Johan could see his breath in the cold air was coming in great gasps. Arkady motioned vigorously for Johan to join him outside.

Johan padded quietly into the front room that served as kitchen, dining room, and bedroom for his boys. Franz and Abe slept on wooden benches that during the day were used to sit at the table. He hurried into his wool coat hanging on a hook by the door and slipped on his felt boots. By the time he opened the door to go outside, Arkady was waiting for him on the porch.

"Mr. Funk, sir!" panted Arkady. "I came as quick as I could, that I did, sir, as soon as I heard."

Johan put his finger to his lips as he pulled the door shut behind him. "Shh, quietly Arkady," he whispered. "The boys worked hard today. We don't want to wake them. Take a breath and calm yourself. Now, what have you heard?"

Arkady took a deep breath. He was a big, strong man, a simple peasant with hands the size of pitchforks. His eyebrows bristled like two pieces of barbed wire guarding his deep-set eyes; his full beard was thick and black as soot. He glanced awkwardly at the man who for years had treated him as a member of his own family.

"They're comin' ta arrest ya, sir!" he hissed. "The Bolsheviks. They're comin' ta get ya!"

Johan was stunned. "Arrest me? But why? What have I done?"

"I don' know, Mr. Funk. They don' need no reason." Arkady paused. He did not want to speak the truth of what he had heard. The charge against his employer was ridiculous in its falsehood. "It's on account of ya havin' helped the Whites during the war, is what they're sayin'. They're sayin' ya sold 'em grain to feed their soldiers."

The Civil War between the Bolsheviks and the Whites had only ended two years before when the last of the rebels had been defeated in the Far East. They had been pushed all the way to Vladivostok before the fighting ended.

"But that's absurd," hissed Johan. "I made a point of helping neither side. I remember I sold all of my grain at the bazaar in Isylkul."

Arkady shrugged. "What's true don't matter to them, Mr. Funk. They're comin' is all I know."

"When?"

"Tonight! I heard 'em talkin'. I was in town. One of 'em said as they should just kill ya and be done with it. Ya gots ta get away, sir!"

Johan was aghast. He felt his face flush. The prickle of fear flowed through his veins to the soles of his feet.

"I'm sorry, sir," Arkady said. He had turned and was already running off into the darkness, into the night, away from the only man to have ever shown him any kindness. That was the last Johan Funk ever saw of Arkady Vargunin. The fear of guilt by association drove him away from Lyubimovka and from his home, to the anonymity of a distant village.

After Johan woke Elizabeth and told her of the danger he faced, she threw some smoked meat and the few buns remaining in the breadbasket—she had intended to bake the next day—into a sack. She worked quietly. Franz and Abe on their beds close by could sleep through a thunderstorm, but she still didn't want to risk disturbing them. As she glanced at them, she realized she would have to deal with the children in the morning. "What will I tell them?" she wondered. Her hands were trembling as she placed the food in Johan's hands. They had quickly decided flight was the only option.

Johan whispered, "It will only be for a few days."

"Where will you go?" she asked.

"I don't know," he said. "Anyway, I can't tell you. They will come and ask you where I am. Would you be able to lie?" He spoke calmly, hiding the icy fear that had taken hold of him with the grip of deep winter. Johan looked at his wife of six years. She matched his height, so as they stood eye to eye, he marveled, even in the soft darkness, at her beauty—her oval face, her full lips, her slightly upturned nose, her eyes, in shadow beneath her pretty eyebrows.

Elizabeth handed Johan his sheep's wool mittens and hat. "God be with you," she whispered as they embraced.

"And also with you," he replied. His kiss lingered on her lips and for a moment he pressed his forehead against hers.

Dressed in his warmest clothing, Johan hurried away from his home. He had no idea where it would be best to hide. He couldn't go to any of the families in the village. He couldn't involve them.

Johan found his feet were taking him toward the forest that covered half of his father's estate. Though it was cold, he was grateful for there was no snow to betray the direction he had taken. He made his way into the bush, seeing the grey, dispassionate trees and underbrush by the light of the moon. Johan looked for an easy path through the bracken, pushing branches out of his way, feeling the slap of those he missed. Occasionally a glint of light reflecting from small puddles of water shone out in the darkness to mark his way where low-lying sections of the forest floor became marshy. Johan moved cautiously lest he sink his felt boots into the mud. He knew what dangers lurked there for him, should his feet get wet.

"Where?" The thought raced through Johan's mind. "Where should I go?"

As Johan walked deeper into the woods, he remembered coming upon a huge boulder years earlier. It had appeared to him to be the size of a small house. Johan had been out hunting wild boar, though without success. He had thought it improbable such a large rock should exist by itself in the middle of a forest on the flat western Siberian steppe. Though he did not know it, the rock had been carried along and abandoned by the retreating glacial ice flow thousands of years before. Now it was surrounded by a thick growth of trees and bushes. Irrationally, he thought, perhaps, if he could find it again the boulder would provide him with the hidden shelter he was seeking.

When eventually Johan found the grove where he knew the boulder to be—the trees had grown thick and clustered around it as if it were the source of all their nourishment—he walked around it to find a way through the thick undergrowth by which he might reach it. Finding a spot, he stooped under the low bushes until he reached the boulder's base. Crawling along the edge of the rock, he found an old den dug under its side. He could not tell whether it was the lair of wolves or some other animal, but it appeared to be abandoned. Scooping the loose dirt away, Johan enlarged the opening. Being dry and sandy, the ground was easily moved. Satisfied, Johan crawled into the den. It was just large enough so that, when he squirmed around he could lie in a fetal position with his head toward the opening. Looking out, he could see, through the treetops, a splash of stars overhead.

"God help me," he prayed. "Protect Elizabeth and the children."

Hidden in the hole under the rock, Johan huddled closely, wrapping his arms around his knees to preserve warmth. The temperature was close to freezing and he was already chilled. Feeling the weight of the rock pressing down upon him, in time, he slept. His dreams were haunted by menacing images of men with wolves' snouts and slavering fangs, of being lost in an impenetrable wood, and of running from rolling boulders which threatened to crush him.

It was when he awoke in the bright sunshine of the next day Johan realized he hadn't brought anything to drink. He knew there was no stream nearby; there were none in the wood. Nor could he remember how far he had walked in the forest after encountering the marshy ground. Fear of discovery kept him in his den. He could not go tramping about in the bush looking for water when the sounds he made might be heard by the curious or the watchful.

"Perhaps," Johan thought, "I'll venture out tonight."

He ate his wife's provisions, some ham in a bun, with a mouth becoming increasingly dry. He wished for a dill pickle from the barrel in the cold room under the kitchen floor.

That night, his second in hiding, Johan heard yapping in the distance and feared the Bolsheviks were searching for him with dogs. In the frigid dark, his blood froze as he listened to determine if the sounds were getting louder. Were they on his trail? It was only when the barking morphed into a chorus of howls that Johan realized he was hearing a pack of wolves on their nightly hunt. Afraid the wolves, too, might find him in their den, he crawled out and searched for a stout branch. Finding one, he crawled back into his lair, reasonably confident he could ward off any wolves that might come. Against Bolsheviks, on the other hand, he knew he was defenseless.

As Johan lay in his keep, he was reminded of another time when he and his family had hidden in the woods. It was in the days of the civil war when the fighting had finally reached their village, in late October 1919. Johan remembered the date clearly because little Katrina was born on the 20th of October. She had been only a few days old.

Members of the White Army had appeared in their village. They had looked a sorry sight, with filthy uniforms and ruined boots. The men seemed past the point of exhaustion. Their officer had demanded they be fed. There couldn't have been more than twenty or thirty, so a large makeshift table was set up using planks on sawhorses in a shed formed by a long, simple upside-down v-shaped roof. The shed was used to store the many implements the family used in farming the land. The soldiers had been surprisingly polite and very grateful for the warm meal the women had quickly cobbled together. Some time later, hearing gunfire in the distance, the soldiers had wearily risen from the table and trudged off to the east, toward Omsk, the political center of their rebellion against the Bolsheviks, a city that had become a seething mass of refugees seeking to escape the bloodshed. It would fall, with little resistance, within the month.

As the artillery of the advancing Red Army to the west and the retreating White Army to the east blasted each other's positions, the family had run into the forest. They had burrowed under a fallen tree. While Elizabeth tried to calm the children, Johan had broken branches and laid them overtop to better conceal them. Six-year-old Franz had thought it quite a lark. He had had to be shushed repeatedly, because whenever a shell screeched overhead he had let out exclamations of wonder. His young mind could not understand the fear of discovery that had fastened clamp-like on his parents' hearts. Abe, aged three, had been less enthusiastic and had clung to his mother's side. While she nursed baby Maria to still her cries, Elizabeth instructed Franz to care for Wilhelm, who was only one at the time. Fortunately, the bombardment had lasted only a day. The Red Army had swept through their area unhindered and the family had been able to return home, no worse for the wear.

On the third day, Johan's thirst began to torment him. He had drunk little the day of his flight and now his dehydration worked against his fear of discovery.

"They won't take me," he mumbled through dry lips. But he began to feel light-headed and knew if he didn't drink some water soon, he might die, hidden and unfound by those he loved and by those he feared.

Johan never knew how he came to be there, but on the morning of the fourth day after Arkady Vargunin's warning, he was found by his father by the well in the anteroom connecting his father's barn with his house. Johan had managed to crank up a bucket of water before passing out on the floor.

Johan recovered quickly from his ordeal. Elizabeth told him during his absence no Bolsheviks had appeared at her door.

"They did not come, Johan," she said with relief.

"But then, what am I to make of it?" he said. "The threat, the warning?"

Elizabeth's thoughts were more to the point. "What were you thinking, hiding as you did?" she scolded. "Why didn't you hide in the barn, or at the neighbors? You could have gone to your cousins in Friedensruh. They would have gladly helped you! As it was, you could have died!"

Johan did not go into hiding again, but it was many months before he ventured to make the two-kilometer journey to Isylkul, where the presence of the police niggled like a pebble in his shoe. Over the years, the pebble became smaller, but it never left completely.

Four years after his flight into the forest, in the fall of 1927, Elizabeth persuaded Johan of the need to get out of Russia. The past was painful to think about; their future was too uncertain. They had heard stories about thousands being allowed to leave the Soviet Union in recent years. Her cousins in Canada kept encouraging them to come. It was time to make the move.

After the harvest was completed, Johan and his eldest son, Franz, traveled to the regional capital, Omsk, to apply for exit visas. But though Johan and Franz went to the government office daily for a fortnight, they were rebuffed each time. The stone-faced bureaucrats barely looked at them. "Go back to your farm. No more exit visas are being granted," was all they would say.

Chapter 4

February 1928

After years of revolution and civil war, the breadbasket of Russia was empty. The country was on the brink of ruin.

Faced with widespread famine, in 1922, Lenin introduced the New Economic Policy. Peasants were to be taxed on what they grew. Instead of forcibly requisitioning food, taxes were set at a lower level. Farmers were allowed to sell their extra produce anywhere they wished. This provided the incentive needed to return farm production to pre-war levels. What War Communism had almost completely destroyed, this new policy allowed to thrive. However, this experiment in state sanctioned capitalism was to be short-lived because, though light industry benefitted from the boom created by expanded farming, heavy industry did not.

In December 1927, at the Fifteenth Congress of the Communist Party in Moscow, it was announced the country was taking a new path to recovery. The years of the New Economic Policy, when limited private enterprise was encouraged, were ended. Rapid, state-run industrialization became the immediate, pressing aim.

It was called the First Five Year Plan. To ensure the success of his plan, in January 1928, Stalin ordered all local party and state officials and their procurement agencies to use any necessary force to obtain as much grain as possible from farmers. The grain was required for export to raise the currency needed to fund the nation's rapid industrial expansion. In order to ensure the enforcement of his new directive, Stalin personally visited the regions of West Siberia where he knew the previous autumn's grain harvests had been good. He saw for himself how farmers, whose one aim was to make a living for themselves and their families, found ways to sell their grain at prices higher than the pittance the government was offering. Stalin formulated his strategy and signed directives that were quickly and efficiently put into action.

During the winter of 1927 to 1928, Franz Funk had avoided any unnecessary trips to Isylkul. He and his children's families had plenty of canned and dried food in storage. The harvest from their gardens had been plentiful. Pigs had been butchered and a frozen carcass was hung in the attic of each home. Because they were self-sufficient, the need to travel the icy, wind-swept road seldom arose. Insulated in Lyubimovka, they heard little news beyond the gossip of friends at the church in Friedensruh. Consequently, when Franz and his hired man Ivan Buryshkin decided to take a wagonload of grain to the bazaar in town one Saturday morning, they were unaware of the trouble that would greet them.

It was a beautiful winter morning. The wind was light and the temperature had risen overnight. Little rivulets of water trickled here and there between diamond-encrusted banks of sun-gleaming snow, gathering up the melting droplets that combined to form puddles. Inexorably, the water forced its way under ice and through mud toward the drainage ditch beside the road.

The wagon had been loaded the day before, so as soon as the three horses were hitched, Franz and Ivan were ready to go. The troika walking side by side welcomed the warmth of the day. The horses were eager to pull after having been cooped up in their stalls. As Ivan urged the horses onward and they left the farmyard behind, Franz could already see where ruts in the road would become channels of mud should the thaw last a few days. The runners that replaced wheels on the wagon and transformed it into a sleigh for winter travel sloughed through the rotting snow. Bells attached to the harnesses jingled a happy tune in time with the horses' steps.

"It's a fine day for a trip to town," Franz said, admiring the sparkle of sunlight on the bright white landscape. "After days in the barn, it is good for the horses to stretch their legs a bit."

Ivan flicked the reins to encourage a little more speed. The horses swished their tails as they pulled and pointed their ears forward, enjoying the fresh air and the open road. Loud explosions erupted beneath their tails.

Ivan chuckled and said, "You can always tell how happy a horse is by how loudly it farts."

Franz laughed at the joke.

The two men talked for a while about chores needing to be done in preparation for spring planting. Machinery required maintenance. Plowshares needed sharpening. Soon the journey lulled them into a pleasant feeling of shared solitude and they rode the rest of the way to town in silence. Though they were boss and employee, their relationship had been fashioned by years of camaraderie; they were comfortable with each other and respected each other for the skills and knowledge each brought to the work of the farm.

Franz always enjoyed the trip to Isylkul. He marveled at the flatness of the steppe and the vastness of the blue sky above it. Occasionally he would spot some wildlife. He often saw a deer or two nibbling the bunch grass growing there. They would flick their tail and bound away, ever wary of the hunter's bullet. He'd often seen a coyote nose down, looking for mice and gophers. It was common to see a hare; he was not surprised to see one now, on the east side of the road, hopping in panic across the snowy field at the sight and sound of the horse-drawn wagon.

The two kilometers to Isylkul were quickly passed. As they drew near to the outskirts of the town Franz and Ivan could not help but notice in the distance a group of men standing in the middle of the road. As they drew closer they saw the men were armed and by their uniforms knew they were members of the local police.

Without thinking about it, Franz began to hum a tune under his breath.

> Beneath the cross of Jesus, I fain would take my stand.
> The shadow of a mighty rock within a weary land;
> A home within the wilderness, a rest upon the way
> From the burning of the noontide heat
> And the burden of the day.

It was an old hymn he knew by heart because it had been sung in church at many Sunday services for as long as he could remember. It was one of his favorites. For a brief moment he remembered the days ten years ago when the guns of the civil war had roared in the distance, to the west of his village. Each evening the family had gathered for prayer in his great-room. They had sung hymns of comfort and encouragement as the sound of the guns grew louder and the family's anxiety mounted. This hymn in particular had brought strength to the family. Now Franz hummed the tune as a prayer for mercy, or a talisman with the power to ward off evil.

As the wagon approached the group of men, one of them, a large man dressed in a dun colored greatcoat with its buttons fastened to the neck and wearing a visor cap with a red star prominently displayed stepped forward and held up his hand. As Franz looked at him, he had the uncomfortable sense he had met the man before. There was no time to dwell on the premonition, though. The wagon came to a halt as two policemen grabbed the horses' halters. The horses shook their heads up and down, snorting and blowing after the effort of the journey, nervous at the strangers who held them and the menacing energy they emitted.

Franz's eyes scanned the policemen. The men holding the horses were dressed in an assortment of sheepskin and woven wool greatcoats. On their heads they wore black sheep's wool astrakhan hats. Their boots were caked with mud from the early melt. Each man had a rifle slung over his shoulder and a bandolier filled with bullets hanging from one shoulder down across his chest. Their dark eyes, buried deep in their swarthy skulls beneath shaggy eyebrows, were fixed on the two men seated on the wagon.

Close beside the road was a copse of larch trees. Franz noticed a few men were standing around a large bonfire. They appeared to be armed like the men in the road, though their Mosin-Nagant rifles were leaning on a log in a helter-skelter array. However, these men wore the drab uniforms and budenny caps of the Red Army. He could just make out a large red star with inset hammer and sickle sewn onto the front of their peaked caps.

Despite the sunny morning, most of the men on the road wore their earflaps down. They were a slovenly looking bunch and from the expressions on their faces they looked as if they were bored and unhappy to be put on such a menial duty as stopping farmers along the road. Nevertheless, as the policemen took control of Franz's horses, the soldiers — Franz now saw there were five of them — picked up their rifles and shuffled onto the roadway.

Questions flitted through Franz's mind. "Why is the Red Army here? Why are the police blocking this road? Why are they stopping me?" He had not long to wait to find out.

A policeman wearing a black leather greatcoat and black leather gloves walked to the side of the wagon. He had a sharp nose tilted to one side; it had been broken in a fight the policeman liked to remember because his adversary had fared much worse. His wide, thin-lipped mouth was surrounded by a neatly trimmed black mustache and goatee. Unlike the others on the road, he wore a pistol holstered on a belt around his waist. Franz noticed the deference with which the policemen and soldiers treated him. Isylkul was a small community and Franz thought he knew the faces of the men on its police force. He had never seen this man before.

Franz could see the look of disdain on the officer's face as he surveyed the wagon. He lifted a corner of the heavy blanket covering the cargo, removed the glove on his right hand and ran his fingers deeply through the smooth grains of wheat. He seemed to enjoy the sensation and paused for a moment before withdrawing his hand.

Still looking at the grain, he commanded, "Comrade Citizens, you will step down from the wagon."

Franz and Ivan moved quickly to obey. As he stepped onto the road, Franz slipped. Ivan had climbed off of the wagon first and was able to grab hold of Franz's elbow so he would not fall. Franz regained his balance. He looked gratefully at Ivan.

"Your name?" the officer said curtly, looking at Franz.

"I am Franz Funk."

The tall policeman, who had stopped the wagon, stepped forward as recognition dawned on him. "I know this man, Comrade Major. This one," he said pointing at Franz Funk, "is a bloody German kulak! I met 'im an' his boys a few years ago. They said they was Dutch, but ev'ryone knows they're goddamned Germans." He spat at the ground by Franz's feet. "They have a khutor a coupla kilometers up the road."

And then Franz remembered. This was one of the men who had appeared at Isaac Dueck's door one day during the Great War. He had said his brother had been killed at the Front and he had wanted to avenge his death. Franz's heart sank at the realization. The hatred the man felt for him was palpable.

"So this wagonload of grain belongs to you?" asked the Major.

"It is my grain," Franz said. He shifted uncomfortably and tried to concentrate. He couldn't place the major's accent; he only knew it was not local. The man spoke very proper Russian.

"Where are you taking it?"

"We're..." began Franz, but he was interrupted by Ivan.

"Comrade Major," broke in Ivan, "we're takin' this grain ta the government depot in town. We are fulfillin' our duty ta supply the tax on our wheat from last year's harvest."

Franz looked at Ivan. He was uncomfortable with the lie but knew it was the safest answer to give. One never knew how the police would respond to the notion of a little private enterprise. During the past few years they had tolerated it, but they could be fickle and policies often changed without notice. Still, he would have preferred to tell the truth.

The police officer turned his attention to Ivan. "It is this man's grain," he said pointing at Franz. "Who are you?"

"I work for 'im," replied Ivan proudly. "My name is Ivan Ivanovich Buryshkin. Mr. Funk is a good man and an excellent employer."

The policeman looked back at Franz.

"That would be a first, wouldn't it, kulak!" he said with a sneer. "The snake always charms the mouse before it strikes." The Major slapped his glove across his gloved left hand. "Today is bazaar day. You were going to the bazaar to sell your wheat. Yes?"

"We have been selling wheat at the bazaar for years," said Franz innocently.

"Selling your grain to anyone but the government is illegal," declared the Major.

"But, I didn't know..." Franz began.

With an impatient gesture, the major interrupted Franz. "Kulak Funk, I am arresting you under Article 107 for the crime of speculating on the price of grain."

Two policemen came on either side of Franz and took hold of his arms. The soldiers standing in a patient ring around the unfolding tableau stepped aside as Franz was marched by them. The policemen walked briskly, propelling Franz toward a motorcar parked on the further side of the trees. It was a black Model T Ford, purchased from the Ford factory in Trieste, Italy.

Looking at the leader of the platoon of soldiers, the Major said,

"I want one of your men to accompany this wagon to the grain depot. Make sure there is no side trip to the bazaar. All of this grain is to be delivered to the government agent." As he turned to leave, the Major glanced at Ivan, "If I were you, I would find another way to put vodka in my cup."

A soldier clambered up onto the wagon seat beside Ivan. His face twisted in a humorless smile as he looked at Ivan. From his gap-toothed mouth, his foul breath smelled of sour cabbage and alcohol.

Ivan watched as Franz Funk was pushed into the back seat of the car. The tall policeman got in beside him. The Major sat in front. Ivan heard the strange sound of the kerosene-burning 2.9-liter engine clattering to life. It wasn't long before the breeze carried the smell of its exhaust to him. The horses shied, snorting and throwing back their heads at the unfamiliar smell and sound. Ivan called out to the horses to calm them as the car drove onto the road and sputtered away. He firmly pulled back on the reins lest the team get it into their heads to stampede. When the smoking vehicle was far down the road he eased on the reins and lightly flicked them over the horses' backs. The troika started pulling and the wagon moved off. The unexpected percussion of sparks in the bonfire accompanied the tinkling of the harness bells. The remaining soldiers and policemen stood in the snow and watched Ivan's slow progress toward town before returning to the comfort of the fire.

The initial shock of his arrest soon wore off, but it left Franz feeling weak in the limbs. Nevertheless, riding in the back of the police car, he could not help but marvel at the experience. He was hardly aware of the policeman at his side as he listened to the sound of the motor and felt the comfort of the cushioned seats. The vehicle seemed to glide over the road, though its comfort was little better than his wagon when bumping through potholes.

Indeed, Franz had only seen an automobile once before. One day, the previous summer, a motorcar had passed the farm on its way north along the road. It had briefly stopped in the yard so the driver could ask for directions. He had honked the horn loudly — it had sounded like a horse's neigh — engaged the gear and driven away in a hurry when the children began crowding around the vehicle, running their hands along its gleaming black metal sides and gazing at it in wonder. The children had run along beside the car until its speed was too great, then stood panting and watching in amazement until the distant dust of the road hid it from their view. They all felt they had just witnessed and been part of an earth-shattering event.

Franz's reverie ended as the motorcar drove into Isylkul. From one end to the other, the town was less than one kilometer in length. Franz knew his way around it and could easily find the shops he frequented. There was Franz Voth and Abram Wiens's farm machinery business, Peter Neufeld and Johann Heide the shoemakers, and Heinz Rogolski the homeopath. Rogolski also gave excellent massages to loosen sore muscles. They drove past Johann Fuhrmann's butcher shop, then the post office. Soon Franz saw the industrial district: the railway station and its warehouses for collecting grain and other farm produce, the platform where benzene and petrol were pumped from railcars into barrels and hauled away, the lumber yards where one could purchase building materials, when they were available. The driver slowed the car and turned onto another road. They drove past the bazaar, a large empty space where, since the towns inception, locals could set up stalls to sell their wares and their produce: eggs, butter, fruit, vegetables, whatever was in season. They had in years gone by even sold horses, cows and sheep at the bazaar. Communist restrictions now made that trade more difficult. Gazing out of the window, Franz could see many vendors were already serving customers, though there were fewer of both than last fall.

The car pulled off of the road and drove through an iron gate onto a yard on which stood the large stone remains of what had once been an imposing building. Looking up through its vacant windows Franz saw blue sky, for there was no roof. He recognized the ruin immediately as old Hildebrandt's mill. It had once been a beautiful structure, a landmark in Isylkul. However, with the coming of the Bolsheviks the mill had fallen idle after its owner was arrested as a capitalist and died of typhus in prison. Eventually vandals set the building on fire and it burned to the ground. Though he had not seen the ruin, Franz had heard about the fire and that little of the old mill remained aside from parts of its limestone walls and a large cellar that had somehow escaped the flames. The cellar had become infamous in the years since, alternating for some as a place of refuge and for others as a place of violence.

The driver got out of the car and walked over to a small brick outbuilding. He entered it, but soon returned with another policeman who shuffled along by his side. This policeman was so tall he had had to stoop in order to prevent his head from banging into the lintel as he exited the building. He towered over the driver. His long arms hung slack as he walked. His swarthy face was wrapped in a bearskin rug of a bushy black beard because of which his thin pink lips seldom saw the light of day. His eyes, when they turned toward Franz, had a vacant look. He looked like a man whose conscience was dead, buried, and long since forgotten.

The policeman seated in the back with Franz opened his door and stepped out of the car. He came around the back and opened Franz's door. As Franz got out, the bearskin sneered and prodded him to go ahead. Franz's stomach turned over as he walked ahead of the man toward the ruined mill. The other two officers leaned on the car and watched. They were unconcerned Franz would do anything to escape. He was unarmed, an old man, and there was nowhere to run.

Franz looked at the crumbled walls. Little else remained. Any pieces of wooden debris left after the fire had long ago been used to heat the houses of those brave enough to cut it into manageable pieces and steal it away. Franz thought of old Hildebrandt and the stimulating conversations they had enjoyed as his wagonloads of grain were being unloaded. Hildebrandt had been a good friend and a smart businessman.

Franz didn't have time to daydream. He saw he was being chivvied toward the cellar beneath the mill. It had once contained many rooms Hildebrandt had used to store any number of tools and other things. As Franz descended the cement steps to the cellar's heavy wooden door he saw the mill's floor—the cellar's ceiling—had been repaired with wide pieces of planking. The door creaked open and he was shoved along a short hallway where a guard used his key to open another door. As the door gaped open, the bearskin grabbed Franz's elbow and propelled him within.

It was some time before Franz was able to see anything at all, but he was instantly aware of the room's repelling rank odor. Franz put his hand to his nose in a vain attempt at deflecting the smell. Slowly his eyes adjusted to the darkness. But even then, he could see neither the size nor shape of the room, nor what was in it. There was no light in the room except for a few weak rays making their way in through a gap beneath the door. They allowed Franz to see he had perhaps a meter of space before the human shapes began. A low murmuring of voices greeted him. Franz took a step and quickly tripped over a prone form.

"I'm sorry," he apologized.

"So am I, brother," said a resigned voice. "There's no room to walk. I cannot in good faith welcome you to this place, but at the same time, know you are welcome. You will discover, as I have, we all share a common burden here in this prison. We are farmers who are unwanted in this land we have these many years called our home."

Franz got down on all fours. With some difficulty—his left knee was very arthritic—he tried to make himself as comfortable as possible.

"I wonder if this is what the Bible meant when it says the servants of the kingdom shall be cast into the outer darkness!" said a sarcastic voice on the other side of the cell. "Although, if truth be told, this is very much the inner darkness!" He was the only one to laugh at his attempt at a joke and his laughter had the sound of madness to it.

"Shut up!" shouted one voice and several others muttered their agreement.

"God is punishing us," came another voice. "We have been selfish. We have not loved our neighbors as ourselves. We have lived in wealth while our neighbors have lived in squalor. God is punishing us," he repeated matter-of-factly.

"Keep your angry god to yourself, Johann," said another voice.

Johann grunted. "This is God's judgment. We must pray; we must repent of our sins," he insisted, though more quietly.

Franz recognized the voice.

"Johann? Johann Neufeld?" Franz was shocked. "You are here, too, Johann?" He had known Johann for years. Johann farmed a large piece of land to the south of Isylkul. Though he didn't care for some of Johann's fundamentalist theology, he knew him to be an honest man and an accomplished farmer.

"Is that you, Franz Funk?"

"Yes, Johann."

"Come over here, Franz. Follow my voice. I'm over here by the back wall. The damn guards have covered the window again. They like to make life miserable for us, though sitting in this shit-hole in the dark is perhaps a bit better than sitting in it with a bit of light to help us to see our misery."

Slowly Franz crawled toward the voice of his old friend. In the blackness, he discovered the straw-strewn floor was covered with men, some lying, but most of them sitting in the crowded room. Shuffling along with his hands in front of him, Franz touched each man he stumbled upon, never knowing whether he would encounter a foot, a leg, an arm or a face. Each time he apologized for disturbing them. In any other circumstance they would have laughed and called it a grown-ups' version of blind man's buff. Some were angry with him, but most understood that in this dark place, finding a friend was an important blessing. At length, Franz and Johann, who had kept calling out to him all the while, were together.

"Make room for my friend, brothers," Johann said to those around him. "Come on, make room."

The men close by grumbled, but cooperated all the same, crowding together in order to create a small space. At long last there was a spot where Franz could sit with his back against the wall. Franz leaned against it and heaved a desperate sigh. After all that had happened he was confused and disoriented.

"What have they accused you of, Franz," asked Johann in a low voice.

"Speculating on the price of grain," said Franz disbelievingly.

Johann grunted, "Same with me."

"Since when is it a crime to sell grain at the bazaar? We've already fulfilled our quota to the government!" said Franz.

"They came to my farm and searched all my buildings. Of course I had grain stored for the spring planting. They confiscated it and accused me of speculation. I was arrested on the spot."

"How can this be? What are they thinking? My God, I have grain in my attic. Every good farmer plans ahead." Franz's voice died away as the incomprehensible nature of the police actions left him completely at a loss.

Johann continued to talk in a low voice, but after a while Franz heard little of it as he fell into an exhausted sleep, his nostrils filled with the smell of old charred wood, of human excrement, unwashed bodies, and fear.

Chapter 5

February 1928

When Ivan Buryshkin returned to Lyubimovka, he immediately sought out the two sons of Franz Funk.

Ivan found Johan in his barn. Johan was feeding his chickens. Their coop was on a platform hung above the cows. It was a good place for the hens, because the heat rising from the animals below kept them warm when winter temperatures became very cold. Johan loved spending time in his barn, listening to the comfortable crunching sounds of his cows chewing their cuds, or the snuffling of the horses nosing their grain. He found even the cackling of the hens was soothing when the world outside the barn became too confusing and threatening. The politics of the nation brought turmoil, but nature held its steady, nurturing pace.

Johan's son, Franz, was also in the barn bedding down the livestock. He was immediately sent to fetch his Uncle Peter. Franz ran through the sheltering walkway connecting the barn to their house—the walkway was made by stuffing straw into a woven framework of thin branches; during the winter the straw provided fuel to heat the house. Once on the road, he soon reached his uncle's farm.

When Franz returned with Peter, Ivan was forced to repeat his tale in more detail before the brothers fully understood what had happened to their father. Peter and Johan were shocked and perplexed.

"But we have sold grain at the bazaar for years now," said Peter. "The government didn't object then! Why now?"

Ivan merely shrugged his shoulders miserably.

"Do you know where they've taken him?" asked Johan.

And of course, Ivan did not know, for, as he explained again, the policemen took Franz away in a motorcar. It was much too fast for him to follow. And anyway, he explained again, he had had no choice but to go straight to the government grain depot.

As Peter thought about it, though, it seemed obvious. "They've probably taken him to the police station at Isylkul."

It was late in the day by the time Ivan left Peter and Johan. He hurried to Franz Funk's barn to complete chores that should have been done long before. Ivan enjoyed his work, frequently reminding himself of how fortunate he was to work for a man like Franz Funk, who treated him with respect and valued his opinions.

Usually Ivan would stop to hand feed an animal or to stroke its head or neck, but not today. He quickly rubbed the horses down, threw hay and barley into the mangers, and filled each water trough with water carried from the well in the anteroom. He shoveled manure into a wheelbarrow and dumped it on the frozen pile outside.

The cows lowed impatiently, not understanding the delay of their evening milking. Their udders were heavy with milk. As he milked the first cow, Ivan was forced to slow his pace, for he knew a cow senses agitation and as a result its milk will be slow to come. In its unease, the cow may whip its tail about and might even kick at the bucket into which the milk flowed. His fingers worked the teats in a comfortable, rhythmic motion. When he was finished, Ivan looked with satisfaction at the foamy surface on the milk in his pail. He poured the milk into a funnel that strained the milk before collecting it in a large milk can.

Ivan set his three-legged stool in the straw beside the second cow. Her name was Blossom. She was a gentle creature and produced a full pail of milk twice a day. He leaned his head against the cow's side and began to milk her. As the familiar routine took hold of him, his hands seemed to do the work of their own accord. After the stress of the day, he finally began to relax.

Ivan's mind drifted back to the day he first met Franz Funk. His friend, Vitaly, had introduced them. Franz was looking to hire another farmhand. Ivan had been apprehensive, but was immediately reassured by Franz's smile and open demeanor. He had laughed easily and spoken clearly about his expectations as he showed him around the farm. Ivan remembered his first look at the huge brick house with its attached brick barn. He had never seen the like before. Inside the barn had been so organized and tidy. He knew then he would do everything in his power to live up to Franz Funk's standards. And when he had received payment for his first week's work, Ivan had been overwhelmed with his boss's generosity. He knew of no one who was paid as much for their labor as were Franz Funk's workers.

Ivan recalled the first time he and Vitaly were invited into the Funk's home for the midday meal. Ivan had several acquaintances that worked for other Mennonite farmers. None had ever received such an invitation. It was his second day at work and they had been replacing some rotten fence posts. After washing up with soap at a sink, Ivan had walked down the hallway, gaping through the doorways leading into grand rooms on either side. He had looked into Franz and Anna's large dining room and stared at the beautiful furnishings: the linen tablecloth, the fine china plates, cups, and saucers with their colorful flowered decorations, and the gleaming silverware. Of course, Ivan's wife, Vera, had told him of what to expect. She had been hired to help Anna with the housework. It was she who polished the silver as part of her weekly duties. They had eaten at a more humble table set in a room off the kitchen. The food had been hot and delicious. Since then, Ivan ate at the Funk's table on most days when he worked at their farm.

Yes, Franz and Anna Funk were the most generous people he had ever met. The thought that the communists should imprison Franz was intolerable. Sitting on his stool, with a stream of hot milk raising thick foam on the surface of the milk in the pail between his knees, Ivan decided that he could not stand idly by. He must do something to help his friend and employer.

Anna Funk wept when she learned the news that her husband had been arrested. She was a frail woman of seventy-eight years, and she could not cope with the thought of her husband locked in a communist prison. A sleepless night passed, and Franz did not return home. The next morning the family gathered together to decide what must be done. All of Franz's children and their spouses were seated in an uncomfortable circle in Anna's living room.

"We need to know how long they intend to keep him," began Peter.

"Also, he will need food," added Anna. "The food in prison, if any is provided, is terrible. You cannot even call what they give people in there food."

Everyone understood this fact. They had all heard stories about the conditions in prison from acquaintances that had had the misfortune of having spent time there, and the good fortune of having been released.

"But, who should go?" asked Peter, embarrassed to even ask the question. "I'm sorry, but I cannot. They might arrest me as well. Who knows where they will ascribe guilt. They may decide to arrest the whole lot of us men."

He glanced around the circle at the other men in the room. Johan could not meet his eye. Nor could Cornelius Froese who seemed busy examining a callous on his left hand. Both were wrestling with the desire to act and weighing the personal danger it involved. Both were losing the struggle.

Cornelius's wife, Sara, sat silently by her weeping mother's side. She placed a protective arm around her shoulders.

Fear held them all hostage.

"I'll go," said a quiet voice.

Everyone looked at Elizabeth.

"No, Elizabeth, you cannot. It's too dangerous; too stressful." urged Johan. "You are pregnant."

"Who else is there?" argued Elizabeth. "Peter is right. If any of you men go, they could arrest you out of spite. They don't need a reason. Anna can't go. She's too frail. Why shouldn't it be me?" She drew a quick breath. "I was sixteen years old when my father, Abraham, died. I still miss him twenty years later. Franz has been a loving father to me from the moment I came into this family. Someone has to go and it might as well be me." She paused; surprised at the words she had spoken. She did not consider herself to be particularly brave. "Anyway," she continued after a moment, "they are less likely to arrest a woman. Especially a pregnant one."

And so it was settled.

Elizabeth was seven months pregnant. It would be easy for her to smuggle food to her father-in-law. She packed some sausage and a few buns in cotton bags and pinned them to the inside lining of her thick fur coat. Being well on in her sixth pregnancy, her belly was bulging prodigiously. Her dress hung loosely at the front, away from her legs.

Putting on her coat, Elizabeth went out into the yard. Johan placed a stool on the ground next to the wagon and gave her his hand for support as she climbed up onto the wagon and plunked herself down on its seat.

"Under this coat, I could hide an elephant," smiled Elizabeth as she tried to make herself comfortable on the wooden bench.

All of the family stood in the yard as Johan guided the horses out onto the road. Before they drifted miserably back to their homes, the family prayed for the safety of Elizabeth and Johan, and for Franz whose fate they did not know.

The road to town had never seemed so long, nor the wagon so bumpy. Along the way, close to Isylkul, Johan spotted the remains of what had been a large bonfire beside a copse of larch trees. He thought, from Ivan's description, this was the place where the police had arrested Franz. He wondered that there was no one ready to stop them on this day and was grateful for the empty road.

When they arrived at the police station, Johan and Elizabeth found a line of women standing in the cold, patiently waiting to ask about their husbands' whereabouts.

"It looks like the police have been busy," said Elizabeth sarcastically.

While Elizabeth joined the line, Johan tended to the horses, rubbing them down with a rough blanket and absent-mindedly fiddling with the harnesses.

"Not your Johann, too," Elizabeth said, surprised to meet her mother-in-law's friend, Esther Neufeld in the line. The women hugged tightly to comfort and draw strength from each other.

It was hours before Elizabeth finally stood in front of the desk clerk, who looked at her blankly with disinterest. She steadfastly refused to accept his evasive answers to her questions. Eventually, he looked for Franz Funk's name on a ledger and told her he had been placed in a temporary prison in the cellar of the burned-out Hildebrandt mill. The station's prison was over-full.

With a deepening feeling of dread, Johan and Elizabeth rode the wagon to the mill. They knew the way well for Hildebrandt had ground many of the their wagonloads of wheat into fine flour before his arrest closed down the business. When they arrived, Johan pulled the team of horses to a stop in front of the guardhouse.

With a determined look, Elizabeth got down from the wagon and entered the shack. She quickly sized up the guard and respectfully asked to be allowed to see her father-in-law. The guard in charge was inclined to turn her away, but in the end, after some initial stonewalling, he saw she was pregnant. He thought of his own wife who would soon give birth to their third child and had pity on Elizabeth. He was a Cossack and, uncharacteristically, affectionate and gentle with the women in his life. Whereas his Cossack comrades considered it their duty to beat their wives and children on a regular basis, he never raised his hand against his family. Furthermore, he did not particularly approve of what he saw happening at the prison where he worked though he had no choice in the matter. He and his comrades were merely carrying out their assigned duties. There was no question of disobeying orders.

"Mother, wipe your tears. I'll get someone to take you to your father."

He called across the yard to his comrade guarding the cellar door. "She wants to see her papa. Let her in."

Johan was instructed to remain seated on the wagon. He watched nervously as Elizabeth slowly walked across the yard.

Elizabeth lifted the sides of her long coat as she descended the cement steps. She needed to be careful not to catch her toe on the hem, lest she'd trip and fall. She felt the bags of food brushing against her knees and worried the guard might notice an irregular bump in the way her coat hung and moved as she walked. He was certainly staring at her, though his eyes seemed fixed on the part of her body that was above her waist.

When Elizabeth got to the bottom of the stairwell, the guard turned the key and the outside door creaked open. Inside the dank corridor she waited apprehensively while the guard opened the cell door and shouted into the darkness, "Franz Funk, ya has a visitor!"

Franz groped his way through the crowded cell and greeted his daughter-in-law with a close embrace.

"Ya has five minutes," said the guard.

To Franz and Elizabeth's surprise the guard walked to the door leading outside, leaving the two of them alone in the hallway. He leaned against the lintel and ignored them completely, looking out into the bright sunlight.

Elizabeth got right to business. Speaking softly in German,

which she expected the guard would not understand, she asked, "Are they feeding you? Are they treating you well?"

Franz shrugged. "They gave us some gruel last night, water with a few cabbage leaves floating on top. Nothing so far today, but from what I'm told, they usually get around to giving us something most days. There is a bucket of water for us to drink from."

Glancing back at the half-open door where the guard stood with his back to them, Elizabeth quickly unbuttoned her coat. She began undoing a pin while whispering, "Here, help me. I've brought you some food."

"Elizabeth, you are an angel sent from heaven above!" Franz could hardly contain his joy.

Keeping one eye on the guard, Franz bent down and quickly unfastened the bags he found there.

"Thank you, Elizabeth," said Franz quietly. "Thank you." He stuffed the bags under his coat.

"Do you know when you will be released? Have they told you anything?" asked Elizabeth.

"I know nothing. They tell us nothing," replied Franz. "It is in God's hands. Now, you must go. I have to get back in the cell. I don't want the guard noticing my extra padding." He smiled as he patted the bulge in his jacket. "Elizabeth, you are an answer to my prayers. Thank you again." He paused and with as much conviction as he could muster said, "Don't worry. This will soon be sorted out. I'll be home soon."

And with that he turned and was lost in the darkness.

"I will come again," Elizabeth promised.

But he did not hear her. It was just as well, for though she came each week thereafter, she was not allowed to see him again.

It would be fifty-one days before Franz Funk was released from the makeshift prison in the cellar of what had been the old Hildebrandt mill.

Shortly after her father-in-law's homecoming, Elizabeth gave birth to a baby girl. The child, named Sarah, lived a few months and then, as if overburdened by the demands placed upon the living, reaching for another more welcome light, she died. The hearts of Elizabeth and Johan were broken and buried with her in the hard coldness of the little Siberian graveyard where they wept her leaving.

As expected, shortly after arresting Franz Funk the police made a search of the Funks' estate. They justified their intrusion on the grounds that Franz Funk was suspected of speculating on the price of grain, and therefore he was probably hoarding it as well. Grain was found in his barn and was immediately confiscated. Next the police inspected the attics of all of the families of Lyubimovka. They knew it was a sure thing, for seed grain was always stored in attics until the spring planting, to keep it dry and to provide insulation against the winter's cold.

Despite their fear of the police, Peter and Johan were incensed when the police began seizing their grain.

"How are we to plant our fields?" Johan protested as the wheat and barley were being shoveled into bags and loaded into the waiting carts. "We need that grain! You cannot leave us with nothing!"

"Not our problem," said a policeman as he stomped down the stairs from Johan's attic. "Get out of our way, or we'll bag you and throw you in with the rest of it." He laughed in derision.

Johan fumed but was silent. The other policemen also found something to laugh at in the comment. But, looking at the officer's lifeless eyes, Johan knew he wasn't joking.

When Peter tried to object, another stone-faced policeman cut him off saying, "Take it up with the magistrate. We have our orders. It's all perfectly legal."

Seeing the policemen marching toward her home, Elizabeth had told her children, to hide in the imagined safety of the forest. "I will call when they are gone," she assured her frightened children. Now she sat wiping her eyes, knowing the grain being carried from her attic meant hunger in the coming year.

The next day, when Franz's hired Russian workers came to work at the farm, Ivan and Vitaly conferred together. They weighed the pros and cons, and in the end decided they must do what they could to secure their employer's release from prison. He had shown them kindness; it was time for them to return the favor. That evening they walked the two kilometers to Isylkul.

Vitaly knew where the magistrate lived. He had known Igor Pasternak since childhood. As adults they had shared stories over more than a few bottles of vodka before Igor was appointed to his present position. The men made a stop at a shop before arriving at the magistrate's house.

The shop owner, Leonid Polzin, was a small man with the face of a weasel—the effect accentuated by brown whiskers bristling straight out from his face on either side of his pointed nose. He sold whatever scraps of metal or other odds and ends he'd 'found' while on his nocturnal wanderings about the town and surrounding villages. Because he was often gone, the shop was open only irregularly. Vitaly was well acquainted with Polzin and knew on this day his shop would be open. As a sideline, or, perhaps, as his main line, Polzin sold locally distilled vodka. It was strong stuff, the quality of which was never guaranteed. A bottle of Polzin's spirits would be required for what Vitaly and Ivan were about to request.

Igor Pasternak lived alone in a simple three-room house on a dirt lane surrounded by a decrepit picket fence. In the back yard grew a garden full of healthy weeds that outstripped the struggling vegetables by two to one. Though he liked to think of himself as a gardener, in keeping with the vegetable that was his name, Pasternak planted plenty of parsnips and potatoes but harvested few. He was a starter, not a finisher.

After his guests rapped politely on his door, Pasternak welcomed Vitaly warmly, as an old friend, and shook hands with Ivan. They were soon seated around his table. Glasses were fetched and the vodka was poured all around. It wasn't long before the talk became loud and animated.

Vitaly brought up the question of his employer, Mr. Franz Funk, and what a fine and upstanding man he was. The magistrate grew silent and said it was illegal to be employed by a kulak, after which Ivan and Vitaly only grew more vociferous in the defense of Mr. Funk, speaking earnestly of his constant even-handedness and generosity.

The magistrate had never before seen two Russian peasants defend an employer so vigorously—and a German kulak at that! He looked at them, first with suspicion, then with a touch of amusement, and finally with envy. At heart, Igor Pasternak was a decent man. He was not a party member, but he was a pragmatist who would do as he was told. "If only we had had more employers like this man, Franz Funk," he said morosely, "Russia would not be in the sorry state it is today." And though his two guests didn't know the state to which he referred, they were inclined to agree nonetheless. The three lifted their glasses and drank to a better Russia.

Softened by camaraderie and alcohol, Pasternak assured Ivan and Vitaly it would not be long before their employer was again as free as a field mouse. Franz Funk was a kulak whose elimination, as stipulated by state policy, was only a matter of time. But his time could wait.

"Leave it with me, comrades." he sighed as they walked out his door. "I'll see what I can do."

It would be seven long weeks before the convoluted wheels of communist justice turned to the extent that a key was put to the lock of the door of the basement cell in which Franz Funk was imprisoned and he again saw the bright light of day. In the meantime, Franz knew nothing of the efforts being made to secure his release.

Trapped in the crowded, dimly lit, claustrophobic prison cell, days and nights blended together and Franz's hope began to wane. He fell into a despair that deepened with each new descent into the complete darkness of night or the artificial darkness of the blocked window. He no longer hummed his favorite hymn; indeed, apart from pleading with God to show mercy, he found his faith quite inadequate to give meaning to his present circumstances.

Occasionally Johann Neufeld would rant about their need to repent of their sins lest God consign them all to the eternal lake of fire on the Great Judgment Day. But Franz was unconvinced. "I have no fear of hell," Franz remarked grimly. "Hell is here and I'm already in it."

One day Franz asked his friend, "Do you really think God requires an eternal hell as well as the temporal one in which we find ourselves here and now?"

The theological argument that followed was inconclusive, but it helped them to ease the boredom of the day.

"Of course there is an eternal hell," asserted Johann. "There must be punishment for people like these guards who torment us, and their communist god, Stalin, whose devilish orders they obey."

Franz was doubtful. "I agree they are the ones who are responsible for our suffering. But when it is our time to stand before God, will we not all have our own sins to be ashamed of? As I am confronted by the unspeakable holiness of a loving God and as I am flooded with gratitude because of His grace that covers my sins, will I then also at the same time be vengeful enough to be concerned about the sins of the others who have harmed me? And do you think their experience will be any different? In the humbling presence of Almighty God, I am convinced my own failures will be enough of a burden to consider. I will then have neither the courage nor the need to wish God's vengeance upon others. Remember, the Bible says we have all fallen short of God's glory."

Johann was aghast at Franz's argument. "You cannot mean to say God will treat these butchers with the same grace as you and me! Does that mean you forgive them?"

Franz merely shrugged. "I don't know if I am capable of such forgiveness. But the Apostle Paul wrote every knee will bow and every tongue will confess Jesus Christ is Lord. Do you think once some have made that confession God will say, 'Good! Thank you for your worship. But, unfortunately for you, your worship comes a little too late. Now, off to hell with the lot of you?' It just doesn't make sense to me. I choose to believe God's judgment is characterized by his mercy, which is informed by his grace. They don't deserve it, but neither do we. I believe Christ did not die for the few but for all."

"Yes, but they must choose to accept his salvation and be baptized," Neufeld sputtered.

Of course, they couldn't come to any sort of agreement. The Bible was open to both interpretations and they each chose the one that suited them.

Conditions in the prison cell were deplorable. But more crushing than the darkness, the hunger, and the smell was the fear permeating everything and leaving everyone numb with anxiety. Each morning the cell door was opened and a guard called two names. The names' owners followed the guards through the door and up the cement staircase. Once outside, the prisoners' hands were tied behind their backs. The guards then harangued and cursed them, calling them enemies of the Russian people—tight-fisted kulaks who exploited the peasants and workers for their own selfish ends.

"We'll show you what a tight fist feels like," they'd taunt, after which they would beat the prisoners, all farmers like Franz Funk, with fists, boots and clubs.

Finally, the prisoners would be made to kneel. A guard would stand behind each, pointing his Nagant revolver at the back of their head. The sentence of death would be spoken loudly. Through the window in the cell wall the prisoners could hear everything happening on the outside where, in the silence following the proclamation of death, a prisoner might be weeping or pleading for his life. Then, two shots would ring out. One prisoner would slump to the ground, his head bloody and shattered. The other prisoner, emotionally shattered but alive, would be returned to the prison cell. The guards had had no intention of killing both prisoners. It was their little joke, their sadistic game. It was their most brutal torment, for the prisoners knew one prisoner would always be returned. But they never knew who would die and who would be spared.

One morning Franz heard Johann Neufeld's name called. He looked fearfully as the dim outline of his friend disappeared through the door, followed by another prisoner whose name Franz knew, but with whom he was not acquainted. It seemed like hours until the familiar shots were heard. Franz waited in a terror of anticipation to see if his friend returned. When it was the other prisoner who stumbled into the cell, Franz wept inconsolably at the senselessness of it all and for the loss of his friend.

The next day, Franz Funk's name was called. On trembling legs he followed the guards outside. It was raining, but even so, Franz's eyes were immediately drawn to the red stain in the snow where Johann Neufeld had died. Franz felt his body go numb. He was immediately dizzy and nauseous. He did not feel the beating he received, nor was he aware of the slushy cold on his legs when he was made to kneel in the snow. As if from afar he heard the curses directed at him and the two deafening shots coming almost simultaneously from behind. He saw the snow erupt in front of him where a bullet buried itself in the ground. Too shocked to feel any relief, Franz saw the body of his prison-mate lying on the ground beside him, it's limbs still juddering their death throes. At the guards' command he stumbled blindly back to the cell where he found he had wet his pants. Franz curled himself into a ball on the cold cement floor. Blackness overtook him.

It was only later, when he was home, that Franz was tormented, not by the question, "Why was I arrested?" but by the question, "Why was I spared?"

On the day of his release from prison, Franz was met by the tall, bearded police officer. Johan and Peter were supporting their father between them, so weakened was he by his ordeal. The officer was walking across the yard, but when he saw the Funks, he stopped. Being directly in his path, the Funks were forced to walk around him.

The policeman stared at them as they made their slow way along. As they came abreast of him he sneered, "Enjoy yer freedom, kulak. It ain't gonna last long." As his sons helped Franz up onto the wagon, the policeman said, "Remember my name fellas. Sokol Volkov. That way, when we meet agin, there won't be any need fer interductions." He laughed at his own joke and went on his way.

The trauma of the entire experience left the patriarch of the Funk family shaken to the core. Nightmares ruined his sleep; his health until then robust, was broken.

Chapter 6

July 1929

Another goal of the First Five Year Plan was to force all of Russia's farmers off of their own land and onto collective farms. Naturally, those who had prospered during the years of the New Economic Policy as a result of their own efforts resisted such a loss of their freedom. And so the arrests of successful farmers intensified.

Farmers who owned several head of cattle and horses, used hired labor, or leased land were labeled kulaks. Specifically targeted for liquidation, they were stripped of all political rights. When local soviets endorsed the "voluntary taxation" of grain supplies, kulaks were powerless to object for they had neither the right to speak nor to vote. Once the motion was passed, and it always was regardless of show of hands for or against—the will of the Party always superseded the will of the individual or the group—grain must either be delivered to the government depot or it was collected by force.

If the farmer had the amount of grain to fulfill his tax quota, upon delivery he may well be greeted with instructions saying his tax had since been doubled. If he was unable to meet the quota and had no money with which to pay the arbitrarily assigned tax, he would be forced to auction off his assets. At any time, his farm might be seized and he could be imprisoned. His family then would be thrown out onto the street and neighbors were threatened with consequences should they think to help them.

Any farmer caught selling grain at the bazaar or in a private transaction, any farmer caught storing grain for any reason was arrested and punished under Article 107. The law against speculation on the price of grain became the noose making it impossible for farmers to legally pursue their vocation.

If a farmer who had been labeled a kulak attempted to voluntarily join a collective, he was often turned away. With no recourse and no justice, farmers struggled to comply. For some, the burden simply became too heavy to bear.

The arrest and imprisonment of Franz Funk the previous year cast a dark shadow over his family. Though they had rejoiced at his homecoming, the obvious toll of the experience was clearly evident. Lyubimovka no longer provided the safe haven it had once been. The political battering rams of the communist dictatorship had thrown down their imagined protective fences, ransacked their barns, and nearly taken the life of their beloved patriarch. Thoughts of emigration increasingly became their only source of hope and salvation.

As Johan and Elizabeth Funk struggled with the new, harsh reality of their lives, they attempted to keep from their children the extent of the difficulties they faced. The younger siblings were told nothing. But as children will, they sensed the tension in the home. They knew their parents were anxious about something. The uncomfortable silence around the kitchen table, the interrupted conversations cut short, the worried looks all worked together to confirm their suspicions.

The exception was sixteen-year-old Franz. As the eldest of their children, Franz was treated as an adult and so was made fully aware of the family's challenges. When his parents argued, he always agreed with his mother. Franz felt strongly about the need to leave the Soviet Union and whenever the opportunity arose, he argued convincingly with his father.

The subject of their uncertain future was a regular topic of conversation between Johan and Elizabeth. Elizabeth was deeply afraid and pessimistic about the direction in which Russia was going while Johan held on to the hope of better times to come.

"It is impossible that this should continue," Johan would maintain. "The Bolsheviks are making such a mess of things the populace must rise up against them. They will be forced to change their ways and govern more reasonably."

But Elizabeth would have none of it. She had relatives in Canada. The glowing letters about the freedom they enjoyed to live and worship as they wished had been arriving for years now. They urgently encouraged their Russian relatives to join them.

"We must emigrate to Canada!" Elizabeth insisted. "There is no future for us here!"

Johan felt helpless in the face of his wife's desire. The door had been slammed in his face; where was the key now that would open it?

"What can I do about it? They refused us two years ago when so many were being allowed to leave." Indeed, tens of thousands of Mennonites with foresight had been allowed to emigrate. But not all had been allowed then, and none were being allowed now. "What's going to change their mind? You know what people are saying. No one is getting out anymore! We must believe things will improve. We must think positively about our future here. What other choice do we have?"

Even as he said the words, Johan wondered at their foolishness. But he knew not what else to say.

Whether they spoke in hushed voices in the evening when the children were asleep in their beds, or aloud at mid-day when the children were at lessons in the schoolroom in their grandparents' house, the discussion invariably degenerated into a heated argument. Elizabeth was terrified of what she foresaw in the coming weeks and months. The arrest and torture of her father-in-law had destroyed any illusion their family would escape the notice of the communist monster. More than anything else, Elizabeth wanted to leave the Soviet Union. She was determined to emigrate to Canada where her relatives lived.

"How can you possibly think life will get better for us here?"

Elizabeth was exasperated with what she perceived to be her husband's naivety and shortsightedness. On this occasion she was kneading dough for a batch of buns and as she became more animated her strokes became stronger and stronger.

"The Bolsheviks have been terrorizing this country for twelve years now. You've read the letters from the south: famine, disease, arrests, people being thrown into jail for no reason at all and never being heard from again, exile, murder!" Her voice was rising now. "They're closing churches and arresting ministers." Her cheeks were streaming tears. "They won't allow us to teach our faith or our language to our children! We have to do it in secret! For God's sake, Johan, we have to hide the fact we have a schoolroom in your parents' house! If the children are in the classroom, they tremble behind closed curtains if a Bolshevik so much as shows his nose on the road through our village.

Now they've made a law so that the grain you raise is not your own. And they nearly killed your father. Our world is crumbling around us and you think our lives are going to get better?"

"But that's just the point!" Johan replied. "How can it get any worse? Things have never been this bad here before. They cannot possibly arrest us all. Someone has to be left to farm the land. Surely they will see that!" Johan could not bear the thought of having to leave the land he loved, just as he could not bear to see his wife's distress. "Anyway, our church is still open," he added lamely.

Elizabeth pounced on his naivety. "Yes but for how long? Johan, are you blind or do you simply live in an imaginary world of your own making where all the shit we live with will one day magically turn into roses?"

Johan cringed at the profanity passing his wife's lips. He blushed at the insult but did not allow the argument to descend into personal attack. He was a patient man who as a matter of course always tried to avoid conflict. He knew, though, he could not defend his illogical hope for a better future against the truth of Elizabeth's words. His desperate optimism defied logic. Yet, in the absence of a tangible alternative, he hung on to his argument.

"Sure, the communists may be getting stricter, but I tell you, it cannot last. People have to live." He spread his hands in a gesture of supplication, as if these words also held some weight of undeniable truth.

"Of course people have to live," Elizabeth replied, her voice quivering with emotion. "But apparently the Bolsheviks don't see it that way. Look at what they are doing to us! How many farmers have been bankrupted? How many have lost their farms? You've heard the stories; you know some of those people! Their villages aren't that far away. How long will it be before it is our turn?"

Elizabeth's eyes pled with Johan to understand. He could not meet her searching gaze, but slumped hopelessly onto the bench by the table upon which she worked.

Elizabeth placed the well-kneaded lump of dough in a large bowl, covered it with a linen cloth, and put it on the warm stove to rise before she continued her assault.

"And now the Bolsheviks are going to force us all onto collective farms! You know the talk about the collectives. It is not enough they've taken away our right to own our own land. Eventually, they're not even going to allow us the freedom to live on the little that's been allotted to us! Is that what you want? Do you want us to live on a collective? Do you want to work for the communists and have your days and hours dictated by their godless ways? Do you want your children to be forced to attend a communist school? Is that the kind of life you want for Franz and the other children? Well? Do you?"

Elizabeth held her apron to her face and sobbed into it uncontrollably. Johan attempted to calm her.

"Of course I don't want to be forced onto a collective farm. But, don't you see? The idea of forcing farmers onto huge state farms is ridiculous. It's not practical. How will they motivate farmers to work land they don't own for a harvest they won't profit from?"

In the heat of the moment Johan forgot Russia's history was the sad story of that very systemic abuse. Peasants had been farming land owned by their lords for a thousand years and subsisting on the leavings.

"And for how long will they get away with closing churches? It's absurd; what they are doing makes no sense and goes against everything an orderly society believes! People simply won't stand for it! More than that, God won't allow it!"

"Oh, Johan you are a dreamer!" muttered Elizabeth when she was able to control her sobs. "How do you think we will be able to resist? I could name you a dozen churches that have been forced to close. You yourself know what is happening throughout the Mennonite colonies. Is God stepping in and working a miracle? No! He is silent. And the people can do nothing but stand by and watch as men with guns arrest their ministers and nail the doors of their churches shut. Do you think we are special and it will be any different here? Do you think God will answer our prayers while he ignores theirs?"

Johan was stung by Elizabeth's words of doubt and despair. But she was not finished.

"Your own father has been imprisoned and tortured for weeks because he didn't know someone has decided to make it illegal to sell wheat at the bazaar. What other new laws do we not know about that can get us thrown into jail and worse?"

Elizabeth's voice rose again in anger.

"Johan, we live in a country where it is illegal for us to sell our own grain! We have already been told a government agent is coming to the farm to supervise when we harvest our apples and plums. We have to hand over everything we grow to the government for whatever they decide to pay, if they pay anything at all. What will be left for us to eat next winter? And if starvation isn't enough, what do you think will happen when Bolsheviks with guns are standing at the door ordering you to move your family onto one of their collectives? Will you say, 'Thank you for the offer, but we'd prefer to stay here?' Do you think they'll smile and leave? Are you so stupid as to think they won't throw you in jail or shoot you like a dog, like they shot all those men when Papa was in prison? Johan, for once be reasonable! We must get out of this country!"

And so the argument would go, round and around, and Johan knew Elizabeth was right.

That summer things came to a head for the Funk family and the dream of emigration weighed more and more heavily upon them as their last resort. As the weeks went by the one question on their minds became, "How?"

One day the cousins were playing in the forest behind their grandparents' home. As they romped through their childish inventions—hiding and chasing games and wrestling in the grass—their play led them to a patch of wild strawberries. A truce was called while everyone busily picked the sweet fruit. The day was sunny and warm, and they were all happy as they munched on their unexpected treat.

No one later could remember who it was that started it, but soon strawberries were being thrown back and forth, and were being mashed on faces and arms. The children began running in all directions, either chasing or being chased, accompanied by much hooting and hilarity.

Abe was running after Wilhelm through a tangle of bracken and pine bows when they came upon a large birch tree in a small glade. It was not the tree, though, stopping them in their tracks and making their blood run cold. Hanging from a sturdy limb by a rope tied around its neck was a corpse. If it hadn't been that the man was suspended in mid-air they might have thought him to be asleep. His face looked at rest, his hands hung limply by his side, his shoes lay neatly side-by-side on the ground beneath him. But he was dead, of that the boys were instantly sure. The fact he was unbothered by the flies buzzing about his face was proof enough, for in their childish minds they thought, "Surely he would swat at them if he were alive." But who was he? The boys had never seen him before.

The corpse swayed in a sudden gust of wind, a macabre pendulum lazily swinging in a tiny arc. Frightened, Wilhelm and Abe ran as if their lives depended on it. They ran heedless of the slapping bows and branches stinging them until they were gasping for breath, their lungs burning. As they ran, their terrified minds imagined the corpse flying after them, the noose tight around its neck and the rope-end flapping wildly behind. Indeed, they swore afterward they had felt the corpse's breath on the napes of their necks.

They found their father in the yard with his brother Peter, and howled their discovery even before they had come to a skidding stop.

The men looked at them in surprise.

"What is it?" said Johan sternly, his hands steadying Abe.

"In the woods!" shouted Abe with Henry nodding vigorously beside him. "A man! He is hanging from a rope on a big birch tree."

"He's dead!" added Wilhelm. He was still breathing heavily, but in the presence of the adults his fear was gone, replaced by a feeling of importance for the news they brought.

"Of course he's dead," countered Abe savagely, angry at his younger brother's interruption. "You'd be too if you were hanging from a tree with a rope around your neck!" He imitated the sight, holding an imaginary rope above his tilted head and sticking his tongue out the side of his mouth.

"Abraham!" Johan barked.

Johan and Peter followed Abe and Henry back into the woods. The men paused briefly, looking up at what misery had wrought. After a few moments, Johan climbed the tree and cut the rope while Peter held the body so it wouldn't fall. Removed from its indecent aerial display and laid upon the ground, the body seemed, to Abe and Henry, much smaller and pitiful. A stretcher was improvised using poles cut from nearby saplings and a blanket they had brought with them.

Reaching the farmyard, Johan and his brother placed the body in a wagon. They drove it to the neighboring village where Johan thought the man had lived. There he and Peter learned the communists had confiscated the man's farm the week before. Without a family—his wife and infant son had died in childbirth a year ago—and now without a home, the farmer had seen no future for himself and had taken his own life. In retrospect, a neighbor realized he had missed the warning signs of the man's deep despair.

It was only a few days after the discovery of the body in the woods that Peter Funk and his family made a hasty departure from Lyubimovka. Their leaving came about like this.

As an elected member of the local soviet, Peter was obliged to attend the properties of recalcitrant farmers and demand they deliver their allotted amount of the "voluntary" grain tax. He hated the assignment and did it half-heartedly, knowing the order was criminal, state-sanctioned thievery. One day, when asked by the head of his committee why there were so few deliveries from his area, Peter had little to say other than that farmers were reluctant to obey the order. After a moment's thought, the chairman took a pistol from his pocket and placed it on the table in front of him.

"It is either the grain or this," he said, pointing at the weapon. "Take it with you and, if necessary, use it."

Peter attempted to refuse but the chairman was insistent. Faced with the ultimatum, Peter resigned from the committee on the spot.

The day after his resignation from the local soviet, Peter received a clandestine visit from a sympathetic member of the committee. The man came in the dark, late in the evening. He found Peter in his barn where he was attempting to cure one of his cows suffering from a bad case of bloating. The cow had eaten too much wet clover and was now in serious trouble. If Peter did not act, it would suffocate from the pressure of the gases being generated in its belly. The cow was in agony, lying on its distended side and could not get up. Peter held a bottle of kerosene to the cow's mouth and forced its jaws open. The kerosene quickly drained down the cow's throat. Peter stood back, waiting to see if his treatment would have any effect. He knew if the condition was not reversed quickly, the cow could be dead within the hour. As he watched, Peter was beginning to think he would be forced to use his knife to open a hole in the hollow of the cow's flank through which the compressed gases in its rumen could escape.

"You were foolish to take a stand against the committee's policies as you did," said a voice. "The chairman is furious."

"Ah, Vasily Aslanov, my friend. You gave me a start. I didn't hear you come in. How are you?"

"You are in danger," said Aslanov, ignoring the friendly greeting.

"Well, the chairman left me no choice," said Peter. "I will not be the representative of a government that sends me with a gun to rob my neighbors on behalf of the state."

Aslanov made to interrupt, but Peter continued.

"Families are being left in poverty. They have no grain for food during the coming winter or for next spring's planting. What will happen to them?" He paused. "Stalin will be the ruin of us all. Tell me, what will you eat this winter when all the grain has been shipped to the cities? We are fortunate. We still have a few animals that haven't been requisitioned. We will be forced to kill and eat them. And when they are gone, there will be nothing left. You heard the stories of the famine coming from the Ukraine only a few short years ago. If the government has its way, that will soon be our lot as well!"

Peter stopped speaking. The enormity of the suffering he foresaw was too much to consider.

Vasily was quiet for a time.

"Ah, look," Peter said, pointing at the cow. "Its side is beginning to flatten. The kerosene is doing its job."

There was a gurgling sound and the cow let out a loud belch. Peter bent over and patted its side. "Here, help me get it to stand."

Aslanov appeared not to have heard. "Yes, well," he began. He looked at the neat barn, the clean stalls. The thought occurred to him, "This barn is cleaner than most peasants' izbas." And then aloud, he said, "Peter, there has been a warrant issued for your arrest. It is only a matter of hours before they will come. Perhaps even this night."

Peter felt the blood drain from his face. His knees felt weak so he leaned against the stall for support. "I guess I should not be surprised." After a moment he looked Vasily in the eyes and extended his hand. "Thank you, my brother, for warning me." They shook hands and embraced warmly. "And now you must go. Obviously no one must know you were here."

"I will be careful," murmured Aslanov. Once more the two men looked in each other's eyes. "There is an old proverb," Vasily said. "When you meet a man, you judge him by his clothes; when you leave, you judge him by his heart." He paused. "You are a good man, Peter Funk."

Embarrassed at the compliment, Peter looked at the cow as it successfully struggled to its feet. It burped up a cud and began chewing contentedly. He heard a rustle of straw on the floor and the creak of the iron hinges on the barn door. His friend had gone.

Later, when Peter was alone with his wife, Ruth, he told her of his impending arrest. As they discussed what was to be done, there was a light knock on their door. In walked Johan. In Lyubimovka, doors were never locked and the family did not stand on formalities. Everyone was always welcome in each other's homes. Johan had come to ask a question of Peter, which he promptly forgot when he saw the expression on Peter and Ruth's faces.

As Peter explained the situation, Ruth roused the children and began packing whatever clothing and cooking utensils they could carry. She wrapped and tied everything in bundles using the handmade quilts from each bed. Their son Jacob looked on sleepily. Ruth brusquely gave him instructions and he disappeared into the bedroom to help dress his younger sister.

"We are leaving this night," said Peter.

Johan stood in stunned silence after Peter had told him all. "Surely not!" was all he could say.

"Only last week Cousin Nicholas and his family left for the Amur region in the Far East. I have managed to keep some money here in the house. We will use it to buy train tickets; we will join them there. No one knows me in the Far East. We should be safe for a while. And then, who knows? Perhaps we'll chance a winter crossing over the frozen Amur and escape into China. Maybe from there we can even get to North America. Think of it, Johan!" Peter continued, suddenly enthusiastic. "Freedom from Stalin, from communism, from this godforsaken country!"

Johan could hardly take in his brother's words.

"Will you take us to Maryanovka?" Peter asked, referring to a rural stop on the Trans-Siberian Railway a few kilometers east of Isylkul. "They might be watching the station in town. We can board the train at Maryanovka in the morning and buy tickets from the conductor. He will not know us."

Johan began to think of all that needed to be done. "What will you take along for food?"

"We have a few things. We'll manage," replied Peter. "Fortunately, Ruth baked this morning."

Ruth was stuffing a mound of buns and a ham from the cold storage into a wicker basket.

"I'll hitch the horses to the wagon," offered Johan as he turned to go.

"Use ours," Peter insisted.

"No, my team knows my voice. They'll respond to me better. It is going to be a long journey in the darkness," said Johan as he ran out the door.

The next week, on one of the last days of July, the Funks got word Grandfather Franz was to be arrested again.

Chapter 7

July 28, 1929

Sokol Volkov did not forget his threat against Franz Funk.

Volkov was an embittered man whose life had been scarred by many encounters with people in authority, none of which had been pleasant. Franz Funk, though a simple landowner and a side-note in Volkov's life's experiences, was merely further proof to his resentful mind that all that was wrong with the world was the consequence of the actions of the greedy and the corrupt, the rich and the powerful.

As a young boy, Volkov had been beaten for failing to fall facedown upon the ground on a day when the Tsar's entourage had raced by his village in a dusty procession of horse-drawn carriages. Volkov lived by a dirt path upon which nothing of note ever traveled. The morning they had been told the Royal Entourage was to appear he stood by the side of the road bathed and dressed in a clean shirt and trousers— his clothing had been washed for the occasion, the first time he and they had been cleaned in months. When the boy saw the approaching splendor of the uniformed men, the prancing steeds and the gilded carriages, he quite forgot the lesson with which his mother had drilled him, the show of obeisance required of everyone in the presence of their monarch. In awe, Volkov had stood alone among the groveling villagers, mouth agape, hands clutching the hair on both sides of his head, watching the spectacle. A guardsman had stopped his horse and given Sokol such a clout on the head with the shaft of his lance that Volkov had lain unconscious for a day. Despite the injury to his head, he remembered the event clearly. After awakening, as he lay recovering on the dirt floor of his parents' izba upon his bed of straw, the seeds of hatred of the upper classes began to germinate in his soul.

Years later when he was a teen, Volkov saw two peasants hung for grazing their animals on land owned by the Tsar, land that otherwise lay empty and untended season after season, year after year. He had been forced to watch as his friend's father had struggled at the end of the rope, his life choked off before their eyes. The Cossack guardsmen had forbidden the grim, horrified villagers from removing the bodies from the gallows. The hanging corpses were to serve as a reminder and a warning to those who thought they could thumb their noses at the Tsar's commands. And so the hot days had passed while the bodies swayed lazily in the summer breezes and black ravens pecked out their eyeballs. Finally, a group of angry peasants cut the bodies down and gave them a decent burial.

"Them Cossack buggers won't be back," was all they said when questioned by other worried villagers.

As a soldier on the front lines in the war against Germany, Volkov had endured hunger and cold while aware of the fact his officers had sold his regiment's supplies to pad their own pockets. Worse, time and again he saw his comrades being mowed down by German machine-gun nests they had been ordered to advance upon. Along with thousands of other weary, disenchanted men, he deserted when the opportunity presented itself. The long journey back home took months.

The moment Volkov crossed the threshold into his mother's izba, she informed him his younger brother, Vasily, the apple of her eye, had been killed in a battle against the Germans. A friend's son who returned from the Polish front had seen it happen and brought the sad news only the day before. Exhausted, ill, and weak from hunger though he was, he was forced to listen to her wailing.

"My Volodya, my beloved Volodya is dead. He has been torn from my breast! Oh God, oh Virgin Mary and all the Saints hear me. My poor Volodya, my dear baby is dead! My poor heart is broken!"

Volkov's distraught mother was intent upon revenge. "It was a German gun, a German bullet; damn them all to hell! May God curse them with everlasting fire!" she raged.

Volkov swore on the family ikon, the picture of the Holy Mother of God enshrined in one corner of his mother's two-room log house, he would avenge his brother Vasily's death. He would seek out and kill a German. For a few weeks Sokol sat in the izba, drinking the peasant's kvass, and vodka, when he could get it. He was obsessed with the injustices his family had suffered. It did not take much for his anger to boil over.

A friend told Volkov about a rich estate north of Isylkul owned by a prosperous German family. Sokol plotted his revenge. A few days later he and a few friends set off for Lyubimovka. They had no plan of action other than to find and kill a German. Arriving, in the village, Volkov banged his fist on the first door that caught his attention.

The German who opened the door was already on the ground when Franz Funk and his sons had interrupted them. Funk had insisted the people of Lyubimovka were all Dutch. There were no Germans among them. Volkov still remembered his confusion at the time, and his humiliation a few years later, when he discovered the people at Lyubimovka were indeed German. By then he had joined the local police force and was rising within its ranks. He gritted his teeth in frustration every time he thought about the debacle. It had been a complete disaster. Nor had his comrades let him live it down.

"You shoulda killed him while ya had the chance. German, Dutch, what difference does it make? They're all the same," they harangued him. "None of 'em belong here."

"I shoulda killed the bastard right there and then," Volkov would growl in agreement.

Though his friends laughed at him for his gullibility, Volkov's mother was less forgiving. Her simmering resentment of his inaction was a canker on his heart, for of all the people in his life, he loved her alone.

So now, Sokol Volkov decided, was the time for Franz Funk to pay for his lie and the humiliation it had caused. Now was the time for the death of his brother to be avenged.

It was quite simple. The government was making the arrest of kulaks a priority. The fact of their existence was reason enough. Volkov would make sure Franz Funk was on the list.

It was Franz Funk's old friend, Makar Gribkov, who brought him the news.

Gribkov had been the owner of the inn at Isylkul used by the travelers as they made their way along the great Trakt Road traveling between European Russia and Siberia. He fed them, stabled their horses, and provided clean beds for their repose. When the Trans-Siberian

Railway arrived in 1906, his inn was inundated with wealthy passengers enjoying the exotic pleasures of travel by rail to the exotic Far East. Though his stables saw less use, his tables were often full.

As a prosperous merchant, Gribkov was rewarded with the appointment of mayor of Isylkul. In this capacity, he and Franz Funk became acquainted through conversations on matters of business. The success of each fostered a mutual respect that carried through the years.

With the coming of the Bolsheviks, the tourist trade dried up. Gribkov was relieved of his duties as mayor. He was forced to lay off the workers who staffed his inn. Over the last years, he, his wife, and son struggled to keep the inn open, serving the few customers who occasionally entered their doorway. Nevertheless, Gribkov's connections to the village grapevine remained healthy and he knew what he must do when he heard his friend Franz Funk was scheduled for arrest.

The Funk family was just returning from attending a Sunday evening service at their church in Friedensruh. Johan had directed the choir, as he did every week. Franz and Anna were walking along the path to their house after having complimented Johan on the choir's singing and the fact his daughter, little Katrina, even as a seven-year-old child was clearly singing with the confidence and gusto of an adult. She had a promising future as a soloist for the choir, Franz had commented. As Franz and Anna climbed their front staircase, they were surprised to see sitting on the veranda, in the deep shadow of the overhang, Makar Gribkov.

"What brings you here, my friend?" asked Franz after initial greetings were done and Anna had excused herself to leave the men to their conversation.

"I'm sorry, Franz, there is no way to say this easily," murmured Gribkov. "You are to be arrested again."

Franz swayed as though he had been struck across the face. Neither man said anything for a few moments.

"I cannot go through that again," Franz said. He stared numbly into the night sky. He saw the moon gently rising over the darkened steppe. He sensed danger in shapes and shadows close by and far away. He sank into a chair, leaned forward and, elbows on knees, supported his head in his hands.

At that moment, Anna opened the door to offer the men some tea. Noticing their tension she hesitantly asked what was amiss. The story was quickly told.

"What will we do?" asked Anna rubbing her forehead. Her mind was blank. She could not comprehend the thought of her husband in jail again. "You're sixty-nine years old! Can't they leave you alone?"

"You must go into hiding," suggested Gribkov after a while.

At that moment a figure emerged from the darkness. All three on the veranda gave a start. It was Ivan, Franz's hired man. He had come back to the farm to check on a sick horse and wanted to let Mr. Funk know the animal was improving.

"Beggin' your pardon, Mr. Funk. Mrs. Funk. Sir." Ivan nodded to each in turn. "I didn' mean ta startle ya." He hesitated a moment and then said, "I couldn' help but hear what ya wuz sayin'. Pardon my impertinence, but what if Mr. Funk was ta come an' stay fer a while at my place? Just 'til th' police ferget about 'im."

"That's very kind of you, Ivan, but I wouldn't want to endanger you or your family," said Franz.

Gribkov liked the idea. "I think you should consider it, Franz. I doubt the police would ever think to look for you there."

Anna jumped on the suggestion. "I'm sure they won't search for you in Ivan's village, Franz! They'd assume you're far too proud to stay in the home of a common laborer," she said, grasping the thread of hope Ivan offered. Anna looked at Ivan. "You know that's not what I think of you, Ivan. I hope you're not offended."

"No, Mrs. Funk," Ivan said. "I know you don' hold ta those sentiments. You've bin most kind ta me and my Vera."

"Then it's settled," Anna said with finality looking at her husband. "You'll go and stay in Ivan's home. When the police come here I'll say you've gone to Omsk." She did not wait for Franz to reply. "I'll pack a few things for you."

"Vera won't mind?" Franz asked. He felt numb with disbelief.

Anna soon returned with a small suitcase of clothing and a basket filled with food. Franz and Anna held each other in a long embrace. Neither could think of any words of comfort. They knew what arrest meant and platitudes, however well meaning, could not measure up. There would be no promises, only the willingness to persevere and to hope.

Finally, Ivan and Franz Funk set out. The route to Ivan's home took them along the road north, away from Isylkul. As they walked, both men regularly looked over their shoulders to see if anyone was coming. A police wagon would make quite a racket as it bumped along the rutted road, but policemen on horseback were another matter. Eventually they turned off the road and followed a dirt track toward the east. Small bushes and a few larch trees grew alongside it so at times they felt some protection from the imagined eyes taking note of their course.

It wasn't long before they came to a small collection of huts with dusty yards surrounded by fences in various states of brokenness. The contrast could not have been greater for Franz, when he compared Ivan's meager dwelling with his own magnificent home. The izba's floor was dirt occasionally made shiny and hard by the application of a watery soup of diluted cow's manure. It reminded Franz of the floors they found in the houses they first lived in during the early years at Lyubimovka. How the women had complained. The izba's one room served as kitchen, bedroom and sitting room. At night it also served as a pen for Ivan's calf lying in one corner while he and Vera slept on their straw pallet in the other. Franz wondered why Ivan and Vera lived in such poverty, given the wages they had been paid over the years.

Over the next few days, while Ivan and Vera were at work, Franz tried to keep his mind occupied by reading his Bible and praying. He was drawn continually to the account of the sufferings of Job. "Is God testing me?" he wondered. "Has he given Satan permission to bring me to my grave? Should I curse God and die?"

He thought of the turmoil of the past year and the decade before that: revolution, civil war, government policy allowing strangers to take what he owned without recompense and to requisition all of a farmer's crops under the guise of a voluntary tax. There was no logic to be found in the radical changes happening in his country. Why would a government persecute its own law-abiding citizens? From one perspective he could understand the arrest of ministers and the closure of churches. After all, Jesus had predicted his followers would experience persecution in this world. But he was an honest farmer. What had he done to deserve prison? He could think of nothing. It made no sense to him at all.

Thoughts of his imprisonment haunted Franz. He mourned again the murder of his friend, Johann Neufeld, and the others who were executed. He trembled as he remembered his own brush with death at the hands of the capricious guards. He lay awake for hours listening to Ivan and Vera snore in their slumber. When he finally descended into the blackness of sleep, his mind conjured images from the dark, crowded, smothering chamber and the execution ground, of his hands being tied behind his back and of blood in the snow.

Franz found himself drawn to the family ikon portraying the patron saint of Russia. Saint Seraphim looked so peaceful hanging on the wall in the gold-embossed wood frame. Looking at it Franz repeated the words of the psalmist over and over, "The Lord is with me; I will not be afraid. What can man do to me?" seeking truth and comfort in the words, craving the presence of God in his crumbling world. Yes, he had learned to fear evil. And he knew what man could do to him.

The question tormenting him was, "My God, my God, why have you forsaken me?" In his prayers he railed against God, "The communists steal from us, they arrest us; they torture and kill us. I understand. This is the way of the world. But the least you can do, my God, is give me the assurance of your presence. I want to feel your reassuring presence! Where is your peace that passes all understanding?" he cried in anguish. And in the darkness of his doubt, he remembered Christ in the garden on the night before his crucifixion, and he remembered Jesus' words upon the cross. He realized, "This is how he felt." The insight brought him a little comfort, but did nothing to dampen his fear.

The threat of returning to prison filled Franz with terror. He trembled when he thought about it. It took all of his willpower to maintain control of himself. Throughout the day, alone in the izba, Franz felt at any moment he might weep. He felt exposed in the hovel beside the road. He had to stop himself from giving in to the urge to run out onto the steppe, to flee as far away as he could go.

Afterward, when he had regained his composure, he would chuckle at the thought of trying to run in his aged body. "I think my bones would rattle apart if I tried to run," he said to the dog lying by his feet.

At other times Franz cowered by the small curtained window and peeked out to look along the road, on guard lest a policeman should surprise him at the door. His fear quite got the better of him for his prayers were met by silence. There was no earthquake, no holy fire, no answering whisper to show he had been heard. The God of Elijah did not come to his rescue. Rather, it seemed to Franz Funk God had abandoned him completely.

On Friday evening Ivan returned to his izba with news that today the police had come to Lyubimovka looking to arrest Franz. As Ivan spoke of what had happened, Franz quickly sat down, afraid, yet encouraged by Ivan's demeanor.

"You woulda bin proud of Anna," he said. "I was in the yard when they knocked on 'er door." His face lit up with pleasure at the recollection. "She didn't bat an eye. She looked the policeman straight in the face and said you wuz in Omsk visiting relatives. Twice!" He chuckled. "After she said it the first time, the policeman didn' b'lieve her. No, she said agin, you wuzn't there. You wuz in Omsk an' wouldn' be back fer two or three weeks. That's what she said!"

Franz was surprised his wife could lie so convincingly. They had always made it a practice to be people who spoke the truth. "What are we becoming," he thought. His gratitude for what Anna had done for him quickly swept away his moral compunctions.

"There wuz two of 'em." Ivan continued his story. "They came an' asked me where you wuz, an' I said you wuz in Omsk, just like Mrs. Funk done. They poked aroun' the farm awhile, lookin' to see if you wuz hidin' in the barn or someplace else. Didn' take long an' they got tired of it an' left."

Franz felt elated. If the police believed Anna's story, they wouldn't return for, perhaps, two more weeks. Maybe, he thought, he could chance a visit to his home. He had to do something to relieve his tension, to escape the small hut that had become his prison. He missed Anna terribly and felt he must see her.

"In that case," Franz announced, "I shall go home. If they think I'm gone for another week or two, I can go home!" He laughed, the weight of the world removed from his shoulders. "Who knows? Perhaps they will forget about me and the whole thing will be over and done!"

The next morning, seven days after he fled, Franz walked home to Lyubimovka. He had wanted to leave the night before, but a summer thunderstorm had struck and it had been too dangerous for him to go out onto the flat steppe. There was no point, he reasoned, to have run from the communists only to be struck by lightning! The air was clean and fresh after the downpour. As the morning glow lit up the horizon, he thought he had never seen such a beautiful sunrise. Hope filled Franz's heart, and his step, as he went along the lane, was light despite his sixty-nine years.

It was Sunday. The Funk family was gathering in their various yards to form a convoy of horse-drawn wagons to go to church. Abe was helping hitch a team to his family's wagon when he saw his grandfather approaching on the road. He watched as Franz jumped the shallow drainage ditch that followed the road through the village. His grandmother was coming down the steps of her house. Abe smiled as he saw his grandfather hurry toward his wife.

When Anna saw her husband coming toward her she gave a short cry, which Franz upon hearing thought to be a cry of delight. Anna covered her mouth with her hand and her eyes flooded with tears.

"Oh, Franz," she cried, "you shouldn't have come!" Her face was crushed into his chest as he hugged her tightly. She pulled away and said again, "Franz, you shouldn't have come! What were you thinking?"

Franz was shocked by her words.

"But, why not?" he asked, fear making his voice high and thin. "Ivan said the police have already come. Surely it is safe for me to be at home for a few days at least. They won't come back so soon."

"But that's just it," said Anna miserably. "The policeman yesterday said they would be back in a day or two. I don't remember what else he said, only that they would be back and they would find you." Her words were running together and she began to cry. "I don't think they believed me. They don't believe you went to Omsk. They're coming back! They might even be coming today!"

Franz was stunned. He leaned on a post of the fence bordering their walkway. He felt faint. Anna was talking, but he could no longer understand her words. They were becoming a strange jumble of sounds. His heart was pounding. His face felt numb. Anna's image became blurred. Blackness overtook him.

As Abe watched his grandparents at the gate, he saw his grandfather fall heavily to the ground. Expecting him to move, to try to get up, Abe ran toward his grandparents' house to help Franz. But Franz did not move.

He heard his grandmother scream for her sons to come. "Help! Johan, George, help! Franz has fallen! Something is wrong with him! Help me!" She knelt over her husband's fallen form and knew not what she could do for him.

By the time Abe reached his grandparents' house, his father had already lifted Franz's limp body. He helped his father support his grandfather, one on either side of him, Franz's arms across their shoulders, as they carried him up the stairs. As they maneuvered themselves through the door, George Willms came huffing up the stairs and took over from Abe.

"Thank you, Abe," his father said. "Now go outside and wait with the others."

In a daze, Abe walked back down the stairs. He clung to the weathered newel post and stared up at the doorway out of which he'd come.

Abe's brother stood beside him.

"Did you see that?" said Wilhelm. His frightened eyes were wide open. "I didn't know Dad could run so fast!"

"Shut up!" said Abe. "Don't you know what's happened? Grandpa's dead! I know he is! He's not moving! I don't think he's breathing! He's dead!"

Still clutching the post, Abe slowly sank down onto the bottom step. He hid his face in his outstretched arms and began to sob.

Chapter 8

August 4, 1929

Franz Funk's favorite possession, aside from his well worn Bible, was his gramophone. Made by Deutsche Grammophon in Hannover, Germany, he and Anna had come upon it in a shop on Nicholsky Prospekt during a visit to Omsk, before the Bolshevik revolution emptied the store shelves. They were both amazed and delighted by the sounds coming from the machine after its mechanism had been wound and the stylus was lowered onto a shellac record. The wooden box housing the mechanism was artfully inlaid and highly polished; the amplifying horn speaker was of thin, burnished brass. Franz decided to make the purchase.

Franz's favorite sound disk was a 1924 Victor recording of Sergei Rachmaninoff playing his Second Piano Concerto accompanied by the Philadelphia Orchestra directed by Leopold Stokowski. He had been surprised to find the recording at the bazaar in Isylkul. Franz did not know how such a thing could happen, but surmised the record had been plundered from some aristocrat's home. Its cover was missing and the disk had been scratched, but the music it played seemed to him to come straight from the heart of God. He loved the tumultuous serenity of the story it told.

While Franz lay on his bed, Anna wound the mechanism and placed the stylus on the disk. She knew the music would comfort her husband. He nodded to her gratefully.

The stroke Franz had suffered the day before left him unable to speak and unable to understand much of what was said to him. His right arm and leg were paralyzed. He lay in his bed unable to comprehend what had happened. The music of Rachmaninoff soothed him. It brought him back to a time when, as a child, on a hot day in Chortitza he had lain in a shallow stream staring at the blue sky above while feeling the steady flow of cool water washing over him from head to foot. Franz closed his eyes and felt the tension leave his body.

Since the hour of their father's stroke, Franz's children and grandchildren had become a steady procession of visitors. They saw him lying on his bed and watched his steady breathing. Aware of his infirmity and unable to express themselves with words, they tenderly touched his arms and caressed his hands. They kissed his cheek and offered bites of food and sips of drink, both of which, more often than not, he refused. Where they could, they helped Anna to keep him comfortable. At seventy-nine years of age, she was too frail to move him. While one helped take care of his bodily needs, another straightened or changed the bed-sheets. They looked at their ailing father and prayed fervently for the restoration of his health. But their faith was tempered with realism and they despaired, knowing there was little hope for his recovery.

It was in the midst of the family's misery, a couple of days after their patriarch's stroke, that young Franz came home with the most unexpected good news. He had been in Isylkul on an errand for his father and had decided to stop at the bazaar—his grandfather had often given him a few kopeks to spend there on anything he wished and he had brought a few along in his pocket. At the bazaar Franz discovered a Mennonite family selling their household goods. The reason why soon came out in conversation and he raced home to tell his family.

"Some families from Slavgorod have left Russia!" Franz could hardly contain his excitement. "The government issued them exit visas!"

"What?" said Johan, astonished. "When?"

"A week ago!"

"This is some rumor you've heard. Can it be true? Who told you this?" Johan could not believe his son's words.

"It's true," insisted Franz. "I was at the bazaar. There was a family selling bedding, plates, furniture, everything! I think their name was Goetz. They're from Uncle Nicholas' village. They said the families who got out sold everything they had and went to Moscow determined to leave the country."

Franz laughed.

"The women with their babies sat in the hot office until it began to stink from all the full diapers. After a couple of days of this, the people in the office couldn't sign the papers fast enough to get rid of the smell and crying babies. The Goetz's are going to go to Moscow to try the same thing. They said they've heard of other families planning to go as well."

The next day, Johan traveled to the Goetz's village to confirm the story his son had told him. When he returned, Elizabeth met him at the door.

"It is true!" he said, as Franz came and stood beside his mother. This was the news Elizabeth had been waiting for.

"Then we must go," was her firm response. "We must go to Moscow. They succeeded. We will, too. We have to leave this godforsaken land."

Johan stood quietly for a long moment. He looked out at the fields with their ripening grain—it looked like this year's crop would be a good one. How could he walk away from it and from all that was familiar to him? He saw Pavel Dmitrienko herding the village's cows down the street, bringing them home for the evening milking. The cows plodded along. Pavel rode his horse behind them. Johan had observed this ritual every morning and evening all the days of his life. He watched one cow walk into its owner's yard.

"The cow knows where its home is," Johan thought. "It will walk straight to the barn where it is kept and know which stall to enter. It is content. Where is our home? Where will we have peace?" He looked at his wife and son. There were tears in his eyes. "Yes," he said, "we will go to Moscow."

That night Johan and Elizabeth went to inform his mother they were leaving Lyubimovka. As they entered the room where she sat beside her husband's bed, Johan's sister, Sara, and her husband Cornelius were on their way out. Sara was crying.

Johan looked at his mother. Wisps of grey hair framed her wrinkled face. Her back, as she sat, was stooped, but her gaze was clear and strong. Her fingers—knuckles swollen by arthritis—worked a set of needles as she knitted what looked to be a pair of woolen socks. She was using wool salvaged from old socks that were worn past repairing. Long practice had taught her hands to work unsupervised.

"How is father?" Johan asked.

Anna paused in her knitting. She looked at her husband, then at Johan and Elizabeth.

"He is dying," she said softly. And then she added, "I know why you are here."

Johan heaved a great melancholy sigh.

"Sara told me about the people in Moscow," his mother continued. Johan's resolve crumbled. "They are thinking about leaving as well."

"You cannot be left here alone," he blurted. "We will stay." The words came in a rush and he meant to say more, but his mother cut him off.

"No, Johan. No," she said firmly. "You must not stay. There is no future for you or your children here in this country. You must leave."

When Johan made to argue with her, she stood and refused to allow him to speak.

"Do not think to change my mind. I am an old woman. I have had a good life. This is where I belong. You must go and find a place where you can make a better life for your children."

"But what about father?" Johan asked.

"Vera will help me. And Ivan. We will manage." She looked at her husband sadly and took his hand in hers. "My beloved Franz is not long for this world. And when he is gone, perhaps I will soon be able to follow him."

Anna felt Franz's hand squeeze hers. He had opened his eyes and he was looking hard at Johan. He was trying to say something. His lips were forming a word. Johan leaned down close to his father's face.

"Go," his father whispered, "go."

The next morning Johan got out the box in which he kept his family's savings. After he had counted the kopeks and rubles, he quickly realized there was not enough money to pay for the unknown costs of railway tickets, exit visas, and ship's passage, not to mention food and lodging during their stay in Moscow—and who knew how long that would be?

It was quickly decided, aside from the few things they would take with them, the family's belongings would need to be sold at the bazaar in Isylkul. Household items, farming tools, everything must go. Each member of the family looked longingly at things precious to them as they were taken away. It was especially difficult to part with their beautiful musical instruments: Johan's guitar, Franz's violin, Abe's mandolin.

"We must sell them," insisted Johan. "The communists would only confiscate them. They'd never let us take them out of the country."

Selling the horses was also difficult. They were calm, steady animals that had served the family well. Abe thought of the many times he had ridden the workhorses to the pond for a swim. He would hang on to their tails while they paddled and frolicked in their own way in the water. What fun it had been. And then there was Franz's prized gelding. The horse was fast; he had won many a race with him—had also been thrown by him and knocked unconscious when the horse baulked during one such race; his brothers racing to his rescue had thought he was dead for sure—and Franz cried as his horse was led away by his new owner.

Elizabeth wept silently as her grandfather's clock—her one possession connecting her with her family in south Russia—was loaded onto the wagon. She had seen her sisters and their husbands only a few times over the years, when they had come to Lyubimovka for a visit. "Will I ever see any of them again?" she wondered as the gravity of their move sunk in.

Still, with nearly everything gone, there was deemed to be insufficient money for their anticipated needs.

One day, Johan and his eldest son were standing by their barn, worrying about the unknown that faced them. Two men they had never seen before came onto their yard and approached them. They shook hands and greeted one another.

"We understand you're selling out," said one. "Going away are you?" It was a rhetorical question. The speaker knew the answer.

Johan was alarmed. Their leaving was not exactly a secret. But no one knew beyond their circle of acquaintances. The family had been careful not to draw attention to itself at the bazaar. But strangers approaching them, knowing they were leaving, could mean trouble. Who knew how the authorities would react?

The second stranger noted Johan's alarm.

"Not to worry," he said to Johan. "We're very discrete."

"Yah, we ain't no friends with the Bolsheviks," said the other. He eyed Johan and then decided to continue. "We have a proposition for you."

Johan looked from one to the other. "What is it you want?"

"We'd like to buy your crop. You see, our fields aren't lookin' too good. Don't think we had as much snow in winter as you. Our fields dried out too soon. And, well, you know the kind of taxes we're goin' to have to pay. We're likely not goin' to have enough grain to do it. So, we're just thinkin' ahead. Since you're leaving, maybe we could harvest yours." He paused to let his words sink in. "It's just goin' to rot in the field otherwise."

The other stranger added, "We can pay cash. We have the money with us."

Since communist regulations made it impossible for Johan to sell his land or buildings, this was the best scenario he could have hoped for. His heart skipped a beat as he wondered what the men were playing at.

"Are you serious?" he asked.

One of the men took a large wad of rubles out of his pocket. "Yes, sir, we are."

Johan looked at the men more closely. They didn't look like farmers, though their story was a good one. He thought, "If they're farmers, then I'm the mayor of Isylkul." Yet, who was he to quibble about legalities? At this point, leaving was all that mattered and the money would go a long way in helping them pay for the journey.

A price was soon settled upon and the money exchanged hands. As the men left the yard, Franz let out a whoop and ran to tell Elizabeth. Johan walked quickly to catch up.

"Surely," he thought, "we now have more than enough money to make it to Canada."

The time soon came when Johan and Elizabeth and their children were ready to leave Lyubimovka. The evening before they were to go, they had gathered in Franz and Anna's great room to say their farewells. The whole family had been there: aunts, uncles, and cousins.

Johan and Elizabeth had said good-bye to his father earlier in the day. He wept silently as they bent to hug him. Though he could not respond to their soft words, they knew he understood the finality of their meeting. Each of the children kissed their grandfather on the cheek and said good-bye. The older ones knew they would never see him again; the younger ones in their innocence and tears did not.

Johan had decided the best time to leave would be in the middle of the night. Anna insisted on seeing them off. Standing strong in the midst of her departing family, she gave each a tight hug. Anna wept freely, but tried to smile through her tears. It had been agreed, should Johan and his family still be in Moscow when Franz died, he would return for his mother.

"Don't worry, Mother," Johan reassured her. "I will come back for you. We will not leave you here. You are going to come with us."

Anna hugged Johan again. His words cheered her, but they also brought more sadness, because if they came true, it would mean her dear husband was dead.   Anna again hugged each one in turn: Johan, Elizabeth, Franz, Abe, Wilhelm, Maria, and Katrina.

"Yes," Anna said, wanting to believe the words. "I will see you all again in Moscow. And if not in Moscow, then in heaven."

Going out into the dark of night, the family clambered onto the wagon that would take them to the railway station. It belonged to Cornelius and Sara. Johan and Cornelius sat on the driver's seat. Everyone else sat on the wagon bed.

"Children," warned Johan, "when we get close to town, you are to remain silent. Not one word, do you hear?" he repeated. "We don't want to arouse any suspicion. Now, crawl under the blankets and try to sleep. Cover yourselves completely. If anyone happens to glance at our wagon, they must only see two men going about their business."

Elizabeth helped the family to get as comfortable as could be managed on the wooden slats amongst their bags and boxes of possessions. She lay down with them and covered herself. "Okay, Johan," she muttered, aware of her own discomfort.

Johan looked back at the bed of the wagon and nodded, satisfied everything was in order. Cornelius flicked the reins and the horses willingly pulled away toward the road. Aside from the clop, clop of the horses' hooves on the hard ground, all was silent. The bells had been removed from the horses' harnesses to lessen chances of their passing being noted.

Johan gazed up into the sky. All of the familiar stars in their constellations were keeping watch over their flight. "I wonder what stars we will see in Canada," he idly thought.

Johan looked back one final time at the home he was leaving. He saw his mother, Anna, still stood on the steps to her home, her frail figure backlit by the kerosene lamp on the stand behind her. She looked small and vulnerable. Anna waved a lonely hand before turning and disappearing into the house.

Part 2
Moscow

Beneath storm's vestment, on the seaway,
battling along that watery freeway,
when shall I start on my escape?

Pushkin
—Eugene Onegin

Chapter 9

August 25, 1929

Together with a group of men and women who were anxiously waiting for distant relatives to arrive, Peter Froese stood on the platform of the Yaroslavsky Railway Station on Kalanchyovskaya Square north and east of Moscow's nearby city center. It had become his habit since word of exit visas and passports being issued by the government jolted the desperate Mennonites of Siberia to action, as surely as if a great dam had been breached. The floodwaters—which would soon also include Mennonites from south Russia, and, indeed, Russians of German extraction from all corners of the land—were increasingly overflowing the gap and daily more and more refugees were pouring out of the Trans-Siberian railcars. Bags around their feet, surrounded by their excited children, the bewildered, determined adults needed all the assistance they could get as they adapted to life in the unfamiliar surroundings of the city of Moscow. No matter what their hopes and expectations were, he knew from experience they were in for a long struggle.

In the days following the abdication of Tsar Nicholas II in March 1917, Peter Froese dedicated his life to the lofty goal of ensuring the well-being of the Mennonites in Russia. He and other like-minded leaders moved to Moscow where they lobbied the fledgling government as its new policies were being formed. He worked out of an office appropriately called the Menno Centre, helping to coordinate relief shipments from North America when famine devastated the Mennonite colonies in south Russia. He was chairman of the All-Russian Mennonite Agricultural Union. Each of the organizations in which he participated was eventually dissolved by government action and most of their members were imprisoned. Peter Froese did not know it on this day, but by the end of October, he too would be arrested and sentenced to years in exile, away from his Russian wife and their young children.

Peter Froese was a tall man. The confident smile on his clean-shaven face and his clear gaze belied the stress under which he lived. He knew he was being watched. Everything he did was seen and recorded by members of the Joint State Political Directorate or GPU, the feared secret police.

On this day, as the train from Novosibirsk and points west sighed to a stop in Yaroslavsky Station, Froese watched as another group of tired travelers gathered on the platform. He knew immediately they were Mennonite refugees because of their clothing and their language. They were not dressed as typical Russians and he could hear them loudly speaking their Low-German dialect. Inwardly Froese cringed. He wished his people had more tact. The authorities were getting antsy about the number of refugees coming to the city. Each week hundreds of them were arriving. He had lost count of the number, but thought it might soon be in the thousands. It was only a matter of time before the militia or the secret police began to act, and from experience he knew that was never good.

The group on the platform swelled to about eighty or so. Other passengers leaving the train muttered and glared at the crowd as they maneuvered around them on the narrow platform. Soon bags were shrugged onto shoulders and children were corralled. As the refugees made their wide-eyed way to the exit doors some were met by excited relatives. Bundles were immediately dropped as the new arrivals were joyously greeted. Others in the group watched these meetings enviously, wishing for such a warm welcome and the comfort of knowing someone familiar with their strange new surroundings.

Froese joined the chaotic assembly and introduced himself.

Johan Funk was relieved to finally be able to leave the train. The trip from Isylkul had taken a long four days and nights. Sleep had been difficult. The cars were crowded. Crammed together on hard wooden benches, the family had had to use shoulders and laps as pillows. Katrina had eventually become over-tired and cranky. Elizabeth had developed a migraine. Maria and Wilhelm were anxious after leaving their familiar surroundings in Lyubimovka, and had become clingy with their weary mother who longed only for a dark room and a comfortable bed.

As her children stepped off of the train Elizabeth called to her oldest sons. "Franz, take Maria's and Wilhelm's hands. Do not let them out of your sight. Abe, take Katrina. Katrina stay close to Abe," she called fearing Katrina might be run over by a train rumbling nearby, its boilers rolling, but its wheels still, as steam gushed from its whistling safety release valves.

As the new arrivals continued their way along the platform, Franz and Abe were excited and ready to face whatever came next. They took their younger siblings in hand and drew their attention to the magnificent station in which they found themselves. They stared and pointed at the large, ornate hammer and sickle atop the building's tall peaked roof and at its gabled windows standing out like two eyes espying their arrival. An octagonal spire topped by a red star towered at one end of the station. The other end of the station looked like the guardhouse of a medieval castle, with arched windows through which, Abe imagined, men with guns were watching them closely. He was tempted to make a joke, but thought the better of it when he saw his little sister was already frightened by the noise and the strangeness of the vast station.

The children paid little attention to the emotional greetings happening around them, as far-flung relatives found each other after long and tense absences. The Funks knew no one in Moscow and so they expected no such welcome. It was Franz who called his father's attention to the man approaching them. He was wearing a black fedora and light grey overcoat. The man was somehow different in his bearing than everyone else; there was a calm surety about him. When he cleared his throat, everyone turned their eyes to him.

"Welcome to Moscow, brothers and sisters."

There were a few murmured words of thank you and not a few looks of suspicion. Communism had taught everyone strangers were at best not to be trusted, and at worst to be feared. Children's hands were more tightly gripped; coat lapels were tugged together in instinctive gestures of self-preservation. Who was this man who spoke their language and met them as though they were expected?

"My name is Peter Franz Froese. I am here to greet you and welcome you to Moscow. I will not keep you long. I can see you are tired by your long journey." He paused and smiled as his words elicited cautious nods. "I am also here to help you answer the questions of where you will sleep tonight, and what you will eat tomorrow. This is a big city, and as you might imagine, the authorities are not all that interested in your presence here."

Froese smiled again. He knew at the moment the trickle of refugees was an irritant to the government. When the trickle turned to a raging torrent, which he knew it would, the government's reaction would be much stronger.

The refugees who now surrounded him visibly relaxed as his kind words were understood. The fact he was a Froese perked their ears. He was one of them.

Trying to gain the trust of the wary travelers, Froese said, "You may have heard of me through some of my work helping with famine relief, or that little agricultural magazine we published for a while."

There were sudden murmurs of recognition. In his excitement someone whispered to his neighbor this was Abraham Froese's son, "You know, the Froeses from the Memrik settlement on the Volshya River. They came originally from the Molotschna." His neighbor nodded vigorously as the connection was made.

Froese looked around to see if any workers or other passengers who were not connected with this group were still loitering on the platform. Seeing none, he continued. "Somehow, our communist leaders find relief committees and agricultural magazines distasteful." He chuckled. "Feeding the hungry and providing advice on how to improve our farming methods are considered to be anti-revolutionary activities in this new Russia, this Union of Soviet Socialist Republics."

Several of his listeners laughed at his words. Their cynicism allowed them to see the humor in what he said. Others looked uncomfortable and glanced here and there to see if anyone was listening beyond their group. They thought this man to be careless. He could be arrested for such comments.

Johan, too, was a little unsettled by Froese's speech. Nevertheless, he admired his bravery and forthrightness. Froese wasn't afraid to say things as they were, even here, in this public place.

"And that is why you are all here, yes?" continued Froese. "You, like all the rest of us, have been pushed to the limit and have had enough. You want to get out of this country that has been our home for one hundred and fifty years. It is time for all of us to move on and find a new land, a new home. We are like Moses in Egypt standing before a stubborn pharaoh, asking to let his people Israel go. What we all need is permission to leave."

Everyone was nodding their heads now. Froese's words struck deep and their truth raised the spirits of the tired travelers.

"Yes," thought Johan, "we will stand before Stalin and demand he let us leave this country." And in his heart he quaked, for he knew now that they had left Lyubimovka it would be very difficult to go back. "Once it becomes known," he thought, "what we are attempting—to get out of Russia—what will the local soviet in Isylkul have to say about it if we are forced to return because we have failed?" And he thought, "No, we will not fail. We cannot."

"But enough of that for now." Froese was smiling again. "Before we can shake the gates of the Kremlin, we must find you beds upon which you can lay your heads and we must get you ration cards so you will have bread to eat. You will need much strength for what lies ahead."

And with that, Froese gave each family the name of a person to contact and the address of a home in which they could stay. He had a list of dachas to the north of the city, unoccupied summer homes, where the refugees could find accommodation. Of course, some of those who had been met by relatives were already assured of places to stay, so they gratefully declined the offer.

After each family had anxiously read their assignment, Froese again called everyone's attention to himself.

"It is vitally important each family present itself at the militia headquarters in Perlovka. You must register your presence in Moscow with the local authorities. There you will receive your ration card. Without it, you will not be able to buy any bread or milk." He paused. "At least, not legally. You may be able to find a farmer willing to sell you some vegetables or something on the side, but I strongly recommend you resist that temptation. Black marketeers and their customers are regularly arrested and imprisoned.

"I would suggest when you apply for your passports, go as a group. The Soviets will not deal with you as individuals for you are nothing to them. You must take advantage of the strength of your numbers. You must force them to listen to your appeal by virtue of the fact that you are many."

Faces grew long at the reminder of the task to come. But Froese smiled and his composure was reassuring.

"For now, go and find your lodgings. Get settled. Rest. Together, and with God's help, we will bend the will of Stalin and soon find freedom in a new land."

Everyone standing in that ragged group of hopeful refugees felt their hearts swell at his words, and their resolve to accomplish that which they had come for hardened. And each thought and prayed fervently, "God willing, the land to which I am bound is Canada."

Chapter 10

August 25, 1929

It was twilight by the time the Funks arrived in Perlovka. A stiff breeze was coming out of the south. It bent and swayed the tops of the fir trees growing plentifully in the area. The setting sun was turning the scudding clouds a roiling array of oranges and reds.

The transfer to the northbound train—a recently completed line from Moscow to Yaroslavl—had been straightforward because it left from the Yaroslavsky Station, wherein they had arrived. The twelve-kilometers trip passed by quickly. Everyone was tired because of the long days of travel, and tense from wondering what kind of accommodation waited at their destination. Most of the people with whom the Funks were traveling left the train at Perlovka. The rest continued on north and got off at communities with names such as Tayninka, Kljasma, and Pushkino. Over the next several months, all those communities and more would be over-run with refugees seeking shelter.

After leaving the railway platform, the Funks walked along the dirt roads of Perlovka, stopping occasionally to ask for directions to the dacha to which they had been assigned. The community presented itself as a shabby suburb of Moscow, though once it had been the playground of the rich. Those days were gone as surely as was the Tsar, dead and buried. Dachas that had served as summer retreats now provided roofs over the heads of those who could come up with the usurious prices charged, though as often as not the roofs were in a state of alarming disrepair. Johan quickly became confused in the hodge-podge of lanes branching off of the main road, ominously named Dzerzhinsky Ulitsa, after the Polish nobleman who for years had been in charge of Lenin's secret police—Dzerzhinsky died of a heart attack in 1926 and since then it seemed every community had dutifully renamed a road in his honor. Those passers-by the Funks met were distant and uncommunicative.

They had little interest in talking to a strange family lugging bundles and boxes of possessions on the darkening forest road.

Johan and Elizabeth were becoming discouraged and thinking they may need to bed down for the night in the forest when they met an old babushka. She was a small granny with a stooped back. Her face was thin and wrinkled with the lines of age on skin that had seen too much sun. A drab kerchief draping almost down to her bare feet covered her hair. She smiled shyly when Johan politely asked in Russian about the dacha the Funks sought, and kindly led them to its front door. Her home was nearby.

In the dim light, Johan could make out the gingerbread scrollwork decorating the dacha's windows and roofline. It gave the house a playful look, though the effect was ruined because some of the scrollwork had come loose and draped down at odd angles. When they entered the dacha, Johan and Elizabeth were less than impressed by its size and condition. It was a small cottage, perhaps fifteen square meters in size, a quarter of the size of their modest home in Lyubimovka. Its furnishings were sparse. Elizabeth groaned at the lack of a stove on which to cook the family's meals. Johan noted immediately there was no Russian oven for heat, should the cold of winter catch them still living there. He sincerely hoped it wouldn't.

The dacha had two double beds with padded mattresses that, in Elizabeth's eyes, had definitely seen better days. However, tired as they were, she quickly laid blankets on the beds. Johan and Elizabeth shared one bed while Maria and Katrina shared the other. The boys lay on rollups on the floor. The night was warm, and everyone was soon fast asleep.

Little Katrina was crying. The morning sun laid a bright patch though the window onto the floor where Abe and Wilhelm slept. Franz was nowhere to be seen. Elizabeth shook off her sleep.

"What is it, Katrina?" she asked.

"I'm all itchy."

As Elizabeth became more awake, hearing Katrina's complaint, she realized she too was itching on her arms and legs. She got up and went to the window where she examined her skin in the brighter light.

She knew immediately what it was.

"Bedbugs!" she muttered. "Ach, Johan, wake up! We have bedbugs!"

By this time everyone was awake and scratching and Elizabeth was incensed.

"What kind of hole have we found ourselves in that we are all bitten by bedbugs as we sleep!" she fumed.

Elizabeth knew what must be done and quickly began giving orders. Franz was just returning from a trip to the outhouse in time to hear his name shouted.

"Where is Franz?" Elizabeth demanded to know.

"I'm here, Mother."

"Good! Where have you been—no, never mind. We have bedbugs. Everyone has been bitten!"

"I haven't any bites," said Peter.

"Well, lucky you!" growled his mother. "Help your father get these mattresses and rollups out of the house. Put them in the yard where the sun will shine on them for most of the day." Looking at the younger boys, she commanded, "Gather as many dried sticks and branches as you can find. We're going to need a hot fire. And girls," she added looking at Maria and Katrina who were examining their arms and legs with stricken expressions on their faces, "Stop scratching. It won't help and you will only make bigger sores that will bleed. See if you can find any large pots in the cupboard over there." She pointed to a cabinet on the other side of the room.

"But Mama," shuddered Maria, "it's so creepy!"

"Never mind, Maria. They're just bugs. Don't make it worse for Katrina. Now get busy."

Finished with her orders, Elizabeth rushed outside to find a suitable place for a fire. Fortunately, in the yard the boys had already discovered a large circle of stones topped by an iron grate. It was obviously the dacha's outdoor fire pit. Soon Maria and Katrina arrived with two good-sized metal pots and a huge dipper. It wasn't long before the boys brought arms-full of wood. Wilhelm excitedly announced a stream ran through the woods close by. A bucket was found and the boys were sent to fetch water. Johan produced a box of matches and a fire was lit.

For the rest of the morning, water was boiled and poured on the mattresses laid out in the yard. Happily, the day produced a hot August afternoon and evening. With any luck, the mattresses might be dry enough to sleep upon that night. If not, everyone was willing to spread a blanket on the grass and dry evergreen needles under the trees. Anything was better than another night spent feeding bedbugs.

Early in the afternoon the owner of the dacha appeared. He was a short man, unremarkable in appearance beyond his flaming red beard. He doffed his visor cap as a courtesy to Elizabeth, who was acutely embarrassed to be found with her sleeves rolled up, her skirt tied above her knees, and most of her worldly possessions spread about in the yard.

"What's this then?" he asked, without introducing himself.

"Bedbugs," was all Elizabeth could say between her clenched teeth.

Hearing the stranger's voice, Johan appeared from the dacha's door. Taking the initiative, he stepped outside and greeted the man. "Can I help you?" he asked. He found the presence of a stranger at his door disconcerting.

Without so much as a reference to the plague Elizabeth had mentioned, the man spoke matter-of-factly, "This is my place. I was told you'd be here. Rent is two hundred and fifty rubles for a seven-month term. Non-negotiable; I won't rent it to you for any less. It's not worth the bother. Pay me in cash today. Take it or pack your things and leave."

"We're happy to pay," said Johan, trying to mollify the brusque man. He hurried into the dacha. Returning quickly with the money, he counted it out into the landlord's outstretched hand.

Stuffing the wad of rubles into his pocket the man looked at Elizabeth. "Mind you look after the place now. Wouldn't want any pests livin' here!" And he laughed uproariously at his joke.

Elizabeth gritted her teeth and ignored the gibe. Getting no response, the man turned and left.

Sometime during the day, a primus stove was found in the dacha's attic. Fortunately, there was kerosene in its tank, so tea was brewed and the last of the rusks—buns baked twice so they wouldn't spoil on the journey from Lyubimovka to Moscow—were eaten.

Later that evening, as she tried to get comfortable lying on a blanket laid over the cushion of fir needles, aspen leaves and dried grass on the ground behind the dacha, Elizabeth grumbled to Johan, "Those mattresses had better be dry tomorrow." After a moment she added, "You are going to have to find food for the family. We have nothing left."

Johan nodded agreement and wondered what the morrow would hold for them. "We will register with the militia tomorrow. Then we will receive our ration cards."

Lying on his back, Johan looked up at the blaze of stars overhead. The limbs of the fir and aspen trees grasped at the darkness in between. He thought of the sky over Lyubimovka and the many nights over the years he had stared at the stars there. These were the same stars; he recognized the constellations though he didn't know their names. Johan wondered if the stars seen in Canada's skies were also these same beacons of light. He thought so, for wasn't Canada also in the northern hemisphere? He marveled at the beauty displayed in the heavens and wondered what lay beyond it. "Where does God abide?" he thought.

Johan's thoughts turned to his father and mother left behind. Not really knowing what to say, he whispered a prayer. He knew his father would die, but did not know when. "And if we are able to leave Russia, and if Father is still alive when we go, what will become of Mother?"

Johan lay alone with his thoughts in the darkness, how long he did not know. Elizabeth lay quietly beside him, her back to him, occasionally moving or sighing a little. It seemed sleep was also avoiding her. Johan turned on his side. Reaching toward his wife, he tickled the nape of her neck. Elizabeth gave a start and, turning, swatted his hand.

"Ach, Johan, I thought it was a bug!" she muttered.

Johan chuckled. He gave his wife a slow kiss. Then, looking around, he saw the children were all asleep in their blankets. He nudged Elizabeth.

"Let's go further into the woods," he breathed into her ear.

The moon was full and by its light they found a glade with a mossy floor. Lying upon their blanket, Johan and Elizabeth made love with an urgency coming from the instinctive, latent fear hidden deep within them that tomorrow might not come.

Which, of course, it did. And Elizabeth knew immediately, upon waking up, that she was pregnant with her seventh child.

Chapter 11

August 26, 1929

The next day Johan, Elizabeth and their children made their way to Number 3 Molodyozhnaya Street, the office of the local militia where they were required to register their presence in Perlovka. Once they were registered they hoped to receive their ration cards. Everyone was hungry, especially the younger children. By the evening they would be ravenous. It was essential the family be given the necessary papers that would allow them to purchase food.

As they walked along the road in the bright morning sunshine, Johan looked about him. Many dachas could be seen amongst the trees of the forest, the decorated slope of a roof here, a window reflecting morning light through the bushes there. From what he observed, the once proud dachas were generally in a state of disrepair, needing the attention that came with the pride of ownership, a virtue Johan knew was in short supply in the new Russia. In the forest, he saw the white trunks of aspen trees standing out amongst the dark evergreens. Except for their green crowns of fluttering leaves stretching skyward in search of light, the lower branches of the aspens were completely naked, barren of leaves. One could see death creeping up their long, elegant columns. Johan noticed some trees had succumbed. Branches once rich in sap were now dry, useful only for the fires of those who would one day cut them down.

When the family arrived at the militia's office, Johan noticed a table had been set up outside on the side of the road in front of the building and a long line of families already waiting to be registered. Adults huddled together while their children kicked at the dirt or scratched in it with sticks. Few were talking and those who did spoke in soft tones. There was no laughter. Johan recognized a few families as having accompanied them on their train from the east. He nodded to them when they made eye contact. Others he didn't recognize, but he heard German being spoken and knew most of the people in the line were Mennonite refugees like his family. Tension was in the air and he soon saw why.

Two members of the militia seated at the desk were asking questions of the family standing before them. The militiamen wore dun-colored caps with red stars pinned on. Thick, dark beards covered their faces. Sharp Slavic cheekbones and dark eyes peered out from underneath the thick eyebrows. Occasionally one of the men wrote something on a piece of paper.

Standing beside and behind the desk was a group of rough looking men. Aside from anything else they may have been wearing, the holstered pistols on their hips, held firmly in place by a belt around the waist with a strap over the left shoulder, drew everyone's fearful glances. Even the militiamen seemed threatened by their presence. They continually scanned the crowd and everyone instinctively avoided their gaze. One of them was looking over the shoulder of the seated militiamen at what was being written.

A man standing in the line in front of the Funks turned and whispered to Johan, "Secret police." He nodded in the direction of the uniformed men. "They're GPU."

Johan knew the man from the train. His name was Jacob Hildebrandt. They had talked a bit about their plans and had instantly formed a bond when they discovered both families were traveling to Moscow for the same reason.

Johan's heart skipped a beat at Hildebrandt's words. "What are the secret police doing here?" he whispered.

He quickly looked to see if his children had heard. He didn't want to alarm them. The children were occupied with their own little game, drawing circles in the dirt roadway. They seemed oblivious to what was happening around them. Only Franz and Elizabeth had heard the exchange.

"They're not here for us," said Elizabeth quietly. "We have done nothing wrong—have we, Johan?" she added suddenly unsure. Was it illegal to leave one's home and loved ones in order to attempt emigration? What new law were they perhaps unaware of?

"See that door over there," said Hildebrandt pointing to an opening on the side of the building. "They're taking men from the line and hauling them in there. I don't know what it's about, but it can't be good. We can't hear what's going on and, of course, the people up front who can aren't going to turn around and tell us."

Johan's heart sank. As he looked at the door Hildebrandt had shown him, Johan noticed some women and children standing forlornly near it. He could see their faces streaked with anxiety and fear.

A commotion drew Johan's attention back to the table in front of the militia office. Two of the secret policemen had come around the table and had taken the man standing there firmly by the arms. As they led him away, his wife began to weep and plead with them to let him go. Grabbing each of her two children by the hand, she followed the policemen as they guided her husband through the doorway and into the building. Seconds later she reappeared as she, together with her children, was roughly shoved back outside. The policeman said not a word but slammed shut the door. The mother and children stood upon the grass looking at the building, stunned by their sudden misfortune.

Quiet returned to the street. Those in the line waiting their turn were silent. Afraid they might be next to be singled out by the secret police, they stood stone-faced, fidgeting, looking at their shoes, at the ground. Tension emanated from the queue like electricity crackling through a high-voltage wire. Those who summoned the courage glanced occasionally at the doorway through which the unfortunate man had disappeared.

"He's the fourth one," muttered Hildebrandt nervously to Johan.

"But, why?" whispered Johan.

"Who knows?" responded Hildebrandt. "Do they need a reason?"

By the time it was Johan's turn to speak to the militiaman at the desk, two other men had been led away, followed by their distraught families.

Johan found he was having trouble breathing. He thought a quick prayer and stepped forward with his family.

"Names?" The militiaman spoke slowly. He licked the stub of his pencil as he waited for Johan's reply. After all of their names had been recorded, the man asked, "Where are ya from?"

"Isylkul. Omsk Oblast," said Johan.

"You have accommodation? Where are ya stayin'?"

Johan gave him the address.

"Reason fer comin' to Perlovka?"

Johan thought for a moment. "What should I say?" he wondered. He quickly decided. Trying to remain as calm as possible, he said, "We are poor farmers. Life is very hard for us back home. We have little education. We are in Perlovka only temporarily while we apply for passports and wait for permission to travel. We have family in Canada and would like to join them there." His hands were shaking as he finished; he clasped them together behind his back.

The militiaman glared at Johan with annoyance. Johan did not dare to raise his eyes to look at the secret police. He felt burned by their scrutinizing gaze. Abruptly the man stamped a paper and gave it to Johan.

"Go two doors down the street to the left. Present this paper and your family will be issued ration cards."

Johan gratefully took the paper from the table. "Thank you, Comrade," he said with relief. Gathering his family around him, he turned quickly away from the office of the militia.

"I'm not yer comrade," he heard the militiaman mutter.

"I hope we never have to do that again," said Elizabeth when they were a safe distance away.

"Ah, but there are many visits to government offices ahead of us, dear," said Johan. "This is only the beginning."

It was only a matter of walking down the street and around a corner before Johan saw where the queue was re-forming a short distance away. The newcomers to Perlovka would need to be patient once again as they waited to receive their ration cards. The self-important, semi-literate apparatchik—the minor communist bureaucrat—who manned the office was in no hurry to oblige the line of families filling the room and spilling out onto the road. Though they presented the required officially stamped paperwork, he examined each document minutely and asked endless questions. He seemed to personally resent handing out the cards guaranteeing the refugees would not starve, as if he were the keeper of the gate and they were attempting to storm his stronghold. In his mind, they did not belong in Perlovka, and should be banished back to the villages from whence they'd come.

Standing patiently as he waited his turn, Johan overheard Hildebrandt speaking with another fellow in the line in front of him.

"God answered our prayers," said Hildebrandt with genuine relief. "I was afraid I would be next to be hauled away by the GPU! As I waited, I prayed fervently to the Lord that He would protect my family and me. I give the glory to God; I made it safely through the militia's line and I will now be able to buy bread for our family."

"Yes," said the other fellow. "God answered my prayer as well!"

Johan turned to Hildebrandt and his friend. "I, too, prayed," he said, trying to contain his anger. "But what about the men who were taken away? We knew one of them. He was on the train with us. Was his name Rempel? He prayed often on the journey through the Urals to Moscow. And the other men who were taken away? Do you think for a moment they were not praying to be protected? Do you dare to suggest God said yes to you and no to them?"

Hildebrandt looked puzzled. He could not grasp the meaning behind the question. "But what then did you pray for?" he asked.

"That I would be strengthened to endure whatever came my way."

Hildebrandt shrugged. "God's ways are mysterious. He is sovereign. He does as He wills. Who am I to question how He works?"

Hildebrandt became uncomfortable under Johan's incredulous look and turned away.

Chapter 12

September 1929

September was a time of slow change. The weather remained warm, though temperatures began to drop at night. The aspen trees mingling with the firs in the forests of Perlovka became somnolent and over the weeks their vibrant greens began to turn to more vibrant yellows so that by the end of the month the forest seemed crowned in gold. The aspen's dying leaves quaked on the evening breezes. Hearing the sound of the rustling leaves, more than one refugee looked out of her window or doorway expecting to see rain. As the yellow leaves fell to the earth in ever-increasing numbers, they created the effect on the ground of millions of gold coins strewn about in a wildly random fashion. But, of course, it was a sham. And the refugees gathered at the gates of Moscow brushed the leaves aside as they foraged for firewood in anticipation of the expected cold of winter, and prayed that they would not still be there to endure it.

After registering his family with the local militia, Johan Funk sought out other men with whom he might go as a group to apply for passports at the government office. It did not take long, for he knew some who had traveled with him on the train to Moscow and there were many others who had recently arrived. Indeed, when he and his companions took the train south to Yaroslavsky Station, Johan was amazed to see the platform crowded with Mennonites greeting each other as more and more refugees joined the rush to the capital. The groups of tens had quickly become groups of hundreds of those traveling together in the hope of being allowed to leave the country of their birth.

Johan was not to know, but thousands of refugees had already arrived in Moscow and thousands would continue to come until the worried Soviets declared it illegal to sell tickets to Germans wanting to travel to the capital city. Even so, the flood continued as desperate people found ways to ride the train to the place they hoped would one day lead to their freedom. All of Moscow's northern suburbs became crowded with refugees looking for shelter. Many families were forced to share small communal spaces. Some refugees, in their haste upon hearing the rumor passports were being issued, simply left everything behind and came to Moscow with little money. It became illegal to hold auction sales and those caught selling their household goods at the bazaar could be arrested. So they came with nothing but their clothes and a few other pitiful belongings. Others had their money stolen by ruthless militiamen or petty thieves. In either case, the unexpected and lengthening time of waiting forced many to rely on the goodwill of family or friends for support. It became common to see refugees begging on the street.

When Johan and his friends arrived at Yaroslavsky Railway Station in Moscow, they walked the three and a half kilometers southwest to Staraya Square where they had been told was the office where they could apply for passports. For hundreds of years, Staraya, or Old, Square, had been used as a flea market. In reality, it was simply the wide street following the wall within the Kitay-gorod kremlin. A kremlin referred to a fortress within the city, of which the city of Moscow had many. The Kitay-gorod fortress was built next to the Moscow kremlin and was the city's commercial centre for centuries, while the Moscow fortress was the Russian empire's centre of government. The Staraya market had thrived for four hundred years within the fortress until the bazaar was dismantled in 1899, thirty years before Johan walked upon its paving stones. In the years before the outbreak of the First World War, the Moscow Merchant Society commissioned the construction of a chain of grand office buildings in the Square that, since the communist revolution, had been taken over for government use.

Walking along Kitaisky Lane on the outside of the six meter-high fortress wall, the group came to an opening where the wall had been partially dismantled. Stepping though, they continued along the road on the inner side of what was left of the wall and came to Number 4. Johan looked up at the massive stone and glass building. It stood six stories tall, with strong symmetric vertical lines, and seemed to occupy the entire city block. It made Johan feel very small. Worse, when he had first seen the building, Johan had spotted a red flag snapping in the breeze on the mast high atop its distant ramparts. Standing on the sidewalk by its front door and craning his neck so he could see upward, the flag was not now visible, but he knew its proud display represented all he had come to hate about Russia. His stomach tied itself in knots as he thought about the corrupt power that seemed to leach out from within the building's very stones. He knew in its upper floors this building housed the offices of the most powerful men in Russia—the Central Committee of the Communist Party of the Soviet Union. His instinctive reaction was to turn and run, but he realized such cowardice would solve nothing.

Johan and his companions looked at each other. Each saw the fear he felt in the reflected in the other's eyes. Gathering their courage they pulled open the tall wooden door and entered the lobby. A guard, with a Mosin-Nagant rifle hung by a strap over his shoulder, immediately approached them. After a few words explaining their mission, he directed them to the first-floor Office of the Foreign Administration Department where passport applications could be made. Surprisingly— for queues were ubiquitous in Moscow—there was no one waiting ahead of them.

"Haven't you heard?" asked the testy apparatchik behind the counter after they had told him their mission. He was a thin, small man. The few strands of gray hair still eking out an existence on his balding head were combed from above his right ear over to the top of his left ear. The glasses perched on the end of his long, bulbous nose showed no signs of ever having been cleaned. "Passports are no longer being issued. The Central Committee gave the order—was it last week? I don't remember and it doesn't matter. No more passports are to be given out."

"But, we know of people who were issued passports only very recently," said Johan, trying to remain calm. He had not expected so sudden and final a rejection.

"Be that as it may, no more passports are being issued. There is nothing I can do for you. Go home, back where you came from."

Johan felt, inside his body, he was beginning to tremble. His worst fears were coming to pass. He had left his home and come to

Moscow for nothing. Worse than that, he had impoverished his family by selling his crop. With no grain, he would have to buy his required "voluntary" tax allotment on the black market at exorbitant rates. He had sold his animals, the family's personal belongings, tools, everything but the bare house and barn.

He took a deep breath. He would try again using the same tack he had used on the militiaman in Perlovka.

"Comrade, we are poor farmers from Siberia." His friends nodded in agreement. "We have little education. There is nothing for us to go back to. We have nothing. It can't hurt for us to apply, can it? Who knows? The government may change its mind again. What can it hurt?"

"That's right. What can it hurt? At least let us apply," his companions chorused in subdued voices.

The office worker said nothing. He stared at the motley group standing before him and noticed a growing line of others who were arriving, likely wishing to make a similar request. After a long pause in which Johan began to feel very uncomfortable, the man spoke.

"Do you have your spravki, your certificates from your regional finance, police and military departments? Can you prove you owe no taxes, are of good character, are exempted from military service?"

The questions were met with blank looks and shaking heads.

"Have you written permission to make the application from your regional soviet?"

More shaking heads and looks of growing dismay.

"What about the Moscow soviet?"

"Comrade," said Johan with his hands outstretched in a plea. "We left our homes in a hurry. Our families are here with the shirts on our backs. Nothing else."

The government employee said nothing. He looked again at the group before him. He wasn't surprised at their responses. Nor had he expected they would have followed the old protocols. An alarming number of people looking very similar to these men had begun appearing in his office in the past month. All had told him the same story. He hoped the Sixth Floor would make up its mind about how to deal with them in some sort of systematic fashion. On his desk there was a growing pile of passport applications, none of which had supporting paperwork. He didn't know what to do with them. President Kalinin had made it clear. No more passports. The order had come from Stalin himself.

The apparatchik sighed. The memory of another group, this one of women and children who had occupied his office came to mind. When was it? July. The office had been sweltering hot. How long had it lasted? It had seemed like days. It had been a group of mothers and their children. It all came back to him. The women had brought nothing with which to care for their brats: no fresh nappies, no food. They had sat themselves down on the floor wherever there was space. It hadn't mattered what threats or curses flew their way. They had simply refused to move until they were given what they came for. He shuddered as he remembered the smell of the dirty diapers and the chaos of howling babies and toddlers. Finally someone on the Sixth Floor had acquiesced and the passports were given. It was Commissar Smidovich himself who issued them. It had taken days before the smell lingering afterward had finally dissipated.

The apparatchik shrugged. It wasn't his decision. His job was to take their information and their money, should the Sixth Floor decide to grant more emigrants their wish.

"Take Ilyinka Street to Nogina Square. Soon after you see the Church of All Saints keep going across the Square until you find a small market. Close by, a photographer has a shop. He will take your pictures. Bring them here when you have them. I'll take your information then."

Johan and his friends broke into smiles of relief. Each of them reached out to shake the government worker's hand. In their palms, they slid a few rubles into his.

"It won't hurt to grease the man a bit," they had decided before coming into the office. Bribery had been *de rigueur* in Russian society for centuries.

"I wouldn't get my hopes up, if I were you. You're fishing in a dry ditch," said the apparatchik as they turned to leave. He shook his head and pulled a thick slice of brown bread and a wedge of white cheese out of his drawer. Being a man of habit, he never deviated from this daily ritual. He opened up a penknife and began cutting at the cheese, while with words of sincere gratitude and with renewed hope, the refugees left the office.

"You're all fishing in a dry ditch!" he shouted as another apparatchik stepped up to the counter to deal with the next group of refugees wanting to apply for passports.

The Funk family visited Nogina Square and had their passport pictures taken the very next day. A week later, Johan and Franz met Jacob Hildebrandt, whose family had also been photographed, at the railway station in Perlovka. Together they traveled to the photographer's shop and picked up the photos. They retraced their steps to the passport office at 4 Staraya Square. The fellow behind the desk scowled when he saw them. Nevertheless, he took the pictures and wrote down the names and pertinent information regarding all the members of the Funk and Hildebrandt families.

"Don't expect anything to come of this," said the man. "You've given the address where you are staying?" He glanced at the words on the paper. "Good. Someone will contact you if your request is granted, which, as I've already told you, is unlikely to happen."

Johan mumbled his thanks.

After Johan, Franz and Jacob Hildebrandt left, the apparatchik leafed through their photos, looking at them one by one. Returning to his chair, he stuffed the Funks' and Hildebrandts' application forms and photos into a large envelope and tossed it onto the already large pile of applications on his desk.

"Something's going to come of this," he thought mournfully. "Oh yes, see if it doesn't."

For the directive had been given that morning that all passport applications already received, and all future requests for passports, were to be forwarded immediately to the GPU. The apparatchik shuddered. He had no desire to ever receive a visit from the secret police. Everyone knew they chose to do their work in the dead of night, arriving in their Black Ravens, knocking on doors, and frightening the daylights out of folks.

"If that were only the worst of it," he thought. "No, you don't want to get noticed by that bunch," he said quietly to himself as he nibbled on his moldy cheese.

Chapter 13

September 1929

Happy their task was completed, and with their hearts washed with the relief of knowing their passport applications had been accepted into the communist bureaucratic machine, Johan and Franz Funk and Jacob Hildebrandt left the Office of the Foreign Administration Department. Their footsteps echoed as they walked over the shiny Italian marble floor of the lobby. They pushed their way through the solid wooden doors and took a deep breath of the cool, fresh air meeting them on the sidewalk. Only then did they realize how stuffy it had been inside the building.

"Well, it's in God's hands now," said Hildebrandt.

"Yes," thought Johan. He knew miracles were few and far between, and silently prayed they would be granted the joy of being the grateful recipients of one. However, his faith was tempered with realism born from experience. It would take more than prayer to rattle open the locks of Stalin's cage.

Looking up at the blue sky, Johan noticed the sun was still high. "The day is yet young. Shall we visit the RUSKAPA office?" RUSKAPA was the Russia Canada Passenger Agency, a cooperative venture between the two countries that since 1923 had helped thousands of Russian Mennonites emigrate to Canada. Working as the feet of the Canadian government on Russian soil, the Canadian Pacific Railroad and Steamship Company medically screened and approved applicants. It also extended credit to those who could not pay for their passage overseas in the company's ships. "Now that our passport applications are being processed we need to register our desire to journey to Canada. There will be the whole matter of tickets to arrange. And entry visas."

The words sounded ridiculously optimistic in Johan's ears. They hung in the air like the possibility of travel to the moon, like a kernel of infinite energy with the power of creation released into the darkness and chaos of their lives.

"Yes," agreed Hildebrandt. "That's the next step. We need to register with them and arrange for credit. With a wife and seven children, I certainly cannot afford to pay, whatever the fare they will charge. I suspect all of my rubles will only be enough to cover the cost of the passports."

After such lofty thoughts as their possible emigration to Canada, Johan was quickly brought back to earth. Looking at his son, he saw Franz was scratching his head. Realizing he had been ignoring his own itch, Johan began to scratch as well. It was only as he felt his fingers scraping over his scalp that he remembered the grim discovery made a couple of days before. Lice. What a nuisance! Elizabeth had been mortified when the insect plague had first been found in their children's hair—what would people think? In Lyubimovka, she had prided herself in her clean, insect free home. By now, everyone in the family was affected. To add to the misery, the bed bugs had returned and fleas had been found hopping about on the floor, making it a true three-ring circus. Johan and Elizabeth were too embarrassed to speak to other refugees about their infestations. It had taken the uninhibited chatter of the children for them to discover there were almost no households free of the insect afflictions.

"God directed the ten plagues at Pharaoh and his people," complained Elizabeth, "so the Egyptian would let the Israelites go to their promised land. Yet, here we live with the scourges plaguing us while the communists drag their heels and refuse to let us go to our promised land. We are afflicted and they ignore us. Surely, God has forgotten us!"

Picking through everyone's hair with a fine-toothed comb had been added to the chores of scrubbing floors and boiling bedding and clothes. Maria had quickly proven herself quite adept at finding the tiny nits and it had become her responsibility to examine everyone's heads before the darkness of evening made such searches impossible.

Nonetheless, everyone's bodies were becoming raw from constant scratching and it had ceased to matter which insect culprits caused the itch. It was all becoming more than a little overwhelming and the words, "We should never have come here," were heard to be muttered by an exasperated, disgruntled sufferer on more than one occasion.

It was only a few city blocks from Number 4 Staraya Square to Number 14 Kuznetsky Most, the building in which RUSKAPA had its office. Kuznetsky Most, the Blacksmiths' Bridge, was so named because at one time the street had run along the Neglinka River to the bridge leading to the largest forge in the medieval city. The river had long since been covered over and the bridge dismantled. But the street had flourished and become home to the shops of many French, English, and Italian traders. As they walked along its sidewalks, Johan was struck with awe by the sight of so many tall neo-classical stone buildings, with their colonnades and large, arched glass windows, though they all seemed quite the worse for the wear of time and neglect. After the Bolshevik revolution, most of the traders had left, but some buildings still seemed occupied. Johan was startled to see an electric sign above the entrance to the large grey stone Passazh Arcade at Number 12 Kuznetsky Most. It advertised the services of a teashop within. He had never seen such a spectacle. He was not to know it was the only electric sign in Moscow, and it had somehow until now escaped the scrutiny of the restrictive communist eye, perhaps, in large part because the palate of its head preferred the establishment's fine teas.

Entering the RUSKAPA office, Johan and his companions saw the room was crowded with people, some standing in groups, others seated, all talking animatedly about their quest to leave the land of their birth, the land seemingly intent now on making their lives as miserable as possible. They were all amazed at the brashness of their actions. They had all left friends and family behind. Some had been able to sell their belongings, but some of the newest arrivals talked of how their auctions had been forbidden. Another, a man named Abraham Penner, spoke of being robbed of the proceeds of his auction. He and his family had no money at all with which to pursue their dream of emigration, yet here they were. Penner's story evoked considerable sympathy. He was directed to speak to a certain Mr. Langemann who had only recently arrived in Moscow from the Ukraine. Langemann was staying in the suburb of Losinka. He had already generously offered to help other refugees with funds. Perhaps he would help the Penner family. Directions were given and Penner left a happier man. And so the conversations went.

Of course, the biggest item of concern was the matter of entry visas to Canada. How did one receive such a golden ticket? Was the government of Canada even issuing them? Some, who had already seen the director, were saying entry visas were not being issued. Was this true? What could it mean? The more optimistic among them shrugged off the rumor and wanted to talk about logistics. How much would emigration cost for a family of nine or ten? And then there were the details of the journey. What train would one need to catch? At what port were ships being loaded? Relatives in the past had gone through Riga, Latvia; was Riga still the port of choice? The anxious refugees mulled over their uncertain future.

Hildebrandt was deep in conversation with an acquaintance he had just happily met when the representative of the Canadian Pacific Railway and Steamship Company, Mr. Ross Owen, called him and the Funks into his office. Preoccupied, Hildebrandt waved them away, so Johan and Franz went in alone. Owen was a large man with a boney frame from which his clothes hung loosely. He gave the impression of a lively coat-rack. His smile was broad, though his long face had a harried look about it. Owen's shiny black hair was slicked straight back and hung over the collar of his checkered shirt at the nape of his short neck. He reached out and, with a firm grip, shook Johan's hand and then Franz's.

When they were all seated, Owen said, "So gentlemen, what can I do for you?"

Johan was pleasantly surprised this Canadian spoke a perfect German. Owen had been in the Soviet Union for a number of years. Most of the prospective immigrants he had met were German Russians. He had come to Russia with a rudimentary knowledge of Russian and German. Immersed in the foreign tongues and with an aptitude for it, he had learned them quickly.

"We would like to apply for entry visas to Canada," said Johan, the butterflies fluttering in his stomach.

Franz added quickly, "And we need to talk about the arrangements required for the journey, the ship and such."

Owen smiled sadly. "Yes. Of course. You and all the people you see out there in the office and a thousand others who've been knocking on my door in the last couple of weeks."

His reply unsettled Johan. The man's introductory comments were not reassuring.

"Do you have family in Canada who are willing to sponsor you?"

"Yes, my cousin lives in Manitoba and has written he and his family are ready to sponsor us," replied Johan.

"That's good, that's good," said Owen. "When the time comes, that will help." He hesitated. "However, I'm afraid what I have to tell you is not the best of news." After a short pause, Owen continued. "The Canadian government has put a temporary halt on issuing entry visas. I am told there are a few issues needing to be ironed out before any more visas will be granted."

Johan and Franz's spirits sank. With nothing to say, they looked at Owen with bleak expressions on their faces. Finally, in an attempt to remain optimistic, Johan said, "We have been told the Canadian Pacific Railway and Steamship Company is offering credit to all refugees it brings to Canada. Is that so?"

"Yes," affirmed Owen. "You don't have to pay a penny for your ship's passage or train travel to your preferred destination in Canada until you are settled and earning a living."

Johan and Franz smiled at this good piece of news. "That is very generous. Thank you!" said Johan.

"Yes, well, first you need to get yourselves to Antwerp." He was referring to the port in Belgium from which his company's ships sailed. "For the moment, neither Russia nor Canada is in the mood to help you in that regard."

Johan and Franz silently digested the enormity of their situation. "Can you speak to someone in your government?" asked Johan tentatively.

Owen laughed. "I could try but they surely would not listen to me. I'm sorry, there is little I can do for now. You'll just have to be patient and check back with us regularly. I'm sure a decision in Ottawa will be made soon."

Johan and Franz looked perplexed.

"Sorry," Owen said, "Ottawa is the capital of Canada. There is one thing I can do. I will add your name to the list of people wanting to emigrate to Canada."

After Johan had carefully spelled the name of each member of his family and watched Owen write it down, the interview was concluded. Owen showed Franz and Johan to the door.

"Thank you for your kindness," murmured Johan.

"Don't thank me yet," Owen replied. "I haven't done anything except give you news you didn't want to hear. Nor do I know when or even if I'll be able to oblige you. Check back with us, though. Don't give up hope. I've heard enough stories to know the hell you people are living in. Canadians by and large are a compassionate people. It's just a few of the politicians that seem to be putting the fly in the soup. And," he added holding up the list, "Your place in the line is secure. You won't get shuffled to the bottom. Don't worry. We'll get you out of Russia, one way or another."

Johan Funk and Ross Owen both knew the promise was an empty one. But it was made with the best of intentions.

"Thank you," Johan and Franz said. "We will come again."

Not wanting to go home after their depressing interview, yet at the same time somehow buoyed by Owen's strained optimism, Johan and Franz decided to walk the few blocks to the center of the Moscow kremlin. They wished to see for themselves the symbolic heart of the communist empire, Red Square. Entering through the Voskresensky Gate, they were immediately struck by the vastness of the Square. It stretched forth before them, a seemingly endless flat space covered by millions of paving stones and surrounded by buildings the likes of which neither had ever seen. As they walked along, they marveled at the beauty of Kazan Cathedral, and at the other end of the Square, the exquisite onion domes of Saint Basil's Cathedral.

"It's a wonder they're still standing," snorted Franz as he considered the cathedrals. "I'm sure Stalin has ideas on how to use the space they occupy for more practical purposes."

Noticing some papers pasted on the wall of the Kazan Cathedral, Franz's curiosity got the better of him. He walked over to see what they were about. He quickly realized they were faded posters. One poster showed a smiling, clean image of a red-clad Soviet worker beckoning a struggling peasant weighed down by all the trappings of the Russian Orthodox Church. He wore an onion dome on his head like a turban, words of the scriptures were printed on his sleeves, and his abdomen was covered in ikons. Hanging by chains twisted about his neck, chest, and waist were crosses and an incense bowl carrying lit candles. A four-bottom plow completed the trinity of images. Underneath was written, "Hey brother, take your caftan, and your dome—put them under the shelf and take the candles from your belly. Suddenly it becomes easier to reach the plough." Beside this poster was another showing a gluttonous priest.

Shaking their heads at the crude images and their message, Franz and Johan walked on. The anti-religious poster brought to their minds the many stories they had heard of Mennonite pastors being arrested and of churches being closed.

"We cannot leave this country soon enough," muttered Johan. He looked around fearing someone had overheard his anti-revolutionary sentiment.

The beauty of Saint Basil's Cathedral drew them on across the Square. As they strolled along, they noticed for the first time there were electric lamp posts installed at regular intervals to illuminate the Square at night. As they drew closer to the old Moscow Town Hall on their left, they saw a small wooden building had been erected in front of it. A long queue of people stood patiently, waiting their turn to enter.

Franz looked questioningly at his father.

"It's Lenin's tomb," said Johan. "The communists have made a shrine to him. These people are making their pilgrimage to honor their dead leader."

"Huh," said Franz in disgust. "They say there is no God but they make a god of Lenin. Despite what the Bible tells us of what the awe-struck witnesses saw, the communists insist Jesus did not rise from the dead and that he was just a man like every other man. Yet they worship Lenin who was a man and whose body is clearly still with us."

Johan put his hand on his son's shoulder. "Keep your voice

down," he said quietly. His son was becoming angry. Who knew if one of the people standing nearby wasn't a member of the secret police?

"Let's go home," said Franz.

Johan and Franz retraced their steps across the Square. They felt dirty, soiled by the communist propaganda they had seen and the feeling of oppression that had overtaken them. The very air they breathed in Red Square seemed corrupted by the ideology that had driven them to leave their home in a desperate attempt at emigration. Only as they left the walls of the Moscow kremlin behind did they begin to breathe more easily.

And so September passed. Johan returned to the Office of the Foreign Administration Department and saw the line was much longer each time he came. The faces of those leaving told him disappointment awaited him there. He also returned to Number 14 Kuznetsky Most, with the same result. He met old friends and made new ones at the RUSKAPA office. They exchanged news and spoke wistfully of the possibility of life in a new land. All of them were becoming more and more concerned. The Canadian government was granting no visas. No passports were being issued by the Soviet government. The situation seemed increasingly desperate.

Chapter 14

October 1929

It was in mid October that the refugees crowded around Moscow learned they were not forgotten in their plight. The world was aware; people outside of the Soviet Union were watching. Perhaps prompted by international pressure, a solution to the bureaucratic Gordian Knot in which they found themselves could be found. Franz brought the news to his family.

"A man from the German Embassy is meeting with our people in the field by Perlovka Station," shouted Franz breathlessly as he burst through the door into the Funks' dacha.

"The German Embassy?" said Johan, astonished, looking up from his work.

"Yes! I heard him say he is from the German Embassy in Moscow! He is here with some other men who have cameras. They are taking pictures and asking questions of anyone who will talk to them."

Johan put down the awl he was using to hollow out the ivory handle of the teapot he had purchased at the bazaar in Perlovka. After buying the teapot he had been approached by a man on the street who was exchanging rubles for American dollars. At first Johan had been uninterested. But, it was a sunny day, the man was a refugee from Siberia like himself, and Johan found himself drawn into a friendly conversation. As they talked, they admired the fine ivory handle of Johan's new teapot. It was intricately carved in an understated sort of way. Looking at the handle, Johan thought of an idea. He willingly handed over the exorbitant rate the man had demanded, albeit a discounted one he was assured.

In his pocket Johan now had a precious American ten-dollar bill. It looked so foreign and exotic and represented to him the real possibility of a new life in a faraway land. When the long, narrow hole he was making extended the length of the ivory handle, Johan planned to roll up the bill tightly and insert it into it. When the teapot was reassembled, no one would ever know what was hidden there. He knew it was a necessary precaution. The forward thinking ones who had emigrated in the years when exit permits were still being given had written letters telling of how at the border to Latvia the guards had taken everything of value from their luggage. "When the time comes, no one will find this ten-dollar note," Johan assured himself.

Grabbing his jacket—it was chilly outside for it was, after all, October 11—Johan joined Franz who was waiting impatiently by the road. They hurried to the Perlovka railway station. There, in the clearing behind the station, they found a growing crowd of Mennonite refugees. The air was full of expectancy, as if something momentous was happening.

And it was momentous. Representatives of the refugees had been meeting with the German Ambassador in Moscow. Messages had been flying between Moscow and Berlin, where members of the Mennonite Central Committee were pressuring the German government to somehow expedite the emigration of their fellow Mennonites from the Soviet Union. Finally, here in their village, was concrete evidence someone, somewhere, was hearing their cries for help. The German Embassy had sent a diplomat to investigate.

Having heard about the gathering, several members of the militia and secret police were also present. They tried to remain inconspicuous as they skirted the edges of the throng, keeping an eye on things, searching for ringleaders, and suspicious about the presence here of the meddling German diplomat.

A chair had been taken from the station and a man was standing upon it as a makeshift dais. He was waving his hands above his head trying to get everyone's attention.

"Hello! Hello everybody!" he called in a loud clear voice.

All around the grassy field faces were turned to the man at its center. Conversations were cut short and only a murmur of sound could be heard here and there. The speaker cleared his throat.

"My name is Dr. Otto Auhagen. I am the Agricultural Attaché at the German Embassy in Moscow. I can tell you my government is very concerned about what is happening to its German colonists in the Soviet Union, and more specifically what is happening here in the communities around Moscow." He paused while his words were received with nods of relieved approval. In their silence, Auhagen saw he had his listeners' rapt attention. "Your representatives in Germany have been talking to our government in Berlin. We know why you are here. We want to help. You are our brothers and sisters, and you are in need. The welfare of every German is the concern of every other German!"

Auhagen was forced to stop as his words were met with loud affirmations and a buzz of exclamations rippling through the multitude.

Auhagen continued, speaking loudly and slowly so everyone could hear and understand. "I am here today to listen to your stories. My government wants to hear from you. We want to know what has driven you to these desperate measures."

There were shouts from the crowd, as some who were only too eager to vent their desperation could not contain themselves.

Waving his hands, Auhagen waited for silence and continued. "I have brought with me reporters from the world press: from the New York Times and the Chicago Tribune in America; and from newspapers in London and Berlin. They, too, want to hear your stories." He began to shout over the now constant noise of exclamations coming from the crowd. "They will tell the world what is happening here in Moscow!" More loud affirmations. "Be encouraged! You have friends beyond the borders of the Soviet Union. Your voices will be heard!" Auhagen felt the energy coming from the multitude like waves battering the shore. He stopped speaking for a time until the exuberant crowd finally calmed to the point where he again could make himself heard. "Now, if you will be patient, I will listen to as many of you as I can in the time I have here."

Auhagen stepped off of the chair and tried to mingle amongst the people. The men and women in the crowd around him were almost delirious with relief knowing the outside world would hear their story. Fading hope had been rekindled in them like oxygen blown over ashes revives sleeping embers. "The Soviets will be forced to listen to us now," was everyone's thought. Auhagen could make no progress through the mob. Someone brought him the chair. He sat down in their midst. An aide stood beside him writing furiously while the newspaper reporters jotted notes and took pictures as the laments poured forth around them. A gate had been opened, the silence was broken, and the cascade of stories could not be held back.

"I was forced to join the collective," said a man who had come from the Ukraine. "They took my land and then thanked me by labeling me a kulak. My family and I were immediately kicked out of the collective. We were left with nothing but the clothes on our backs! A friend had compassion on us and loaned us the money to come here. Leaving this country is our only chance at survival!"

A farmer from a village near Slavgorod in Siberia piped up, "Our whole village was made responsible to pay for the fines levied on those who couldn't meet their so-called "voluntary" grain tax. The fines are exorbitant! Our crop this year was miserable. I could barely meet my own obligation, let alone pay for someone else's. It left me bankrupt!"

"Yes, and it was the local soviet that decided how much grain we had to pay," added a man from the same village. "They cared not a whit our harvest was bad. For them it was all about filling their quota. For us it meant no grain left for bread in winter or for planting in spring. If we starved to death, all the better, was what they thought."

"They arrested our minister," said someone quietly. "They closed our church, locked the doors, and then used our sanctuary as a grain silo!" Tears ran down her pale cheeks.

Another who said he was from the Crimea complained, "I was arrested for no reason and tortured. But at least I was released—who knew why? They arrested my neighbor. He was never seen again. His wife and children were left destitute."

"They're arresting us here in Moscow," said a voice in the crowd. "They're knocking at our doors in the middle of the night! I know of three men who have been taken. And that is only on our street."

Voices were raised in agreement as others counted off the numbers of those they knew who had been arrested. Auhagen's head began to spin with the catalogue of injustices he was hearing.

"There are children dying of measles here, in our neighborhood, in Perlovka," said another voice choked with emotion. "Please help us!"

"We have no rubles left. They took what money we had and refused to give us ration cards. We are being forced to beg on the streets," cried a voice further away.

The stories went on and on, and the good Dr. Auhagen wept in his growing despair at hearing them. And he thought, "Something must be done to help these people."

The militia and agents of the secret police stood around the edges of the crowd watching the litany of the abuses the refugees were suffering rise to the heavens like smoke from the burnt offerings of their lives. They, too, thought something must be done: something must be done to find out who was leading this rabble of malcontents; something must be done to move them back to the backwaters and hick-towns from whence they had come.

The next day, in the afternoon, the Funks' were busy with the daily chores. Water was being carried from the stream and heated. Clothing was being washed and hung on low branches in the trees around the dacha. Firewood was being collected. Everyone had a task, even little Katrina who was stirring a pot of thin soup being prepared for the evening meal.

Looking down the street, Johan noticed a group of young men and women. From their dress—the color and style, their clothing was clean, with no obvious signs of needing mending, and looking recently pressed—he knew immediately they were not refugees. They were coming out of his neighbor's house and when they spied him, three—a girl and two boys—came his way while the others headed toward the dachas across the road.

"Good afternoon, Comrade," one fellow said cheerfully, thrusting out his hand.

Johan said nothing but politely returned the handshake.

"We are from the komsomol at the university in Moscow."

Immediately Johan's guard went up. He had heard of the komsomol, the All-Union Leninist Young Communist League. They stood for everything that was the antithesis of his beliefs.

"We have come today out of concern for your welfare," said the young woman with a thin veneer of sincerity. "We have learned of your plight and feel nothing but sympathy for you." The speaker's companions nodded their agreement. "Your ill-advised adventure in attempted emigration from our great land has put your family in jeopardy. Winter is coming and these dachas are not equipped to protect you from the severe cold it brings. We know you are having difficulty getting entry visas to Canada."

Johan was shocked they were aware of this. How did they know?

"You are going to have to face the facts, Comrade," continued one of the young men. "The decadent country of Canada does not want you." When he saw Johan was about to argue with him, he plowed on. "You can understand our government cannot issue exit visas if you have nowhere to go."

"It's just a matter of time," Johan managed to get in. "Canada will open its doors."

The young woman chimed in, "Yes, but it the meantime, your family will freeze to death, or starve. You cannot expect the people of Moscow to continue providing bread for you when you obviously have no intention of helping to build our great communist nation."

"This great communist nation you speak of has made life intolerable for my family," said Johan bitterly.

"I'm sorry you feel that way," said the komsomol youth. "However, if you agree to return to the home you left, our beneficent leaders will pay all your expenses. Think of it—free train tickets back to the home you left. Do you not wish to return to your friends, to your farm, your land?"

"We have nothing to go back to," said Johan. "We will stay here until we are given permission to leave or until we freeze or starve to death as you put it. Those are our only options."

The komsomol student's face was no longer friendly. Her hostile, penetrating gaze made Johan uncomfortable. "I would advise you to reconsider, Comrade." The word, comrade, was spoken with heavy sarcasm. "Our leaders are losing patience. You could face arrest. You risk imprisonment. You risk your family being loaded into a boxcar and being shipped to a place they may find very unpleasant. Yes, I would advise you to reconsider," she concluded harshly.

With those words left hanging frozen in the crisp autumn air, the trio of komsomol students left. Standing on the path by the road, looking at them walking confidently along, Johan was chilled and shaken.

"What have we gotten ourselves into?" he thought. "We had a farm, we could grow our own food, we had a solid roof over our heads, good friends, a church community, loving family around us. And what have we now? A rented bungalow meant only for summer living, no work, we are dependent on ration cards for food, we have no friends, our family is far away and we meet roadblocks at every turn. And now threats." He turned and walked toward the dacha where his family busied itself with the routine of daily survival.

"Oh God, have mercy on us," he prayed.

Chapter 15

October 15, 1929

Johan Funk was returning to Perlovka from Moscow. He had stopped by RUSKAPA, where the staff had once again been apologetic. He had also made an inquiry at the Office of the Foreign Administration Department. The man behind the desk there was impatient and unhelpful.

"You'd be better off going back ta yer home," he'd growled. His refrain, oft repeated, was an ice-pick in Johan's ears.

Waiting to board his northbound train at Yaroslavsky station, Johan was talking with a friend who seemed to know the broader picture.

"Did you know that daily there are young men who are braving arrest to get into the German Embassy in Moscow to plead our case?" he said.

Johan was amazed. No, he was not aware of such brave deeds being done.

"Yes, that is true. We are not alone in this fight," the man continued with certainty. "Did you know letters have been written to the Central Executive Committee and the Central Committee? Perhaps Kalinin will act on our behalf. And a letter has gone to Piotor Smidovich himself. He's in charge of affairs relating to national minorities. He has a lot of responsibility—God grant he also has a heart." He chuckled at his lame attempt at humor. "I'm told letters have even been sent to Lenin's wife, Nadezhda Krupskaya. And to Maxim Gorky." He nodded in satisfaction at this bit of news. "Perhaps they still have some influence, though I doubt Gorky can do much. He's in exile in Sorrento, Italy."

Johan was surprised at the daring and foresight being shown by some of his fellow refugees. "Who is writing these letters?" he ventured.

"I don't know, and it is better that way. If the authorities question us, we cannot lead them to those who attempt to give all of us hope." The fellow leaned in toward Johan and lowered his voice. "I can tell you people are getting desperate. We are trying to move an iceberg and there is fear we will be crushed beneath its weight. There are some who are threatening to go to Red Square in protest at the lack of action. They say they are determined to remain there until they are given passports or until they literally starve to death. Have you ever heard of such brave determination?"

Johan had not heard these rumors and was distressed at the hopelessness enveloping his people. "How can the government ignore the cries of so many thousands of us?" he thought for the thousandth time. "Something has got to give."

Johan was turning to walk to his train when he spied a familiar face in the crowd. It took him a moment to recall the name attached to the face for the meeting was completely unexpected. It was his old friend, Peter Ens. Though they had lived in different villages, they had attended the same church in Friedensruh. Many times they had chatted while feeding and watering the horses that had pulled the wagons carrying them all to Sunday worship, caring for the animals so they would be rested and fresh for the return trip after the services ended.

"Peter," he said with delight as he reached out to grasp his friend's hand. "It is so good to see you!"

"It is good to see you, Johan. It is such a surprise to see a familiar face. My family and I have only just arrived."

Looking further, Johan could see Peter's wife, Agatha, and their four children coming along. They had very little luggage with them.

The reunion was joyful. In fact, joy filled the air of the station, competing for space with the ubiquitous steam of the idling railway engines. Many refugees were gathered and welcoming the arrival of family and friends who had joined the migration to Moscow from the far reaches of the Soviet Union.

Because few knew when, or even if, their loved ones might come, it had become the habit of many to simply gather at the station and wait. The camaraderie felt by all as they met and talked and waited bolstered their spirits while giving them a purpose during the long, tense, tedious wait for permission to emigrate. It was a daily occurrence becoming increasingly annoying to the railway workers who constantly had to fight the endless crowds standing in their way on the platforms and sitting on every available chair and bench while they tried to get on with their work.

"Welcome to Moscow, my friend!" Johan said enthusiastically. When Agatha joined them, she reached out to shake Johan's hand. The children looked at him shyly. They were quite overwhelmed by all the loud, mechanical sounds and the strange smells greeting them at the huge railway station. It was a new, different world from that of their small family farm in Siberia.

After the initial greetings were completed, Peter Ens's face became serious. "I have some sad news for you, Johan. Or perhaps you have already heard. Your father, Franz, is dead."

Johan was stunned. Tears immediately began spilling over onto his cheeks. "I didn't know."

"Your father died almost two weeks ago. When was it, Agatha?" Ens glanced at his wife. "It was a Wednesday, October 2, I think, during the night." Agatha nodded in agreement. "Your mother said he was peaceful at the end. Those of your family still in Lyubimovka were all with him when he died." Peter paused while Johan wiped his eyes with a tattered handkerchief. "The funeral was held in our church in Friedensruh."

Ens reached for his friend and held him in a strong embrace as he sought to comfort him. He murmured, "Your mother is well. She is a strong woman, despite her age. The funeral was simple. We did our best. The choir sorely misses your leadership. Some have quit singing. Others have stopped coming to church altogether out of fear of reprisals, or they have simply vanished—walked away from their homes to come here, I suppose, hoping to get out, like we have. Auctions are forbidden."

Ens moaned in his own grief of loss. He knew he should be comforting his friend but his own pain had gotten the better of him and he continued.

"We didn't even lock our doors when we left. The peasants are free to loot our home and barns like black ravens on a rotting carcass. We worked so hard to enjoy the comforts we had." He shook his head. "Ah, Johan, how did it come to this?" Realizing the inappropriateness of his monologue, Ens apologized. "But, I shouldn't be telling you this. Not now. I'm so sorry; my mouth ran away with me. These are terrible times."

Johan thanked his friend and, in a daze, boarded his passenger car.

As Johan rode the train north to Perlovka, he remembered his last words to his mother. His grief at the loss of his father quickly turned to resolve to make good on his promise. He would return to Lyubimovka and bring his mother back with him to Moscow. He would rescue her from the madness that had overtaken Russia and bring her to Canada with his family.

The story of Franz's death and Johan's plan to bring Anna to Moscow were quickly told.

"But what if someone recognizes you?" Elizabeth cried.

"By the time I get to Isylkul no one will know who I am," Johan said confidently. "My face will be covered in beard. I've always been clean-shaven. No one there has ever seen me any other way. I'll wear some ragged clothing. I'll pick up an ushanka hat and some old felt boots at the bazaar in Moscow. I'll look for a coat, some ratty old sheepskin even a peasant wouldn't care to wear. With the ushanka's flaps pulled down, with my beard and sheepskin, I'll blend right in. I'll look like any other peasant riding the rails. It won't be a problem."

Elizabeth looked at her husband's stubbly face. He hadn't shaved in a few days and she had grumbled at him that very morning about him looking like a vagrant. "He's probably right," she thought. At the same time, Elizabeth was afraid to see her husband leave. It was a long way to Isylkul. What if something was to happen and he was unable to return? Whatever would she do, trapped here on the outskirts of Moscow with five hungry children to feed and another on the way— her monthly flow had not come for two months now and she was certain she was pregnant—and with no husband to rely on?

Elizabeth sighed deeply. "Yes," she reluctantly agreed, "you must go. You promised your mother."

Elizabeth had told the younger children to 'go listen to the birds' when she had seen her husband's face as he returned to the dacha from his trip to Moscow. While they all went to play in the small wood, only Franz had remained.

Turning to his eldest son, Johan said, "When I am gone, every couple of days you must go to Moscow and check to see if our passports are ready to be picked up. We cannot merely wait to be notified. I don't trust them. They may decide to let us go, but telling us about it would be going the second mile. And when have you ever known a communist to go the second mile for anyone? No, we must be proactive."

Franz nodded in agreement.

"Also go to RUSKAPA and see if Canada is issuing visas. If they begin taking applications, we don't want to miss out. Can you do that?"

"Yes, father," said Franz. He didn't have to be told how important these tasks were.

The next day Johan boarded an express train bound for Vladivostok at Yaroslavsky Station. At Chelyabinsk he planned to get off of the express and take a post train for the rest of the trip. It would be slower than the express because it made so many stops, but it would stop in Isylkul while the express would only stop at Omsk. All going well, he would arrive in Isylkul within the week.

As the train rocked and clattered along its steel track, Johan tried not to think about the fix he and his family were in. Like a drowning man caught in a millrace, he fought the crushing feeling the decision to leave Lyubimovka had been a terrible mistake. He feared for his family's future. The danger to which he was exposing them made him light-headed at times. When he thought about it, the terrible consequences that might yet be reaped if the government remained intransigent brought on waves of nausea. At the same time, though, he was more determined than ever to see what he had started through to the end, whatever end that might be. There really was no going back.

Looking out of the coach's window in order to occupy his mind, Johan marveled at the contradiction he saw between the vast, natural beauty of God's creation and the puny, dilapidated structures built by people. The impoverished villages sprawled intermittently along the track were in sharp contrast to the self-conscious display of wealth he had seen in Moscow. But even the architectural wonders of the city could not compare to the rich colors of autumn in the Ural Mountains: the myriad shades of vibrant yellows, oranges, and golds, the stubborn greens; the towering, obstinate, grey rock formations; the foamy whites and blues of cascading rivers and waterfalls. At night, even the stark, moonlit snow-capped peaks with their ghostly skirts of silent, monochromatic evergreens held more beauty in his eyes than the fantastical onion domes of Saint Basil's Cathedral. Johan drank in the beauty of God's creation and his tormented soul found some rest.

Johan was transferring trains in Chelyabinsk when, on October 19, the Soviet government sent a note to the German Embassy in Moscow informing it four to five thousand refugees would be allowed to leave the Soviet Union. There was one condition. A country must first be found that would accept them. Johan was unaware of the momentous event, but his son, Franz, was not, for the news was quickly spread amongst the refugees waiting at the gates of Moscow.

Elizabeth was ecstatic when Franz told her of the miracle that had occurred. Since there was no time to lose—for who knew if the government may not change its mind—and knowing the cost of an exit visa was 55 rubles per adult over eighteen, Elizabeth gave Franz 110 rubles. She wished him God-speed and sent him back to Moscow. Franz hurried to the Office of the Foreign Administration Department where, when it was finally his turn, he happily placed the rubles before the apparatchik, with whom he had spoken only two days before.

"For our exit visas," he said with confidence. "I understand the government has agreed to let us go. It is only my mother and father who must pay. As you can see from our birth certificates, the rest of us are younger than eighteen years."

The bureaucrat squinted at him through his greasy glasses. "Your father has been designated a kulak. For him and his wife, the cost for exit visas will be 330 rubles... each."

Franz immediately felt his blood boil within him. "You can't be serious!" he shouted, trying in vain to contain his temper. "I don't have that much money! This is all I have, 110 rubles!" He shoved the money across the desk toward the apparatchik.

The communist stared at him and said nothing.

Franz was about to argue further, but realized he would be trying to reason with a stone wall. He snatched the rubles from the desk and left.

Chapter 16

October 20, 1929

Johan Funk arrived in Isylkul in the evening on Sunday, October 20, though he did not know it, for he had lost track of the days. He felt grimy from the sweat of his own unwashed body and from the shabby, oily sheepskin coat he had wrapped himself in for the duration of the trip. He shuddered to think of the vermin living in the thick, impenetrable depths of the greasy wool and knew from the itch under his arms, some had probably migrated and found warm habitation on him as well.

"The first thing I'll do when I get to Mother's is have a good scrub," he had told himself all of this last interminable day of travel. "One thing we still have plenty of is hot water."

Looking through the window of his railway car toward the dimly-lit Isylkul station platform, Johan could see the shadowy shapes of passengers beginning to mill about. There were no welcoming parties here, he noted, though a couple of figures standing at attention in the deeper shadows alarmed him.

"Is that the police?" he thought. He was immediately frightened. It was a knee-jerk reaction, he realized and he quickly calmed himself. "I have no reason to be concerned. I'm just another peasant among many."

Johan stepped off of the train with as much confidence as he could muster. Hunched over in an effort to conceal his face, he slowly walked toward the exit. Having no luggage to occupy his hands, he thrust them deep into his pockets and assumed the languid stroll of a tired peasant. Johan looked ahead and noticed he would be forced to step almost within arm's reach of the two men standing on either side of the exit. Glancing at the one, he gave a start for he recognized him. It was Sokol Volkov. Volkov was suspiciously eyeing everyone who went by him through the gate.

"What are they looking for?" Johan wondered.

Johan knew there was nowhere else to go, unless, he quickly realized, he was to pretend he'd forgotten something on the train and get back on board. But at that moment, a whistle sounded, the steam engine let out a great chuff, and the train began to pull out of the station. Johan knew there was nothing for it but to continue on.

Walking slowly now, for the narrow gate would only allow a few through at a time, Johan pushed his way into the middle of the crush so that, as he passed Volkov, he would at least be somewhat protected by the obscurity of numbers. Nevertheless, as he plodded by, Johan felt Volkov's staring eyes sear him like a flicker of flame and he felt sure he would be recognized. He fought the illogical urge to run and the equally illogical conflicting urge to reveal his identity. He felt like he was walking in thick spring mud. His feet seemed to cling to the floor. It took all his effort to lift them and shuffle them forward, one foot then the other. Time slowed and yet before he knew it, he was out in the freedom of the street.

A feeling of elation grew in Johan as he walked along the dirt road. His steps were suddenly light. He struggled to keep to the same listless pace—he was a peasant, he reminded himself, and peasants were never in a hurry. He looked cautiously about him. There were very few people about, other than the tired travelers making their various ways home.

Strolling along the sidewalk with buildings on his right side and the road to his left, Johan saw his reflection in a shop window and was surprised by what he saw. "I hardly recognize myself," he thought. Shaking his head, he moved on. Looking at the buildings on either side of the road, he thought, "They are all about as shabby as I look. Yes," he said to himself, "nothing is being done to keep things tidy or in good repair. No one cares." He could find no hope in himself for the town and the people he knew there. "It will all eventually go to rack and ruin."

Lost in his thoughts, Johan did not see the man in the darkened doorway as he strolled by.

"Johan Funk!"

Johan heard his name called, but in his sudden alarm, he did not recognize the voice.

"Johan Funk. That is you, isn't it?"

Stopping, Johan turned to see whom it was who had called him.

"I almost didn't recognize you in those duds!"

It was Makar Gribkov. The old friends shook hands warmly. "Come, let's walk," said Gribkov. "No one stands still anymore." He smiled wryly at Johan. "We're all afraid of being overheard. It seems the fashion is to tattle on one's friends and acquaintances—anything to avoid suspicion of oneself. Sad isn't it?"

They walked in silence for a while. "It's all over town that your family left," Gribkov said, more quietly now. "Here one day, gone the next. And you're not the only ones." He paused. "But you probably know that."

Gribkov's hands were thrust deep in his pockets and his shoulders were raised to preserve some warmth around his neck—the night air was frigid. "Volkov was furious. But not as furious as he was when he found out your father had died. He still hoped to get his revenge for whatever wrong he felt Franz had done him, though after all these years you'd have thought he'd have gotten over it. I think he broke a militiaman's head—the fellow who told him the news. I'm told he gave him a backhand that knocked him clean out. He's a right bastard, is our Sokol Volkov."

Johan could think of nothing to say.

After another step or two, Gribkov added, "My condolences, by the way. Your father was a good man, an honest man, a real friend."

Johan murmured his thanks. Then he added, "I never got a chance to thank you for warning Father about the arrest warrant."

Gribkov grunted, but said nothing for a time.

"What are you doing back here? I'm guessing your family is in Moscow? Don't act surprised that I should know. It's common knowledge by now; so many of your people have left." Gribkov paused. "You've come back for your mother?"

When Johan nodded, Gribkov said, "Good."

They came to a cross in the road.

Gribkov said, "This is my way home. I wish you well, my friend. If you need anything in the next day or two, I'll try to give you a hand. It's the least I can do to honor your father."

Johan thanked him for his offer.

"But, don't drag it out," Gribkov said as they shook hands in parting. "I'd collect Anna and get back on the train to Moscow as quickly as I could, if I were you. The militia is getting edgy. Moscow has sent a directive about stopping the flow of German refugees. Apparently the Party doesn't like the egg that's being spread all over its face. All you people clamoring to get out isn't doing our country's international image a favor. And you never know what Volkov might get it into his head to do."

It was late in the evening by the time Johan reached Lyubimovka. The sky was clear and the moon and stars gave the land a glow that lit his way. Not that he needed it; he could find his way home from Isylkul blindfolded, so many times had he made the journey.

He was chilled through by the time he entered the village. Johan saw the darkened homes and was filled with sadness at the memory of what had once been and was now lost. He came upon Pavel and Larissa's home first. It showed no signs of life. Johan had told them of the sale of the crop and offered to pay Pavel to stay on to help with the harvest. But Pavel would have no part of it. If the Funks were leaving, he had said, so would he. "Your secret is safe with us," he had affirmed mournfully. Pavel and his family left Lyubimovka in the early morning hours a few days later. They did not want any farewells. Gratefully, though, Pavel had touched his pocket where he had put the gift of rubles Johan had given him. They would help keep his family fed for a while until they found a home and work elsewhere.

Looking a little further along the road, Johan saw his own house. In his mind's eye he saw again the work it had taken to build it: dismantling a granary on the property of a cousin in a neighboring village; hauling the boards to his property; his son, Franz, spending endless hours pounding straight every single nail salvaged from the tear-down; erecting the walls and roof; and finally moving their possessions from their old mud and wattle house to their new dwelling. The memories cascaded over him: the joy of his children's births on the very bed where they had been conceived; Christmases sharing simple gifts of handmade toys and clothing; family meal times; arguments, songs, laughter, tears. Despite the memories filling him with sentimentality and sad joy, Johan had no desire to go and open the door of his house. It was merely another wooden frame and was no longer his home.

Before he turned up the path to his parents' home, Johan saw the gate where, a few years earlier, a bull had almost gored his stepbrother, George Willms, to death. The memory came to him as if it had happened that afternoon. The village herder was collecting the cattle from each farm's gate along the road to take them out to pasture. The cows were plodding along the street and came to the Willms' gate. Willms was standing nearby, waiting in case the bull needed extra encouragement to join the herd. The bull was a cantankerous animal, but the herder had found most of the time it responded well to his whip. From a distance Johan had happened to look just as the animal turned on its owner. It knocked George to the ground as easily as if he had been a sheaf of straw. Meaning to kill Willms, it had attacked him where he lay. Fortunately, the beast's massive head was wide enough so that its sharp, curved horns pierced the earth on either side of George's chest. The herder on his horse had sent his long rawhide whip snapping at the bull's ears and testicles until it relented. The animal had been chivvied into a corral where it was killed and butchered that same day. Willms had been lucky to suffer only bruises. Johan shook his head at the memory. The bull's red meat had been tough and, shared throughout the village, had set everyone's cooking pots to long, slow boils in order to make it palatable.

Looking at his mother's house, Johan saw it was cloaked in darkness. Wondering whether it was wise to surprise Anna at this late hour he thought to spend the night in the barn. The hay would make a soft bed and, with the heat emanating from the cattle and horses, the night would be quite comfortable. As he approached the barn, Johan glanced over in the direction of his sister Sara's house. Seeing the soft glow of a kerosene lamp in the front window, Johan decided to drop in.

Johan knocked softly on Sara's door. It wouldn't do, he thought, to simply barge in. He didn't want to give his sister and her family a fright. Johan heard someone come to the door and undo a lock. "Yes," he thought, "there is enough fear now that doors are locked at night." In all their years in Lyubimovka, he had never locked the doors of his home. When the door was opened part way, Johan saw his sister and her husband, Cornelius, standing inside, together. Cornelius's hand was on the door and it seemed he was taut as a wound spring, ready to slam the door shut.

"Ach, Johan!" cried Sara as Cornelius opened wide the door. "I hardly recognized you! What are you doing here?" In her shock at seeing her brother, Sara found herself all discombobulated. "Come in! Come in!"

Johan hugged his sister and shook Cornelius' hand. He shrugged off his sheepskin coat and left it outside on the porch.

"Why are you here?" asked Sara as Johan bent over to remove his boots. She looked out into the darkness of the yard. "Are Elizabeth and the children here as well? What has happened?"

"Shut the door, Sara," said Cornelius. "You're letting the chill into the room."

"They are all in Moscow," replied Johan. "They are all well. I am here alone. I've come back for mother. I promised her; I'm going to take her to Moscow."

Cornelius gestured to a chair. "Sit down, Johan. Sara, make some tea."

They were soon seated around the kitchen table. They visited awhile, and when the tea was served, the conversation became more serious.

Cornelius said, "Do you really believe you will be allowed to leave this country?" When Johan didn't reply immediately he added, "You have been in Moscow for months and are you any closer to emigration?"

"I don't know how much closer we are," said Johan. "But I do know that staying in the Soviet Union is not an option for us. We are being squeezed on every side. They will kill us all, if they have their way. What is the worst that can happen? If we die trying to get out, at least we will have died on our own terms, not theirs."

"There are worse things than death," said Sara softly, arguing for and against attempting emigration with the same few words.

They sat in silence for a while.

"How are the children?" asked Johan. Sara and Cornelius had been childless until they had adopted two children into their family. Abie and Tina were brother and sister and came from a neighboring village. They had been orphaned during the civil war when both their parents died of typhus within the span of a month.

"They are well," said Sara.

"And Mother? How is Mother?"

"Her body is frail, Johan. But, I think, her spirit is strong. These months since Father's stroke have been very hard on her. Since his death…" her voice trailed off.

Silence settled again around them. Sara folded her hands and placed them upon the table.

"Johan it is so good you have come—tonight of all nights. Cornie and I are trying to decide whether to join you in Moscow. We have been up for hours tossing it back and forth. We simply cannot decide if we should take the risk."

And so, for the umpteenth time, they discussed the pros and cons of camping out in Moscow in an attempt to force the communist government into allowing them to emigrate. The discussion was emotional and physically draining. Leaving everything for one throw of the dice seemed at once foolish and inevitable. At long last, in the deepest darkness of the night, Cornelius and Sara came to a decision. They would go to Moscow.

And by the time they were ready to leave, two days later, Anna's other children, George and Helena Willms, and Cornelius and Rose Willms, had decided to come to Moscow as well. Lyubimovka, the Village of Love, would be abandoned to the wind and the cold, the snow, the ice, and whatever time and chance brought its way.

It was early when Johan awoke the morning after his arrival in Lyubimovka. Looking out into the darkness, he saw a hard hoar frost had coated every surface with ice crystals glittering in the glow of the dying moon. Further on, Johan noticed a timid light in the kitchen window of his mother's house. It was too early for Vera Buryshkina to have started her daily chores, which told him his mother was awake. Knowing he must not be seen by Vera or Ivan, Johan quickly dressed. Once outside, he pulled the frosty air into his lungs. Fragments of the memories of a hundred mornings such as this flooded his mind. Pushing them aside, Johan walked along the path to his mother's door, knowing there had never been a morning such as this.

Coming to his parents' home, Johan climbed the steps onto the veranda. He tapped lightly on the front door. Trying the latch, he found it unlocked. He opened the door and stepped into the entryway calling softly, "Mother, I'm home." He paused a moment and then said, "Mother, it's me, Johan. I'm back. I've come for you."

There came a rustling from the kitchen. Johan quickly removed his boots and padded down the hallway. He met his mother in the doorway to the kitchen. She had on her flowered silk dressing gown, a frayed remnant of the prosperity that had once been theirs.

"Johan," Anna whispered, her hand coming to cover her mouth. Tears welled in her eyes and overflowed. "My Franz. He is gone!"

Johan gathered his mother in his arms. In their shared sorrow, he wept with her. Holding her, he was shocked by her frailty. She felt as light as a dry leaf in autumn. Johan held her in a strong embrace lest she be blown away by the gale of her grief, for the love that had been her firm anchor for forty-two years had died and was buried beneath the frozen Siberian soil. Johan said nothing, for—for this moment—there was nothing words could say.

Chapter 17

October 22, 1929

The day of departure came too quickly for Anna. She became morose and wondered aloud whether she shouldn't stay in Lyubimovka.

"I am old," she said. "My life is here. My Franz is here." And the tears began to flow anew. "How can I leave my Franz and start a new life some place far away? Who will visit his grave? Who will pick up the leaves and place flowers where he lays?"

When her children argued with her, telling her she had once been a young widow with a house full of children and she had willingly begun a new life then, in a new place, with a new husband, she demurred. "Yes, but as you say, I was young and full of energy. I had a long life in front of me, and children to feed. People do what they have to do to survive. I simply don't have the energy to start over somewhere else. Let me die here."

"No," Johan insisted gently, but firmly. He understood his mother's sentimentality. Her husband was barely cold in the ground. "This is what you must do now to survive. All of your children are leaving Lyubimovka. You cannot remain here alone. You must come with us."

Anna argued weakly that Ivan and Vera could care for her. They had been such faithful and honest workers all these years. "Or perhaps someone from the church could move in with me. The house is large, there is plenty of room." It was only when Johan said if she refused to leave, he would be forced to bring his family home from Moscow and remain in Lyubimovka with her that Anna finally agreed to come to Moscow with him. "I know you're right, Johan," she said. "But at my age it is so difficult to face such an uncertain future." Johan didn't tell her the future she would have faced in Lyubimovka, had they stayed, would have been equally uncertain.

Haste was of the essence. Johan did not want to be separated from his family for longer than was necessary and, if by some miracle their emigration request was granted, it was obvious he needed to be with Elizabeth and the children in Moscow. And he worried his presence at Lyubimovka might be discovered by the police.

"We will leave tomorrow," he said after a supper of cold ham, zweiback and plumi moos, a delicious cold soup made of stewed plums. The local soviet had long ago confiscated all the Funk's grain so the flour for the buns had been purchased on the black market at the bazaar in Isylkul.

"Your father smoked that ham," Anna had tearfully announced while Johan had cut slices and placed them on a plate. They had reminisced about Franz and had wept freely together.

"When your father came back from St. Petersburg—that city they now are calling Leningrad—and told me we were moving to Siberia, I didn't believe him. When he showed me the papers saying he had purchased this village, I told him I didn't want to go. I didn't want to move away from the good life we had in the Ukraine. He said we could have a wonderful life here, and you know, he was right. These past seventeen years I wouldn't have wanted to live anywhere else."

"Yes," agreed Johan, "Lyubimovka has been a good place to raise our children."

"And now we will find a new Lyubimovka where we are free to live as we wish," said Anna wistfully as she dried her tears. "Our cousins in Canada are exuberant in their insistence we come there. They say they do not have any fear of the police or the government. Do you think such a thing is possible?"

Leaving her home was difficult for Anna, but once she had decided to join the migration to Moscow, her only remaining immediate concern was for the farm animals that would be left behind. There was no time to sell them.

"The things I have in this house," she said, "it is all just stuff. But the horses and the cow, what will become of them? The chickens and pigs—who will feed them? They can't stay here in the barn. We can't just leave them."

Johan agreed. "But," he said, "the fewer people who know you are leaving, the better." Later that evening he saddled Franz's favorite mare and rode to Friedensruh. "I will make arrangements," were his parting words to Anna. "Don't worry, the animals will be well cared for."

Anna did not look back as the wagon carrying her and Johan left the yard of her home in Lyubimovka. She was wrapped in a thick woolen blanket to ward off the cold. It was late in the evening and they meant to catch the midnight train. Low clouds obscured the moon and in the darkness, their safety depended as much on the horses' good sense as Johan's guidance. He encouraged the horses into a comfortable walk while in the bed of the wagon, Anna's son, Cornelius, struggled to find a comfortable position for the long ride to the station in Isylkul. He would bring the wagon back home.

The family had spent a long time discussing where and when it would be best to board the train. The Willms brothers wanted Johan to take the train at the station in Isylkul, but Johan at first had argued against it. He did not want to risk another chance meeting with Sokol Volkov. However, Anna's frailty decided things for him. A long, grinding wagon ride in cold temperatures to the next station west of town would simply be too much for her to endure.

Johan had rejected any thought of accepting Gribkov's offer of help. He had not even told the family about his conversation with him. Gribkov was a Russian, and though a good family friend, was not to be trusted. In the end Cornelius Willms had offered to take Johan and Anna to Isylkul. There was nothing for it but to accept his offer, but, nonetheless, Johan had acquiesced reluctantly. The rest of the families— both Willms men and their wives, as well as Cornelius and Sara Funk and their children—all planned to begin the trip to Moscow in the next day or two, as soon as they had disposed of whatever belongings they could in such a short time.

Johan hummed a hymn under his breath as he guided the horses along. Before leaving, Anna had walked through all the rooms of her house, remembering the sounds and smells of her family's days there. Then she had joined Johan in the barn. She watched as he made sure all the animals were well fed and watered. Over the years Anna had spent little time in the barn. It had been Franz's domain; hers was the house.

She stopped at each stall and petted the horses and the cow, recognizing in each the smells her husband's clothes had carried. She asked more than once if the cow's udder was empty. "She will suffer if she isn't milked in the morning," she had worried.

"Don't concern yourself," said Johan, "Ivan will be here in the morning. He will milk the cow and feed the animals. When he sees you are not at home, he will think you have gone to Isylkul for the day and because tomorrow is a religious feast day, he will be in a hurry to return home so he and Vera can go to their church. By the time he returns the next day, the animals will all be gone." Johan hoped that would, indeed, be the case.

Anna said, "I'm sorry we cannot be honest with Ivan and Vera. They have been such good workers. They provided your father with a place of refuge when he hid from the police. Surely we owe them something for that."

"Yes, I am sorry too," said Johan. "But this is how it must be."

Anna nodded and continued on her pilgrimage through the barn. Looking at the chickens she espied an egg or two. She thought to bring them along, but then realized they'd more than likely be broken along the way. So she left them tucked under the cluck's warm feathers. She spread some hay among the chickens. As there was no grain for feed, the birds would need to content themselves picking at what they could find in the dry grass.

As their wagon left the yard, the cow lowed in the barn. Hearing the cow, Anna was content, for her son had said he would make arrangements for the animals' care. And her son was a man of his word.

The road to Isylkul was rutted and frozen. The wagon lurched over bump after bump, but Johan hardly noticed. He was tense with anxiety, fearing they might be stopped and recognized. To his relief, they met no one along the way.

Anna was grateful when they arrived in town. They stopped on a lane not far from the station. She groaned as Johan helped her climb down from her seat on the wagon. Her arthritic frame had been jolted severely and for a time she found it difficult to move her stiffened limbs. She kissed Cornelius on the cheek as he embraced her. "I will see you in Moscow," she said simply.

"Yes," agreed Cornelius, "we will come as soon as we can."

Anna took the small bundle of possessions Johan handed her. It contained the only things he had allowed her to bring. She shuffled along beside him as they walked the last distance to the station.

"Is it necessary, all these precautions?" she complained. "We have to stop in an alley and walk to the station?"

Johan did not want to explain again the need for anonymity. They could not make an announcement of their arrival at the station. The poor walked, and thus so would they.

Johan was again wearing his "peasant get-up" as he called the sheepskin coat, ushanka hat, and felt boots of his disguise. He had chosen Anna's shabbiest coat for her to wear, and a non-descript, ragged kerchief to cover her hair. She looked like a proper babushka, though she would have blushed had her husband seen her dressed so.

Arriving at the station, they found a bench where Anna could rest. Johan dropped the bundle he had been carrying and pushed it on the floor beneath her. "I will be back as soon as I can," he said. He entered the station and joined the line of passengers buying train tickets.

When it was finally his turn, Johan stepped up to the wicket. "Two fares to Moscow, please," he said in his best Russian. He handed the agent his identity card. The man looked at it and abruptly handed it back.

"It says on your card you are German. I cannot sell you tickets to Moscow. We've received a directive. No tickets to Moscow are to be sold to any German colonists. No exceptions." The agent's voice was rough and deep, sounding like it came from the bottom of a gravel pit.

Johan could have kicked himself for his forgetfulness. Gribkov had warned him of this. Thinking quickly he replied, "Did I say Moscow?" When the agent merely stared at him, Johan added, "I'm sorry. I meant to say two tickets to Ekaterinburg. We're going to Ekaterinburg. I'm taking my mother there to visit a relative." Johan chose Ekaterinburg for their destination because it was off of the main line to Moscow. Perhaps it would deflect the agent's suspicion. For good measure he slid a ten-ruble note across the counter. Johan didn't like resorting to bribery, but knew there was no sense in offending the man's corrupt sensibilities by holding to stricter moral scruples.

"Well, that's different," growled the ticket agent with a skeptical look, pocketing the rubles. "Ekaterinburg, eh?" He rummaged in a pile of papers and produced two vouchers.

Johan paid the fare and gratefully took the precious tickets to where Anna waited.

It wasn't long before the train arrived. Johan was relieved to hear the chuffing of the engine as it pulled into the station. Just as he and Anna were collecting their few belongings in preparation for boarding, a commotion on the far side of the platform drew his attention. A group of militiamen were making their way through the crowd of waiting passengers. Johan saw they were stopping people and asking questions. It appeared they were checking tickets.

A family of German Mennonites was among the passengers. They were easy to pick out in the crowd of Russians because of the distinctive clothing they were wearing. When a member of the militia approached the family Johan had a feeling there would be trouble. "Show me your tickets," Johan heard the militiaman say. By this time, the passengers making their way to board the train had begun to give the family a wide berth—it was their instinctive response of self-preservation. As he climbed the steps to his car, Johan had a clear view of what was happening.

The hapless husband nervously handed over his tickets. After they had been examined, the officer said loudly, "No German colonists may travel to Moscow. The ticket agent knows this. Where did you get these tickets?" Something was muttered that Johan couldn't hear. The officer of the militia tore up the precious tickets and dropped the pieces to the ground where they were immediately trampled underfoot. Other members of the militia surrounded the family and, using their rifles, prodded and pushed them toward the exit and out of the station.

Johan's breath was taken away by what he just witnessed. As he and Anna found their seats, he took a last look at the station. There was no sign of the family that had just been denied passage. How fortunate he and Anna were, he realized. He breathed a prayer of thanks. What troubled him, though, was the question, "Where will I be able to buy tickets to Moscow?" He had no answer for that, and he certainly had no intention of going to Ekaterinburg.

Chapter 18

October 24, 1929

Johan Funk was becoming more pensive and nostalgic with each kilometer the train carried him away from Lyubimovka. The finality of separation had not hit him when he and his family had left in August, for then he had had the conflicting hope of a promised return. He might see his village again, but it would mean his father was dead. Now there would be no going back. Johan thought of his parent's beautiful, red brick home, now empty of life. While his mother worried in the kitchen preparing food to bring on the train the night before, he had walked through the house, stopping in every room. He had drunk in the scents and memories found in each, knowing all physical connections with his past were being irrevocably severed.

Johan thought about the picture left hanging on the great room wall. It was the only oil painting he had seen in all the thirty-eight years of his life. He had often stopped to admire the picture, sometimes with his nose almost touching the canvas as he sought to understand the artist's technique. The thick oils depicted with strong, deft strokes the bright spring colors of the orchard growing in the field between the house and the forest of pine and birch beyond. The artist had appeared on the farmyard one day—in the happy years before the brutal color red had begun its oppressive rule over the land—and offered his services. Wearing a large straw hat to shade his head, he had labored at his easel in the bright Siberian sunshine for many days, Johan recalled, though he couldn't remember his name. The painter had captured perfectly the delicate pinks and whites of the apple and plum blossoms against the soft, pale blue of the cloudless sky. Regrettably, the humble artist had insisted on leaving the beautiful work unsigned. The ornate golden frame to showcase the painting had been purchased in a shop on Prince Alexander Prospekt in Omsk.

"He was too self-effacing," thought Jacob. "Such talent needs to be acknowledged."

Johan wished somehow he had been able to bring the painting along—an impractical desire, he knew. It was too cumbersome to carry and too large to fit in a suitcase, even when removed from its frame and rolled up. Sadly, taking the painting with them had simply been out of the question, just as taking anything else beyond the essentials had been impossible. The police and militia were watching for Germans traveling to Moscow. It would have invited immediate suspicion if Johan and Anna were seen to be carrying anything beyond a few possessions. It had been difficult enough getting the large bag of rusks—twice-baked buns—his mother had prepared onto the train and under their seat, essential lest they starve along the way. Johan thought no one had noticed in the chaos of everybody finding their spots and getting settled themselves. He comforted himself with the observation that some of his fellow passengers were also bringing with them large bundles and baskets of possessions. What he and his mother carried was not at all unusual.

The painting had been left hanging above the mantel on the stone fireplace in the great room, along with the comfortable furniture and muted decorations with which his father and mother had decorated their home. They couldn't have risked holding an auction, and, indeed, there had been no time for it anyway. Johan hoped his friend, Nicholas Janzen, to whom he had quietly spoken his intentions after he had visited his father's grave in Friedensruh, would come quickly to collect any items he could use or easily sell. Otherwise, the painting, like everything else left behind, would become the possession of the first person with the temerity to enter the abandoned house—the house the locals had once liked to call the finest in all the country between Omsk and Moscow—and loot its contents.

Nicholas had promised to quietly disperse the animals amongst the Mennonite community of farmers who were in greatest need.

The steel wheels of the train clattered on the tracks below and Johan rocked to its sway as the wagon rolled over small dips and rises in the Trans-Siberian Railway roadbed. They were traveling westward, away from Isylkul toward the distant slopes of the Ural Mountains.

Somehow, along the way they would obtain tickets to the city of desperation, Moscow, on the other side of the Urals.

Johan huffed some warm air onto the frosted pane of glass beside him. Using the sleeve of his jacket, he rubbed a spot clear. Through the small window, Johan peered into the night. The luminous waxing moon lit the monochrome landscape with an argent light that took his eye captive with its breathless beauty. Johan loved the land of his birth—the land did not change, only its rulers. The flat, grey steppe stretched endlessly away beyond sight. Shadowy pines, aspens, birches and larch stood wraith-like, branches stretched beseechingly skyward in the fields. Here and there the stream-slashed earth was cut deep and dark by wandering waterways leading patiently and inexorably to places north, to the Arctic and its frozen seas. Johan knew if he had been a painter rather than a farmer and musician, this would be the scene he would paint. It would, in a multitude of shades of silver-white, present Russia at her very best, where the light of the moon showed the greatest dimensions of her beauty and where, hidden from the light of day, no evidence could be seen of the oppressive brutality now walking upon it.

The thought of what his beloved country had become brought a short, cynical laugh from deep in Johan's gut. It was soundless and without mirth. He shook his head for the thousandth time in disbelief at how intolerable life had become under the communist regime, and at the desperate turn his life—and indeed, the lives of everyone he knew and loved—had taken.

To turn his thoughts in another direction, Johan looked into the dimness of the railcar. He focused his attention on his fellow travelers. The wagon was crowded. It was what had once been considered a third class car—the communists insisted since all were equal, all should now travel in the same austere conditions. Again his cynical snicker escaped him. He had seen the shops in Moscow; shops where he and most everyone else could not hope to even enter. Clearly, some were more equal than others. Again, Johan focused on the railcar. Its wooden benches and floor were filled with weary, sprawling passengers, their tattered packages and baskets of belongings grasped tightly to guard against the light fingers of thieves and pickpockets that invariably were to be found in such a large, ragtag group. Loud snores mingled with the occasional dull mutterings and sighs of disturbed sleep.

156

Johan shivered. The small smoky potbellied stove set in the middle of the car did little to push back the cold. Unrepaired holes in one end wall allowed whatever warmth there was to escape out into the night. Johan had first noticed the holes because of the array of sunbeams piercing the dim air of the wagon in a pattern that evoked the memory of a rose window he had once seen in a cathedral in Omsk—he could only imagine how the holes had been made. Fortunately they were in the wall at the trailing end of the car. The frigid cold of winter had not yet arrived, but there was enough frost in the air to chill ones bones.

A cloud of cigarette smoke blown through the nostrils of an insomniac passenger on the bench across from Johan stung his eyes. The man was slouched sideways against a large, shoddy bundle. He held his cigarette close to his mouth in the fashion of the Russian peasant, between the thumb and index finger of his left hand. The man was staring through the smoke at Johan. Johan felt acutely uncomfortable under his inscrutable gaze.

Johan peered further into the railway car. Though it was night and many of his fellow passengers seemed asleep, plumes of smoke could be seen rising here and there like the smoldering smudge pots that had warmed the autumn night air in his father's orchard enough to keep the fruit from freezing. In the greasy, flickering glow of a kerosene lantern hanging on one wall, Johan could see the disparate wisps merge above the grey forms creating a pungent fog rising to slowly escape through the rose window, pushed along by the currents seeping into the car through poorly sealed windows.

"Perhaps the drafts aren't a bad thing after all," thought Johan wryly. He wrinkled his nose at the acrid smell of the strong tobacco the peasants preferred. That, mixed with the rancid reek of their unwashed bodies, made breathing difficult.

Johan glanced at his mother leaning against him. She was asleep, with her frail head resting on his right shoulder. His arm was numb from its awkward position wrapped protectively around her. He moved it slightly and wiggled his fingers to restore some circulation. He drew her tighter to him. The lines around her mouth and eyes were deep with sadness and exhaustion. Her lips drooped at the corners in a frown. Errant strands of her wavy silver hair lay across her face. In a tender gesture, Johan smoothed them over her forehead. Sleep should bring peace, he thought, but there was no peace in his mother's aged visage. He reached over with his left hand and drew her shawl closer around her.

The familiar burning in the pit of Johan's stomach returned as he remembered the dream that had awoken him. He was not sure when the burning had first begun though he knew it was some time during the early anxious days in Moscow. Now his stomach roiled because of a dream he had encountered in his sleep twice before in the tumultuous months leading up to this day, and he feared the dream would prove prophetic.

In the beginning of his dream, the members of Johan's family were all together. His father and his mother were there. Johan was there with his wife, and their children, Franz, Abe, Wilhelm, Maria and Katrina. Johan's brother, sister, and stepbrothers, and their families were there as well. It was dark, an indeterminate season, though not winter, judging from the lack of cold and snow. Carrying only a few bundles, they were all leaving their village at the start of what could only be described as a fateful journey. He knew not where they were going, but was certain of the need to leave and that there was no question of return. The separation from what had been was going to be final. In the darkness and confusion of the dream their traveling took them along winding pathways through thick forests and over high mountains, beside fast-flowing rivers and across the great distances of the grassy steppes. The days and nights passed by and the paths twisted and turned. The group encountered dead ends and came to crossroads. And with each twist and turn of the way, with each crossroad forcing choices and decisions, a family member disappeared, and then another and another so that with each new dawn, there were fewer of them left to begin that day's journey. At the end, when the unknown destination was achieved, there were left with Johan only his wife and his children. The rest of the family had all vanished.

Reality brought Johan back to the present. He thought of Elizabeth and the children waiting in Moscow. It was eight days since he had last seen them. His stomach twisted as he worried about their welfare. Were they warm? Did they have enough to eat? Were they safe? God forfend the secret police should take an interest in them.

Johan's eyes peered through the murky glass at the pale steppe crawling by. The train was slowing. Was it another post station? Or was it Chelyabinsk where he would have to face the problem of buying tickets to Moscow? Time would tell, but already he had the beginnings of a plan in mind.

In the darkness of the railway carriage, he hugged his mother to him and soundlessly wept. He mourned for her grief and pain, for his dear dead father, for his abandoned home and for his lost homeland.

Chapter 19

October 24, 1929

The ticket agent in Chelyabinsk was proud of the position of responsibility the Party had given him in return for his service in the Red Army during the civil war. He had lost a leg when a grenade exploded in his foxhole during the battle for Perm, and as a result was unsuitable for most jobs. However, sitting on his stool at the ticket counter in the railway station the man was happy. He felt the power of his position and used every opportunity that came along to exert it. When he received the directive to refuse tickets to any German colonists attempting to travel to Moscow, he determined no Germans would slip by his kiosk. He didn't understand the need for such an order, but that did not bother him. Nor did he think about its implications. "If the government says no Germans are to travel to Moscow, then so be it and let the devil take them," he muttered after his overseer had given him his instructions.

After Johan and Anna left the post train that had carried them from Isylkul, Johan looked for as comfortable a spot as he could find in the Chelyabinsk Railway Station in which his mother might rest while he purchased tickets for the next leg of their journey. In an out-of-the-way corner, he found a once ornate armchair that at one time must surely have been someone's treasure, but was now a battered version of itself.

"I will be back as soon as I am able," he said when Anna was safely settled.

Too tired to say anything, Anna merely nodded her head. Johan looked long at his mother as she closed her eyes. He worried about the toll the journey was taking on her. She was thin and her skin was pale; she looked every one of her seventy-eight years, and more.

Johan walked toward the long line of people purchasing travel vouchers at the ticket agent's counter. Standing to the side, in an alcove that allowed him to see the transactions as they were being made as well as hear what was said, Johan watched person after person purchase tickets—some to Samara in the south, others to Ekaterinburg in the north, and many to Moscow in the west. Before each ticket was sold, the agent asked to see the buyer's identity card. Everyone in the queue looked Russian and none were refused a ticket. However, there was one family dressed differently from the others. Johan knew they were German without having to hear them speak to each other. When it was their turn to approach the counter, they were quickly and firmly refused tickets. Johan watched as they picked up their bundles of possessions and bleakly wandered out of the station with the forlorn, confused look of people who are lost and who have no idea how to find their way again.

Johan made his decision. Asking for tickets to Moscow was out of the question, so he would get tickets to a city along the way to Moscow. This would take him off of the express route, but so be it. Better to arrive later than to not arrive at all.

It took him hours to reach the agent's kiosk. With a long line stretched before him, the man got up and left the people standing there while he disappeared into a back room. He hobbled out on his crude crutch without so much as a word of explanation. As they waited, some of the spurned passengers had slowly settled themselves onto their belongings. The women sat and chatted noisily while the men stood with dull looks of resignation on their faces until the agent miraculously reappeared. There was much grumbling and quiet cursing, but none wanted to raise the man's ire lest he take their complaints to heart. Those closest to the kiosk were wisely silent—they were local and knew the man's temperament—and the line moved forward at a snail's pace once more.

"Two tickets to Nizhny Novgorod," Johan said when he finally reached the kiosk.

After looking at Johan's identity card and receiving payment plus a few rubles of tea money, the agent slid the two tickets across the counter toward Johan's hand. "Ya don't look like no German I've ever seen," he said as Johan pocketed the tickets.

Johan smiled. "Spasiba," he said. "I am grateful for your kind service."

The train to Nizhny Novgorod didn't leave until later that day.

While they waited, Johan explained to Anna they did not have tickets to Moscow, but to Nizhny Novgorod, five hundred kilometers east of Moscow.

"We'll get there," he said confidently in response to her querying look. "It will only take a while longer. And you will get to see some beautiful country along the way." Johan explained the reason for their detour—the strategy of the Soviet leadership to stop the flow of German refugees to Moscow by denying them the right to buy train tickets.

"I've seen enough of Russia," grunted Anna after listening to his attempt to put a positive spin on their predicament.

"We will be traveling north to Ekaterinburg," said Johan trying to inspire interest in the journey in his mother. "From there we'll go through the Urals to Perm on the Kama River, then on to Kirov and finally south to Nizhny Novgorod. At Nizhny Novgorod, we'll purchase tickets to Yaroslavl. That's a community north of Moscow. There are plenty of refugees there already and we'll have no trouble getting tickets to Perlovka from there."

Instead of sitting during the hours until the train arrived, Johan decided to stretch his legs a bit. Lately he had noticed inactivity caused his knees and hips to stiffen. He had begun to wonder if he was getting arthritis. Sitting in the cramped railcar for the last two days had been difficult. It was painful for him to begin walking after his joints stiffened up, though the pain subsided when he walked for a while. Strolling along the platform, Johan looked at the building and the remnants of the grandeur that had clothed it when it had been built at the turn of the century. It had once been a beautiful station though now, like everything else, it was suffering from the neglect of indifference that communism had spawned.

Coming to the end of the station platform, Johan noticed a train sitting idle on a siding. It seemed to be made up of cattle cars, flatcars loaded with logs, and other freight cars. There was no engine attached. A group of men seemed to be at work on one end of the train, but Johan couldn't tell what they were up to. Without much thought, Johan walked toward the train, stepping over the sets of tracks between the platform and the siding. The sun was shining and a brisk wind blew from the east. The air was cold and held the promise of a frigid night.

As Johan drew closer to some freight cars, he thought he heard some noises coming from within them. Looking around to see if he was being observed and seeing no one, Johan walked toward the wagon closest to him. Listening, he was shocked to discern human voices. Johan looked again to see if anyone was watching him. There was no one in sight. He rapped on the wall of the freight car.

"Hello?" he said tentatively. "Hello in there."

The car was suddenly silent.

A man's voice said, "Hello? Hello? Is someone there?"

"Yes, hello," said Johan, startled.

"Hello! Can you help us?"

All at once many voices began crying for help. They grew in intensity until someone inside the car was able to assert himself and the car once again was quiet.

"Who are you? What has happened? Why are you in this freight car?" Johan said. He began to tremble as reasons for what he had happened upon began to flash through his mind.

"Can you help us?" cried the same voice. "Can you open the door?"

Johan hurried around to the other side of the car and found its sliding door. A large iron padlock ensured no one without a key would be able to open it. "I cannot open it. It's locked," said Johan. He quickly looked around on the ground but there was no bar or anything else with which he might be able to pry the lock.

"We need food and water!" cried the voice. "I don't know how many of us there are in here but we have barely enough room for the children to lie down to sleep. We have had nothing to eat or drink for two days. We need help!"

Johan's skin began to crawl at the horror he was hearing for he recognized something in the sound of the words being spoken.

"A woman has given birth; the baby died. Another child has died and others are sick. There are elderly people among us who are failing. There is no heater. If help does not come, we will either die of thirst or we will freeze to death!" The voice was hoarse in its desperation.

"Who are you?" asked Johan, knowing the answer but not knowing what to say and unable to help. He knew getting an official from the railway station was out of the question, for a government that would lock people in a railway car—and it could only be the government that would do such a thing as this—was one lacking any sense of compassion or humanity.

"We are Mennonite refugees. Most of us have been staying in Pushkino," said the voice. "Where are we?" Before Johan could reply the voice went on, "They arrested us, the men, and tortured us at the Lubyanka. They stuffed us in small rooms so hot we couldn't breath, day after day, until we signed a paper saying we would 'voluntarily' return to our villages. They even told us they'd pay our way. Then they loaded us into these train cars. Some of us are with our families; other families have been separated. Where are we?"

"Chelyabinsk," said Johan miserably.

"But most of us in here are from Crimea!" cried the voice. And then, after a momentary pause the realization struck. "They're not sending us home; they're sending us to Siberia!" A renewed wailing grew inside the car and the prisoners began pounding on its walls.

"I don't know what I can do!" Johan said, horrified. The pounding grew louder. The people in the railcar next to the one where he stood began pounding on the walls of their car, in a futile expression of despair and hope and anger and fear.

A shot rang out from the far end of the train. Johan looked and saw a soldier coming his way.

"You there!" the soldier shouted. "Get away from that car!" His rifle was in his hands, but it was pointed upward. The soldier began to run toward where Johan stood.

Johan cried, "I'm sorry!"

He ran away from the freight car and the soldier with his gun. He stumbled over the train tracks as he ran toward the station. Looking back he saw the soldier had stopped by the freight cars. He was shouting and hitting the side of the freight car with the butt of his rifle.

Johan continued to run until he was out of the station and on the street. He ran and ran, not thinking of where he was going, but with the one thought he needed to distance himself from the horror playing itself out at the station where his mother waited for him. He ran from his impotence to help and from the knowledge his family might at this moment be in danger of a similar fate. He ran from the soldier who had challenged him and from the fear causing him to run in the first place.

Where was his courage, yet who could challenge such grand brutality? He ran from the certain awareness it was not he, and he ran from the recognition of his drive for self-preservation that was stronger than his willingness to put himself at risk in order to help others in desperate need. And, he ran from the realization that, pray as much as one might, God was not in the business of preventing human atrocities.

It was only much later after Johan came to his senses and thought through what happened that he realized there was nothing he could have done to help the refugees—the prisoners in their wooden rolling cages. Nothing at all. But, regardless of the realization of the futility of the guilt he still felt, it would take Johan even longer to forgive himself for his inaction, and God, for his.

Eventually, Johan made his way back to the railway station at Chelyabinsk. He found where his mother had sat the entire time he was gone. She eyed him unhappily for his long absence, but said nothing. She could see the distress on his face, but when she asked what was the matter, Johan looked away and was quiet.

The train to Nizhny Novgorod arrived noisily. Johan helped Anna up the steps and directed her to an available bench where they sat in silence. He looked in the direction of the siding where the freight train had been. It was gone.

With a lurch, their train began to move. Johan stared long into the darkness while his mother, quickly asleep, snored softly beside him.

Chapter 20

October 27, 1929

In the spread-out yet tight-knit community of Mennonite refugees living in the northern suburbs of Moscow, fueled by stories being told and retold through the grapevine within hours of their occurrence, anxiety was spreading like frost on a mid-winter windowpane. It seemed the communists were becoming increasingly impatient with the nuisance that had planted itself in their capital city. People spoke of being stopped and asked, "Who is your leader?" In the communist mind, it seemed incomprehensible so many people should be able to act upon the same goal without being led by someone. For the most part they were answered with silence and shrugs, for in truth, there was no single leader. When one grandmother boldly answered, "Our leader is God!" her interrogators were confused and disbelieving, for surely God was dead—they had been told so by their glorious leaders Lenin and Stalin. They laughed at her in a display of bravado, but for some it was a false gesture and they wondered if such a large movement of people might possibly know something they had been denied.

Worse, though, were the arrests. Black Ravens, the cars of the secret police, were appearing more frequently in neighborhoods at night. Doors were being knocked upon; angry questions were being asked. Husbands and fathers were being detained, though the arrests were sporadic and seemed haphazard. No one knew who would be targeted next. A few of the men were returned to their families with grim faces. Some told stories of torture, of being crammed into rooms so full of men that new arrivals were passed over top—hand over hand—until at the back of the room they were let down where they could stand in the press, unable to do little else except gasp for breath. Those closest to the doorway refused to give up their place, for there at least was some hope of finding breathable air. Some of those arrested were not heard from again. Some families whose husbands and fathers had been arrested were loaded onto trucks and taken away. No one knew where they went, for they, too, did not return.

One of those arrested was Jacob Hildebrandt. He answered a loud midnight knocking on his dacha's door, and when he could not give satisfactory answers to the secret policemen's strident questions, he was taken away to the Lubyanka, the infamous prison housed in the basement of the beautiful Neo-Baroque architectural masterpiece on Lubyanka Square in the heart of Moscow. It had originally been constructed in 1898, to house the All-Russia Insurance Company. After their revolution in 1917, the Bolsheviks quickly saw other more practical uses for it and the grand building was made the headquarters of their secret police. The Lubyanka gained the reputation as being the tallest building in Moscow, for, it was said by those who entered it voluntarily and involuntarily alike, that from its basement one could see Siberia—for most prisoners who survived their stay in Lubyanka, Siberia by forced transport was their next destination. Hildebrandt was one of those fortunate to be released from his imprisonment. His response to the anxious questions of his family was a somber silence, for he was traumatized and knew nothing of the whys or the wherefores of his experience.

Knowing what was happening in the community of refugees, Franz Funk was filled with anxiety. His stomach churned in his waking hours and his nights were spent in restless wakefulness. Sleep found him only occasionally and then for short periods of time. When he slept, nightmares often plagued his unconscious mind.

In the absence of his father, Franz was carrying a burden no sixteen-year-old should have to bear. He worried about the safety of his father who was risking arrest should he be recognized by the police in Isylkul. He was relieved the Soviet government was finally issuing passports, but his family was being charged what appeared to him to be an arbitrarily exorbitant fee. The cost of the passports had been increased for everyone, from 55 rubles to 220 rubles, but 330 rubles had been demanded of him. He had refused to pay. He thought the apparatchik at the Office of the Foreign Administration Department was trying to take advantage of him because of his age. "He's trying to fleece me because I'm the son," he thought angrily. And so he worried about whether or not his family would be given passports at all, and wished his father were there to advise him.

Elizabeth had been distressed when Franz returned home without the passports. "Such a large sum," she said. And then she had added hopefully, "Johan will sort this out when he gets home. He should be back in a few days."

But Johan had not returned. It was now eleven days since he had left. Elizabeth had been certain Johan would return home on the ninth day. "The Express trains from the east make travel so much faster," she said. "Four days traveling to Lyubimovka, a day at most to collect Mother, four days back to Moscow."

Franz had spent yesterday at the Yaroslavsky Railway Station, waiting for his father to arrive, but he hadn't come. While at the station, Franz heard stories from people arriving and others waiting, like him, that added to his fears: stories about people who had been refused tickets to Moscow; people who had been escorted off of the train when it was discovered they were German Mennonites traveling to Moscow; people who had already been living in Moscow's suburbs and had been forcibly returned to their villages. Some who had been sent home had been determined and resourceful and found their way back onto the trains. They had made it to Yaroslavsky Station. Their stories only served to deepen Franz's anxiety.

"He'll come today," Franz thought as he got off of the train from Perlovka.

The Yaroslavsky station was buzzing as usual. Among those in the station were people returning from their visit in the city. Many had huge grins on their faces.

"We got our passports!" shouted a man, waving pieces of paper in the air.

Other happy Mennonite refugees smiled. "We got them, too!"

Quite unexpectedly, a group of refugees standing close by began to question some who had received their passports.

"Why have so many of you been issued passports?" demanded a man who identified himself as a Lutheran German colonist. "We, too, have been trying to get passports, but not one of us has yet been successful!"

"Are you cheating?" asked a heavy-set Lutheran. "Who have you gotten to in the government? What are you paying him?"

There were murmurs of support from his group of friends.

"That's all nonsense, we've done nothing you haven't done," insisted the man who had waved his passports about. "Just keep pestering them. You'll get your passports," he said, and he ran off to catch his train.

The Lutheran German refugees grumbled amongst themselves. One said, "The Catholics aren't being given passports either. What are these people doing that we aren't?" Unhappily, the group left the station.

Franz had been shocked to hear the exchange. He could feel the desperate frustration of the Lutheran refugees. Their predicament was no different from his. But then he reminded himself, "My family's passports are sitting at the Office of the Department of Foreign Administration." His next thought was, "Father, where are you? Why aren't you here to tell me what to do?"

As Franz pondered these things, a man said loudly, "There is a rumor a transport train is being readied. It may happen any day now." His comment stunned the people who were standing about him. "I have it from a reliable source!"

"Really?" gasped those near him.

"Yes!" he averred. And when they pressed him for the source of his astounding information, he could only say a friend had told him, a friend who had insisted he had heard it from an official at the German Embassy.

Some wondered, "Where will the train pick us up? At which station? Here in Yaroslavsky? Kljasma? Pushkino? Perlovka?" Others asked, "Where will they take us? Will it be Leningrad? Riga?"

One man said helpfully, "I heard in July a train carried some refugees to Leningrad."

This news had the effect of an electric shock on Franz. He was in a frenzy of excitement. Here he was at Yaroslavsky Station to meet his father, but wasn't it more important for him to go to the passport office and finally obtain his family's precious passports, regardless of the cost? If transport trains were actually being prepared, he could not delay. His family must be aboard one of those trains. And, of course, his father knew his own way home to Perlovka; he did not need his son to meet him at Yaroslavsky. Franz's indecision was short-lived. He ran back to the Perlovka platform where the train happened to be in the process of boarding passengers. He found a seat and impatiently waited for the train to depart.

When the train finally started to move, Franz willed it to go faster. The trip to Perlovka never seemed to have taken so long. His heart pounded with nervous energy. "What if they stop handing passports out before I get there? What if there is a huge line of people and all the passports are gone?" he thought over and over. "It's up to me. I cannot fail Father! I cannot disappoint Mother!" But the money to pay for the passports that would get them the chance to be among the lucky ones on a transport train out of Russia was at the dacha in Perlovka. He had no choice but to first go home and get it.

Franz arrived at the Office of the Foreign Administration Department in the early afternoon that same day. There was a long queue of people anxiously waiting in front of him. Elizabeth had been overjoyed to hear the good news the miracle of emigration might be about to happen. She quickly counted out seven hundred rubles. "Some extra, if you need it," she had said with an excited wink. After Franz left she had reluctantly counted out the remainder. There were still a few hundred rubles left. "We'll manage," she reassured herself.

The queue moved slowly, as did everything in the Soviet Union of Socialist Republics, but eventually Franz stood before the desk of the passport officer.

"I've been here before," he said without hesitation, "and I know our passports are ready. The Johan Funk family." Franz put the militia's Certificate of Residency on the man's desk to prove his identity. After the apparatchik had perused it and handed it back, Franz counted out 440 rubles and laid them on the desk. Nervously, he waited to see the man's response. If that was the fee most people were being charged, he thought, perhaps things had changed and he would be able to save his family 220 rubles.

The apparatchik counted the money. He leafed through what seemed to be a ream of papers until he finally took one out. After looking at the paper a moment he slowly and deliberately pushed the money back toward Franz. "It say's here the charge for your family is 330 rubles per adult." The man looked at Franz with hostile eyes.

"But everyone else is paying 220 rubles," said Franz, struggling to control his emotions. "Why are we being charged more?"

"It says here your family were landowners," said the man indifferently. "Landowners pay more."

Franz lost his temper. Months of uncertainty, tension, and anxiety boiled up within him. The blatant injustice that had plagued his life for years past caused his mind to go black. Feeling he was being roughly pushed with his back up against a wall by what seemed to be a blatant bureaucratic cash grab, the emotion welled up from deep within him and he shouted, "Give me our passports!"

"Give me the money!" the uncaring servant of the communist machine shouted back. "You want your passports? The fee is 660 rubles!" he said, loudly cursing Franz and the rest of the people waiting in line.

A man standing in the queue behind Franz poked him in the ribs. "You'd best pay the man, son," he said quietly. He had looked toward the lobby. "The guard is coming. You're causing a disturbance. Do you want to get arrested?"

Franz realized he had no choice. Without another word, he counted out an extra 220 rubles and laid them on the desk. He glanced behind him and saw a guard had entered the room. He was holding his rifle across his chest, at the ready. Franz threw the rest of his rubles onto the pile.

The apparatchik slowly recounted all of the money Franz had given him. With exaggerated movements he put the fee for the passports in his drawer. He deftly pocketed the extra rubles. Finally, he took the Funk family's passports and handed them to Franz.

"Our noble country has no need of the likes of you," he said as he slid two papers across his desk. "You people are vermin and contaminate us all. If you weren't leaving, we would be forced to exterminate the lot of you."

Franz saw the man's mouth move, but didn't hear his insult. At long last, it had happened. In his hand he was holding two passports, one with his father's name on it, the other with his mother's name, his name, and the names of his brothers and sisters. They were the keys unlocking the path to his family's freedom. He was surprised they only listed their names and indicated they had permission to leave the country. He noticed the pictures his family had paid for and delivered were not included on the passports. He wondered at the discovery, but it mattered little. The papers he held were more valuable to him than all the gold in the world, and it filled him with joy.

Franz tucked the passports into an inner pocket of his thick winter jacket. As he hurried back to Yaroslavsky Station, he thought the sun was shining brighter than it had been before he had entered the building. Though the hour was later in the day when one would expect temperatures to chill, he felt the air was warmer. His steps were quicker and effortless. He hummed a favorite hymn, "Now thank we all our God with heart and hands and voices," and thought about how surprised and pleased his father would be when he finally arrived in Perlovka.

Chapter 21

October 28, 1929

The air in and around Perlovka was fairly sparkling with hope. If one hadn't known it was the end of October, one might have been excused for thinking the frigid grip of winter was ended instead of just beginning, and the glorious days of spring were imminent. The same cosmic force that routinely caused the earth to tilt and rotate upon its axis so the sun's warmth increased and decreased as the months of the year went by—the force governing the seasons and bringing forth blossoms and fruit in their time—that same force had caused a tectonic shift in the Soviet government's attitude toward the thousands of refugees clamoring at its gates to be allowed to leave the country. Hundreds of passports were being issued.

Stories abounded telling of how this colossal transformation of government policy had occurred. Some talked about the influence of the Tolstoyans who had been asked to lobby the government. Others told of a letter writing campaign aimed at the members of the Central Committee. There were whispers about an unlikely personal relationship built between a prominent refugee and President Kalinin. People talked of productive conversations with Zinoviev, another high-ranking government official. But gleaning truth from the stories was like trying to contain water in a cloth sack—the details disappeared through the fabric. And those who talked most were left wondering most while caring least, for the fact of the matter was clear for all to see. Passports were being issued and with passports came the possibility of emigration.

Nor were the excited refugees to know the full extent of the diplomatic wrangling being done by German Embassy officials in Moscow on their behalf, or the fact Germany was offering free passports and guaranteed repatriation for refugees—should they be deported from the countries to which they were allowed to immigrate. After years of ignominy following its utter defeat in 1918, German ethnic nationalism was once again raising its proud and confident head. And despite their century long stay in Russia, the refugees were Germans who needed their motherland's help.

People greeted one another with a joy unfelt in months—years—and talked of better times in a better place to come. The fact Canada had yet to issue entry visas was of little concern. The Canadian Pacific Railway and Steamship Company had promised credit; the Canadian government would approve their entry.

"After all," said one bystander in the crowd gathered at the Perlovka Railroad Station, "If the Soviets have said yes, then Canada surely will, too!" He looked to others for confirmation of the veracity of his prediction.

With the prospect of imminent emigration, friends and strangers openly began to speak of the country of their dreams.

"Our relatives in Canada say Canada is a democratic country," said one enthusiastic speaker. "The people choose their representatives in government from a variety of candidates who belong to different political parties. There is open debate without intimidation!"

"People are free there," agreed another. "They go where they want to go; they say what they want to say. Churches are welcomed. The citizens do not fear the police because the police in Canada actually work to protect the people. They are not the government's sledgehammer used to crush political dissent as they are here! Imagine that!"

Many shook their heads at the thought of such an idyllic place. They felt giddy at the very idea they were one step closer to living there.

"What language do they speak in Canada?" asked some who knew little about the country. "Why, German, of course," they were answered by those who were certain of their knowledge. "No, English," they were corrected by those also in the know—which brought feelings of consternation to those for whom the thought of learning a new language was daunting. "There are whole villages where German is the only language spoken," argued others indignantly. Which, when confirmed by those with family members in such villages, immediately lowered levels of anxiety considerably.

"What is the weather like?" a grey-haired grandfather asked.

"The climate and the soil in the Canadian prairies is much the same as our steppes. Wheat and other grains grow abundantly!" a happy farmer expounded.

And on and on the happy conversations went.

News of an impending transport train added to the excitement like a spark to dry tinder, bringing joy and laughter such as had seldom been heard or seen in the crowded northern suburbs of Moscow. Rumor or not, it had to be true.

However, the refugees' joy at the thought of a train sent to take them out of Russia was a double-edged sword; it quickly gave way to feelings of fear and heightened concern. There were too many unanswered questions. Now that the possibility of departure loomed, no one wanted to be left behind. There were many thousands who still had no passports. Some had not yet been able to make their applications. And others, arriving in Moscow without sufficient funds to pay for them, waited impatiently for responses to their wired pleas for financial help from far-flung relatives.

As soon as he had arrived at their dacha the day before, Franz had shown his mother their family's passports. She held them in her hands almost reverently, as an Orthodox Christian might hold her ikon. They represented to Elizabeth a tangible miracle of God and were precious beyond words. She found herself weeping with the joy of the promise they contained. Mother and son hugged each other and the younger children, when they came in from their outdoor play, shyly watched their mother's happiness.

Elizabeth held the passports so her children could see them and exclaimed, "Children, we have been given permission to leave this country!" In as much as their age and maturity allowed each to understand their mother's announcement, there was much clapping of hands and joyful shouts, in part, for the younger ones, simply because their mother's obvious joy was contagious. It had been many months since they had seen her so cheerful. But in the midst of the merriment, Elizabeth's face darkened, though she tried to hide it from her happy family, for she remembered her absent husband and worried, "Where are you, Johan? Please come home!"

The next morning, after a simple breakfast, Franz and Elizabeth discussed whether he should return to Yaroslavsky Station in the hope of meeting his father and grandmother there.

"Wouldn't it be wonderful for you to greet them with the news we have our passports?" said Elizabeth wistfully.

Franz agreed, but still hesitated. Finally it was decided he should wait at the Perlovka station, for the same gladsome end could be achieved closer to home.

"With the rumors of a transport train, it might be best if I stayed closer to home," remarked Franz. "I'm sure those who are able to go will need to have their names recorded. We need to make sure we are on such a list."

"You are right, Franz," Elizabeth agreed.

A chill breeze was tearing the few remaining leaves off of the quaking aspens when Franz took to the road. Bright sunlight reflected off of disks of ice where puddles from the previous day's rain had frozen overnight. Some puddles were shiny mirrors while others were chaotic layers of opaque shards, having been crushed by the busy boots of children who had been out early and had stomped them down in their destructive playfulness. Franz was not bothered by the cold for, having grown up in Siberia, he was used to far worse.

As Franz approached the railway station he noticed a crowd had gathered there. He was amazed for the morning was yet young. Generally, it was closer to noon before the men began to congregate on the field behind the station where in their conversations they rued the past, argued about the present and dreamed about the future. There was little else for them to do as they waited for the wheels of the government to turn in their favor. This time, though, the atmosphere in the crowd was different. Franz could feel the excitement in the throng.

Franz approached an on-looker and asked, "What is happening?"

"Haven't you heard?" laughed the man, who introduced himself as Dietrich Epp. "Where have you been? There is a transport train coming to our station tomorrow morning!"

"A transport train? Tomorrow morning?" Franz was shocked. "What time?"

"Early! At five o'clock!"

"For us?" Franz could hardly believe his ears.

"Yes, of course for us!" chuckled Epp. "We are being allowed to emigrate!" His face was lit with the joy of anticipation.

"Where will the train be taking us?" Franz asked.

"Leningrad, I think, then Germany by boat," said Epp happily. "Germany is opening its doors!"

Franz flushed with excitement and maneuvered his way into the crowd. People were standing about the stationmaster's office door. He wanted to see inside. When he was close enough to catch a glimpse through the doorway, Franz noticed an officer of the secret police was seated behind the stationmaster's desk. Another man, who Franz recognized but whose name he did not know, was standing beside him. He was bent over, looking at what the GPU man had written. Another refugee who seemed visibly upset stood in front of the desk.

"That is not how my name is spelled," said the man, whose name happened to be Grünau. "It's spelled this way." And Grünau patiently spelled his name for the writer.

"I'm sorry, sir," the secret policeman's helper, whose name was Letkemann, said tactfully, "but you have misspelled many of the names."

The GPU agent cursed and said, "Your Mennonite names are incomprehensible! Here, you do the writing, Letkemann."

A man, who had been standing in the line by the door, nudged Franz. "Boy, you are going to have to go to the end of the line. Don't think you are going to jump ahead of all of us who have been waiting long before you arrived."

Franz apologized and made his way back through the crowd. He met Dietrich Epp who asked him, "How long have you been in Moscow?"

"Since the end of August," replied Franz.

"They're making a list of passengers on the transport train based on when they arrived. It sounds like your name should be on it!"

"How do you know this?"

"I was here early. My family is already signed up," said Epp happily. "They're selling passports, too, though I must say they might as well come right out and say they're robbing us. Four hundred rubles each, they are, for the adults, that is."

As his excitement at what he was hearing grew, Franz was

having difficulty keeping up with the man's chatter.

"Are you under eighteen? If you are you can get a passport for free," Epp was saying.

"I'm with my parents and brothers and sisters," said Franz. "We already have our family's passports." His head was buzzing. "Four hundred rubles!" he thought. "Then at 330 rubles, we got a bargain."

"Well then, get in that line and sign up!" the man encouraged Franz cheerfully. "Do you have your birth certificate with you? You have to hand it in. It seems we are to lose all of our identification papers except for what they give us."

"I don't have any of my papers with me!" Franz realized. He turned and ran down the street back to the family's dacha.

Elizabeth was not at all happy the family would not be allowed to keep its birth certificates. She grudgingly gave them to Franz when he insisted they had no choice in the matter.

When Franz returned to the railway station he saw no one was there, aside from the regular traffic of passengers waiting for the next train. Panicking, he hurried to the stationmaster's office hoping he knew what had happened. The door was closed. Franz knocked louder than propriety dictated. Hearing a gruff response, he entered.

"Comrade Stationmaster, I apologize for disturbing you. But can you tell me where the people are who were registering passengers for the emigration train? They were here a little while ago and now they're gone! Do you know, has the list been filled?" he asked, trying to quell the rising apprehension he felt at the prospect of missing out on this golden opportunity.

The stationmaster sat slouched on a chair behind his desk. "Don't know," was all the disinterested man would say from within an amorphous cloud of grey cigarette smoke.

Franz ran from the station. Meeting a man on the road whom he recognized to be a fellow refugee, he asked if he knew where the people creating the transport train passenger list had gone. This was the first the man had heard about the transport. He was surprised and excited at the news and began asking Franz questions so he could learn more. Soon a group formed in the middle of the street. The excited refugees interrogated Franz, but he knew nothing more than he had already told them.

"A train is coming tomorrow morning," he repeated. "Half an hour ago there were people at the railway station making up a list of those who will be allowed on it. I need to know where they've gone." Franz was becoming agitated in his fear-filled frustration.

Someone who had just joined the group and was listening in on the conversation said, "Oh, I know where they've gone. They are at Martin Letkemann's house."

Martin Letkemann was well known to many of the refugees. It was whispered he was one of those actively participating in secret, unofficial negotiations with members of the Central Committee to secure permission for the refugees' emigration.

When Franz and the rest of the scrum that had gathered about him arrived at Letkemann's dacha, he quickly learned the reason for the change of venue. The GPU man writing the list had been so slow, and so incompetent in his ability to spell the Mennonite names being added to the list, that Letkemann had offered to generate the list for him. The policeman had happily relinquished his responsibility. Letkemann had suggested they move to his residence where there was more room than in the tiny station office and the secret policeman had willingly agreed, saying he would bring the necessary passports to the station when the train arrived, at which time Letkemann would see the correct amount of rubles were handed over in payment for the passports.

Franz joined the jubilant queue waiting to be included in the list. When it was his turn to put forward his family's name, he made sure it was known they had arrived in Moscow on the twenty-fifth of August. He handed over the militia's registration papers proving his assertion. "And we don't need to buy passports," he said proudly. "We have already been issued ours!" Letkemann examined the Funk family's passports.

When Letkemann asked for the family's birth certificates, knowing they would not be returned, Franz was uncertain about laying them on the table. It felt wrong to leave them behind. There was a finality to the act that frightened him. Should things go sideways, how would any of them be able to prove their identity or citizenship?

As Franz left the Letkemann's house, the elation he had felt at ensuring the family's inclusion on the list of passengers was replaced with a rising feeling of panic. "The transport is tomorrow morning," he realized. "What will we do if Father still isn't here?"

It was early evening. After adding his family's name to the transport train list, Franz had spent the rest of the day waiting at the station, watching the trains and praying his father and grandmother would arrive on one of them. They had not. Franz noticed a GPU man come out of the stationmaster's office. He spoke with some people who were gathered there. Martin Letkemann was with him. Franz moved closer and listened to what was being said.

"I've just been informed," said the secret police officer, "the transport train will not arrive tomorrow morning at five o'clock."

Franz's heart froze as he waited for the expected bad news; there will be no train. That was, after all, how things worked in the Soviet Union.

The officer continued. "Instead, the train will arrive tonight. Passengers on the list must be here tonight at midnight. They must be prepared to board with paperwork ready to be inspected and the money for passports collected. Anyone who is signed up but is not present will be left behind. The train will wait for no one."

The GPU officer disappeared into the station. Franz was stunned. For a moment the group of refugees to whom the officer had spoken were silent, but the silence was quickly broken by the excited voices of those who realized they had better get busy.

"There's hardly enough time to pack our bags!" said a man.

"My wife is doing the washing today," worried another as he hurried away. "All of our extra clothing will be wet."

A woman who had been standing with him said, "My husband took a last minute trip to Moscow. He was expecting the train to come tomorrow morning. I don't know if he'll be back in time tonight!"

Letkemann said, "We have to let the others know!" He hurried into the station office and returned a moment later with the GPU officer.

"We can use my car," said the policeman.

Chapter 22

October 29, 1929

There wasn't enough room on the midnight train provided to shuttle refugees to Leningrad. During that hectic day, two transport lists had been compiled, one with the names of two hundred families and another with three hundred. Even before the train arrived, everyone knew one would not be enough. The lists contained too many names.

A large crowd of expectant refugees gathered at the Perlovka station long before midnight. They waited quietly, impatiently, hardly daring to breath, lest the promised train prove to be an illusion. When the train arrived, they were shocked to find it was made up of only six passenger cars and a freight car.

Someone noticed a sign on each car, "PERESZELENZY." "Resettlers?" he commented to no one in particular. "We're not resettlers." After a moment he realized the truth of it. "The government doesn't want people who see the train to know it is full of emigrants! They know this whole godforsaken country would be empty in a week if its citizens knew they could leave."

The cars of the transport train were shunted onto a siding where they were eventually packed with jubilant travelers who were first stopped by guards checking, and keeping, their identification papers and rummaging through their luggage. It was a wonder there wasn't a riot, for the passengers whose names were not called grew ever more despondent at being left off of this miraculous ticket.

Letkemann appeared once again to be in charge of his fellow refugees. "We will need more cars," he told the weary looking GPU officer beside him. The officer merely shrugged his shoulders and said there were no more railway cars available. However, in the midst of the chaos of alarmed refugees, an announcement was eventually made telling everyone a second train would be provided the following night.

With the hopeful reassurance they would not be left behind,

teary friends and family waved at loved ones on the train. As the transport pulled away in the early hours of the next morning, they waved, shouted blessings, and promised the expectation of a future reunion.

Many left standing in the darkness of night at the station were envious and wished they were on the train. They prayed earnestly this first fortunate group of refugees traveling to Germany via Leningrad might prove to be the vanguard of many—themselves included—yet to come. They prayed the second transport would materialize that evening as promised. They prayed many more trains would be set aside for the salvation of the thousands whose names were being added to emigration lists in every northern suburb of Moscow, who still waited to receive permission to leave, and they prayed for the hundreds of latecomers who were appearing in Moscow almost daily, coming from every corner of the Soviet Union, united in their dream of escape from its oppressive regime.

Franz Funk was among those who had watched the first train depart. His heart was sick and he felt like weeping. If his father did not return before the next transport arrived, he knew they would not be on it. His mother had at first been excited such a miracle as the provision of an emigration train could have occurred. "First passports and now an emigration train?" she had said in wonder. She had given Franz the family's precious birth certificates and passports, and he had hurried away to add their name to the emigration list. Later, though, Elizabeth had flatly refused to consider joining the transport unless Johan had returned first.

The argument had occurred in the middle of the afternoon when Franz returned home for a quick bite to eat. The uninsulated, drafty dacha was cold. The children were sitting around the small table, bundled in their winter clothing, shivering while waiting for water for tea to boil. Some huddled close to the Bunsen burner and stared at the small flame below the kettle heating up atop its cradle. They felt little of the tiny burner's benefit. When the tea was finally served, they gratefully held the warm mugs between their hands and sipped the scalding liquid.

"I am so grateful we will not need to spend the winter here," said Franz, aware of the empty space his father's absence created and looking to fill it with words. "With no proper stove or fireplace, we would freeze." The Bunsen burner had been turned up as high as it would go. Its small flickering light danced in her children's eyes before being lost in the dimness of the room.

Elizabeth cut a slice of bread for each of her children. They looked at their portions with resigned expressions on their faces. "I'm sorry, children," she lamented. "This is all our ration cards allow us to have." Sarcastically, she added, "Our esteemed leader isn't concerned about how much food children need to grow strong and healthy." She immediately regretted her choice of words. They were unhelpful.

Trying to make light of their situation, Elizabeth smiled. "But if I never see another loaf of this black bread, it will be too soon. Russians don't know how to bake good bread."

Which also didn't help the mood of the children who remembered the delicious white bread she used to bake all too well. Thoughts of her homemade strawberry jam and the rich butter made from cream that rose to the surface of the milk in the pail standing in the cold cellar of their farmhouse in Lyubimovka didn't help either. Nevertheless, they didn't complain about what they had been given. They were hungry and knew there was nothing else to eat.

"The transport will arrive tomorrow morning," Franz exulted after he had washed the last bit of the hard bread down with a swallow of tea. "There's still plenty of time for Father to arrive home today."

Hearing Franz's words, his brothers and sisters became animated with excitement, laughing and jostling each other as they talked about their father's expected return and the train coming to take them out of Russia. They were all more than ready to leave the crowded, drafty, vermin infested dacha that was their temporary home in Perlovka. Wherever the train took them must be better than where they were now. In the midst of their jollity, Katrina spilled her tea and swatted Wilhelm for bumping her elbow. He pushed her harder, as big brothers are wont to do, and Katrina began to cry.

"Go outside children," snapped Elizabeth, losing her patience. Getting a dry cloth, she said, "I'll clean this up. Go listen to the birds. Franz and I need to talk."

After the children had put on their boots and spilled out the door, Elizabeth said, "Tell me again, what time does the transport train arrive,

Franz?"

"Tomorrow at five in the morning."

Elizabeth was silent a moment. "I have something to say." She hesitated as she gathered her thoughts. "Franz, if your father doesn't come today, we will have to give up our place on the train. I will not leave without him."

Franz was not surprised by his mother's words. He would have expected nothing else from her.

"Mother, I have a better plan. If Father doesn't come today, I will stay behind. You and the children must get on this transport. When Father comes, he and I will catch another transport train and join you in Germany." When Elizabeth made to argue with him, Franz raised his voice. "Please Mother, you must take this opportunity to get out with the rest of the family."

"And what if there isn't another train?" asked Elizabeth with quiet intensity. "Then you will be stuck here."

"We'll all be stuck here if you refuse to go tomorrow morning and there are no more trains!" said Franz, trying to keep his voice level and his emotions in check. "You must go!"

"I will not leave you and Johan behind," said Elizabeth flatly.

"But you must!"

"No!"

"Will you at least think about it?" Franz pleaded.

"No, and that's final," said Elizabeth.

With his mother's refusal, Franz had not even told her about the change in the train's arrival time to midnight that same day. Without his father being there, there was no point. When the announcement had come a second train would be added the following day, Franz had felt some light stirrings of possibility. But the thought was growing in him that he and his family might be destined to remain in the Soviet Union. He could feel the opportunity to emigrate slipping out of his hands like a fish fresh-caught from a stream.

When he returned home in the dead of night after the first train had left, Franz found his mother awake.

"Why aren't you sleeping?" he asked her quietly, knowing the answer. When she did not answer, he said, "There is a second train. It is coming tonight."

"When?" she asked.

"Midnight."

And so, while the rest of the family slept, mother and eldest son again discussed what they should do. She would not hear of his idea of remaining while she and the rest of the family left. It was all Franz could do to convince her to at least join the waiting throng at the station that evening. "That way, when Father comes, we'll be ready to leave," he had said with all the optimism he could muster. "I'm sure he will come today." In the end, Elizabeth had agreed. They would pack their meager belongings and go to the station.

As he lay down upon the mattress next to his brothers, Franz thought he heard his mother sniffling. He looked into the dark of the room and tried to still his anxious mind. To divert his attention away from his apprehension concerning the whereabouts of his father, he searched for the excitement he might have expected to feel as he thought about the train his family could take on the first leg of its miraculous trip to Germany. "We will be boarding in a matter of hours!" he thought. He tried the words out, but all Franz felt was dread. His father was missing, and his family would not be leaving Perlovka without him.

Too nervous to sleep, after a few restless hours, Franz decided it was time to get up. A wet snow was falling as he walked slowly to the railway station at Perlovka. He pulled down the flaps on his hat to cover his ears and flipped up his coat collar to provide some protection for his neck. He was in no hurry because the first train of the day would not arrive for another half hour. As he plodded along kicking at the snow, Franz thought about his mother's words. She was very stubborn. And, perhaps, she was right. "We all go, or none of us go," he said to himself. Even as the words left his mouth, he feared the implications of the decision, should they be forced to stay.

Arriving at the railway station, Franz saw a train from Moscow was already unloading. He watched as passengers burdened with packages and bundles of possessions climbed down onto the platform and looked around to get their bearings. "More refugees," he thought.

"They just keep coming." Franz noticed someone was waving in his direction. He looked closer and his heart leaped with excitement. It was Uncle Cornelius and Aunt Sara. Their children, Abie and Tina jumped off of the bottom step of the passenger car and joined their parents on the station platform. Coming down the steps behind them he saw his Uncle George and Aunt Helena Willms. They were quickly followed by his other uncle and aunt, Cornelius and Rose Willms. Rose was carrying a baby thickly wrapped in a warm blanket. Franz was surprised, for he hadn't known his aunt was pregnant.

"It is so good to see you!" Franz said, shaking his aunts' and uncles' hands. He looked at Aunt Sara. He was already a head taller than his petite, favorite aunt. "Is Father with you? Did he bring Grandmother?" Franz searched the crowd even as he spoke the words.

"What?" said Uncle Cornelius in his booming voice. Cornelius Froese was a big man with a voice to match. "Are they not here? They left two days before us. I took them to the train in Isylkul myself. We were going to leave right away the next morning but were delayed because I wanted to make sure all the animals were taken care of first."

The look on Franz's face was all the answer he needed.

"Not here? I can't imagine what is taking them so long," said Uncle Cornelius, "though I did see the militia giving some of our people trouble in Chelyabinsk."

Aunt Sara gave her husband a stern look. "Don't worry, Franz, they'll get here," she said confidently, though what the source of the confidence she felt was, she could not tell. "Your father is a resourceful man. They'll get here."

Franz offered to take his relatives to his family's dacha. "If Father comes, we will be leaving on a transport to Leningrad tonight," he said. "You can have our place. The rent is paid until the end of March."

Franz's aunts and uncles were thrilled to hear emigration was becoming a reality. While they walked to the dacha, Franz filled them in on what they needed to do and where they needed to go to apply for permission to leave Russia.

By evening, Johan and Anna had still not arrived in Perlovka. Praying for one more miracle, Elizabeth packed the family's bags and took her family to the railway station where a transport train was scheduled to arrive later that evening.

"He'll be here," Elizabeth said, echoing her sister-in-law's confidence.

The platform of the station became crowded with passengers whose names on the transport list entitled them to a place on the second train to Leningrad. As the hours passed, the cold followed them. The expectant refugees cheerfully sat on their luggage and huddled together for warmth, talking excitedly about the journey they were about to undertake.

Sitting cross-legged on the wooden station platform, Franz held his youngest sister on his lap and cradled her to add his warmth to hers. He found himself hoping the transport train would not arrive as promised, for his father had not yet returned. Nor did it, for when midnight passed, the tracks at the Perlovka station were empty. There were no officials present to tell the puzzled refugees where their train was or when it would arrive. The waiting crowd grew quiet and the children slept while their parents kept watch.

And while the increasingly anxious passengers on the Perlovka railway station platform wondered at the delay of their promised train, and while they struggled to keep at bay the cold of a late October night, half a world away, the afternoon markets of a global economy in its infancy crashed. The economies of nations were ruined in mere hours. The jobs of millions of workers disappeared as the countries in which they lived sank into depression. Germany, the nation upon which all the refugees' hopes were pinned—heavily dependent on foreign investment—teetered on the edge of bankruptcy.

To make matters worse, the German government in Berlin was made aware of the fact that the day before, on Monday, October 28, the Canadian government, pressured by a prairie lobby weary of Russian Mennonite immigrants and worried about the country's ability to assimilate more of them, decided to put off the acceptance of any new refugees from the Soviet Union until the spring of 1930. In the face of Canada's hesitation, the next day, Germany stepped away from negotiations with the Soviets and discontinued issuing entry visas. Shackled by the Canadian government's decision, the Canadian Pacific Railroad and Steamship Company's representatives at RUSKAPA in

Moscow refused any further involvement in the affair.

Diplomacy had failed. Though they did not yet know it, the refugees waiting at the Perlovka railway station in anticipation of the imminent arrival of their transport to freedom had been handed their final and complete rejection.

Chapter 23

October 31, 1929

Johan Funk stood at the ticket window of the Yaroslavl railway station. He told himself there was nothing to be nervous about and that he and his mother were almost home, that German refugees were as common here as aspen trees in the forest, but he still needed to take a calming breath. "We stick out like aspens among evergreens, too," he muttered under his breath, forgetting for the moment the peasants' clothing he was wearing that had helped him blend in with the ragged crowds of local passengers over the weeks of his journey. "That's our problem. We don't blend in."

It was nine days since Johan and his mother had set out from Isylkul. Johan was exhausted. His hips and back ached from the interminable hours spent seated on the hard wooden benches of the crowded passenger trains. To his surprise, his mother seemed to be taking the trip a lot better than he was. Since their stop in Chelyabinsk, the further they had traveled, the more energetic she became.

When the ticket agent gave him his attention, Johan said, "Two tickets to Perlovka."

The bored ticket agent barely looked at Johan. He shoved two tickets across his desk and took the rubles Johan held out to him. As Johan walked away, he thought, "If only I had met that agent at Nizhny Novgorod."

Purchasing tickets for the train ride from Nizhny Novgorod to Yaroslavl had been an ordeal. As he had done in Chelyabinsk, Johan had stood back and watched to see how thoroughly the agent checked the identification of those buying tickets. He had quickly discovered the Nizhny Novgorod ticket agent was very thorough. Everyone buying tickets was asked for identification, regardless of their destination.

Johan and Anna had arrived at the station late in the evening and it was not until the evening of the next day, when there happened to be a rush of people wanting to buy tickets immediately prior to a train's departure time, that the man became sloppy. Seeing the opportunity, Johan had quickly joined the queue. In his haste to accommodate the press of passengers, the agent had stopped asking for identification. He handed out tickets as quickly as the rubles to pay for them were placed in front of him. Nevertheless, Johan had been tense with fright lest the man should for some reason ask to see his identification card. He hadn't. Pocketing his tickets, Johan had thanked the man for his kindness— almost sincerely—while the agent waved him on so he might serve the next customer. Johan and Anna were barely seated before the train left the station.

But in Yaroslavl it was a different story. Tickets in hand, Johan helped his mother onto the train to Perlovka. As they took their seats, he found himself relaxing for the first time in days. He felt drained from the excess of nervous energy he had used along the way. He had never been forced to be duplicitous before and hoped he would never have need to be deceitful again.

"It won't be long now," Johan smiled at his mother.

"Yes," said Anna. "I can hardly wait to see your family. I'm sure the children will have grown. I'll hardly recognize them."

Franz Funk struggled to his feet. He moved his limbs to work out a cramp that had come from sitting so long in an awkward position. It was crowded on the platform of the Perlovka railway station. Looking at the elderly men and women around him, he wondered how they were managing. "If I'm finding this difficult, it certainly cannot be easy for them," he thought. Yet he heard few complaints coming from the people stranded at the station.

For almost two days Franz's family, together with the rest of the refugees whose names were written on the list of the promised second transport had camped out at the railway station. There was nowhere else for them to go. They had settled accounts with their landlords; new arrivals like Franz's relatives had quickly taken any vacant homes for their own use. A few lucky passengers had found shelter in the station's waiting room, but most had been forced to move onto the field behind the station to wait and sleep out in the open. The local police had been almost polite in their insistence most of the refugees move off of the station platform. Its space was needed for the movement of the regular traffic of passengers coming and going throughout the day. Fortunately, during the days of the refugees' encampment, it had not rained or snowed, though it was cold, especially at night.

Some refugees had lost heart and left the station, thinking the transport they had been promised was simply another fiction propagated by the authorities to torment them. "There never was going to be another train," they said dejectedly as they trudged off to find warm shelter and to make new plans in the pursuit of their dream. The rest of the refugees huddled at the station had refused to give up hope. "Surely a train will eventually come for us," was their stubborn mantra. "The first train came; our train will come, too."

As was his habit, Franz scanned the passengers arriving on each of the trains stopping in the station. There was little else to do in the tedium of waiting. The younger children ran around in the field playing their games and alternately laughing together or getting into fights. Some of the older teens gathered in groups to talk and gossip, but Franz chose to stay close to his mother whose spirits seemed to sink lower with each passing hour. Between her concern for her missing husband, the question of the missing transport, and the cold she and her children were being forced to endure while waiting for both, she was being severely tested. Franz, too, had begun to wonder if his father would ever return. Russia was an enormous country. If something had gone wrong with his father's mission, there was no question of searching for him. He could be anywhere. Franz wouldn't know where to begin looking or whom to ask who would care enough to give him an answer. Even so, he refused to give in to the growing sense of despair percolating in his gut. He continued to hope and to search the crowds of incoming passengers to see if his father and grandmother were among them.

A train pulled into the station going south to Moscow from Yaroslavl. Without expectation, Franz quickly scanned the people who were leaving the train. Seeing no one he recognized, he turned his attention to a group of passengers who were happily being welcomed by waiting loved ones. He watched with envy as they greeted one another with warm handshakes.

Franz heard his mother's voice. "Johan!" she gasped.

Turning, he saw his mother struggling to her feet. Looking where her eyes pointed, he saw a man coming toward them. Beside him walked his grandmother. He looked again to assure himself the man in the grungy outfit was indeed his father.

"What are you wearing?" Elizabeth was asking, befuddled by shock and surprise at seeing her husband so unexpectedly—and at seeing him wearing such a dirty, matted, sheepskin coat. "You look terrible!" Johan and Anna wrapped each other in a tight embrace while Anna smiled happily beside them. In the joy of the occasion, they didn't care if others saw their unseemly, public display of affection.

"Father!" Franz cried, "Oma!" As tears filled his eyes, Johan, Elizabeth and Anna became a kaleidoscope of colors and shapes. He blinked his eyes to rid them of their tears. Wiping his cheeks dry, Franz embraced first his father and then his grandmother. He saw Elizabeth was crying at the same time as a wide smile covered her face. His father, ever the soft one, was weeping along with her. The rest of the children came from their play, were happily surprised, and joined in the merry meeting.

"Where have you been?" scolded Elizabeth, when everyone had caught their breath. "You are late. We were afraid you might never come home." Fresh tears ran down her cheeks. She fished around in her pockets until she found a handkerchief with which she wiped her eyes and blew her nose.

"Don't be silly," said Anna, putting her arm around her daughter-in-law's shoulders. "We were always going to come. It just took longer than we expected."

"Where did you come from?" asked Franz in amazement. "I've been watching people getting off the trains for days! I didn't see you!"

"We came from Yaroslavl," said Johan. "On this train!" Hugging Elizabeth again, he said, "I'm sorry it took us so long to get here—it's a long story." Trying to minimize the difficulties of the journey he said, "Buying tickets was a bit tricky and for a couple of days we were shunted off onto a siding in Nizhny Novgorod. They left us sitting there until another engine was found."

"Yes," said Anna, "but at least we had a good view of the Volga while we waited. What a beautiful river! Johann found a farmer and bought us some food." She didn't need to say his purchase was on the black market. They all knew it was so, except for the younger ones who were too happy to wonder. "We were fine; a little inconvenienced is all."

"Enough of that. We're here!" said Johan. "But, what has happened?" he asked, taking in the crowd of refugees in the station and on the field. Some were milling about. Others were seated or lying around dozens of campfires. "Why are so many people camping at the station? Why are you all here?" he asked with more urgency, looking at each member of his family in turn. "Was there a fire? Has something happened to our dacha?"

"No, Father," said Franz with glee. "We've got our passports! We have permission to leave Russia! We've been given entry visas to Germany! They're right here!" He pulled a packet of papers out of the inner pocket of his coat.

Johan's eyes grew wide. "Really? Passports? And entry visas to Germany?" He took the papers from Franz and examined them closely. "Thank God!" he laughed with a depth of relief he could not previously have imagined.

The joy and surprise of Franz's news brought more hugging and jubilant tears.

"And there is another thing," said Elizabeth when everyone had calmed down. "We've been promised a transport train to take us to Leningrad."

"The first transport left two days ago, on Monday night," interrupted Franz. "It only had six passenger cars, so we were told another transport would pick the rest of us up on Tuesday at midnight. But it didn't come, and a good thing too! We didn't know what we were going to do if our transport came and you hadn't returned with Oma." He went silent, for he didn't want to explain the decision his mother had insisted upon.

Everyone's mood had become somber.

"But here it is Thursday and no train has come," wondered Johan.

"It will come!" cried Franz with certainty. "Now you are here, it will come!"

The return of Johan with Anna worked miracles for Elizabeth who chattered happily with her mother-in-law for the rest of the afternoon. The younger children ran off to play their games, but returned frequently to assure themselves their father and grandmother were indeed there, safely amongst them. Katrina in particular lingered and hugged Johan repeatedly, making up for the loving physical contact she had missed in the days of his absence.

When there were no other distractions, Johan opened a large cloth sack he had brought with him. Franz had seen it, but had not asked what it contained. "For you," Johan said, handing Franz a handsome guitar of a kind he had never seen before. The top and back of its body were slightly rounded and beautifully painted. The frets on the neck shone golden and, rather than being flat as one would expect, the head at the end of the neck was ornately carved and curved similar to the scroll of a violin. "I found it at the bazaar in Nizhny Novgorod. I thought of all you lost when we left Lyubimovka—the precious things you sold— your horse, your violin. I want you to have it."

Franz was speechless. He examined the musical instrument, admiring its artistic design, and then he ran his thumb over the taut strings.

"It's beautiful, Father. Thank you!"

"You are welcome," Johan said with a smile.

Two hours later, a train pulled into the Perlovka railway station. The refugees camped at Perlovka Station craned their necks and saw it was empty. Everyone stood and looked at it hopefully. Might this be their promised train?

After a while, an official emerged from the station office. "Your transport to Leningrad has arrived," he shouted. "Prepare to board."

Part 3
Leningrad

It's time to drop astern the shape
of the dull shores of my disfavor.

Pushkin
—Eugene Onegin

Chapter 24

October 31, 1929

Johan Funk's first thought, when he heard their transport train to Leningrad had arrived at the station, was one of overwhelming gratitude and relief. His gamble which saw his family leaving everything they knew and held dear—their farm, their home and all their earthly possessions, their church, and friends—and of bringing his family to Moscow on the off-chance they might be able to receive permission to emigrate, was paying off. Johan's second thought was, "How am I going to get Mother onto this train?" Thanks to Franz's persistence, the family had passports; she did not. The wave of relief he felt gave way to the familiar burning of anxiety in the pit of his stomach.

To the refugees who had camped at the Perlovka station all the hours of the previous two days, seeing the extraordinary train rolling toward them—the dirty steel and painted wood of its physical structure, the black smoke filled with sparks like fire-flies erupting from its stack—seemed for a brief moment to be the result of a massive conjuror's trick. But the dream that had appeared did not disappear into a shapeless vapor of disappointment. It idled and occasionally chuffed magnificently before them. The dream had metamorphosed into something that could be stroked with a light finger. The sharp squeal of the train's wheels as it ground to a halt was heard, with a sense of astonishment, by all. The reality of the repeated explosions of released steam as it rumbled where it rested could not be denied. The smell of the oil lubricating its great pistons and the axle grease squeezing out of the massive wheel-hubs gave evidence to its wondrous concrete existence.

Johan's family, like everyone else, scrambled to their feet when it was declared the train before them was theirs. Hearing the announcement this transport had indeed come for them elicited cheers and shouts of thanksgiving while families quickly got down to the job of sorting themselves out in preparation for boarding. Elizabeth and the children immediately began going through their pile of luggage. Each child would be given her own bag to carry.

Johan stood still and watched. "Wait!" he said. "There's no hurry. We'll all get on."

Elizabeth looked questioningly at her husband.

"Just wait," Johan repeated calmly. An idea had formed in his mind, born of his experience gained on the trip back to Perlovka.

Johan walked over to where his wife was lifting a bundle to give to Abe. He did not want to be overheard—though in the excitement filling the station like a downpour after drought he knew it was entirely unlikely. Johan leaned close to Elizabeth's ear and said, "I want to see how carefully they are checking our travel documents." He paused as he closely observed a policeman helping a refugee family board the train nearby. "I need to know how thorough they are. We don't have a passport for Mother, and I'm determined to get her on this train with us. I am not about to leave her behind."

Elizabeth's eyes darted to where Johan was looking. She nodded uncertainly.

Johan watched the eager crowd pressing toward the passenger cars. As he scrutinized the boarding process, he was surprised to see there were no members of the militia present. Nor were there any uniforms of the GPU. In passing he wondered why, but in the moment he did not dwell on it because he was struck by the realization the local police were actually helping children and the elderly up the steps and into the carriages. They were handing luggage and other bundles of the refugees' possessions up to men who stood on the platforms by the carriage doors, who then passed them along into the cars. With no militia or secret police present, no one was checking documentation at all!

Johan's heart sang with relief! "It's okay," he said. "Let's go." His family enthusiastically picked up their bags and joined the press to board the train.

There was joy in the air as the refugees of Perlovka patiently waited for their turn to board their train. There was no tension, no second-guessing, nor feelings of regret. Broad smiles abounded and fervent gratitude was spoken to the policemen who lent a hand to each as they mounted the stairs to the possibility of freedom. For the moment it seemed kindness had overcome enmity at Perlovka station.

When it was the Funks' turn to board, a policeman politely gave his hand to each of the younger children while they took the long step from the station platform to the bottom rung of the stairs leading into the train car. Together, he and Johan helped Anna, then Elizabeth, climb the stairs. Johan expressed his thanks and the children waved at the policeman as they entered the passenger car and found seats.

Everyone was settled and their baggage stowed under the wood benches when Johan noticed a tall man wearing a fedora coming along the aisle of the car. He was stopping by each family, checking to find their names on a list he carried, and making notations as he spoke with them.

Franz saw his father's questioning look. "That's Martin Letkemann," he said. He is in charge of the emigration lists. I thought he left on the first train."

A man sitting on the bench in front of the Funks heard Franz's remarks. "I heard Letkemann is waiting for money from the south," he said, turning and looking back at them. "He doesn't have enough to pay for his family's passports. I don't know why he doesn't just borrow some rubles to pay the difference. I, myself, have lent money to some who are on this train."

"He will have his reasons," said Johan noncommittally. He didn't like the smug nature of the fellow and wanted to end the conversation. "I hope Letkemann doesn't make things difficult for us," Johan quietly remarked to Franz.

When Letkemann stood before the Funk family, he looked at them dubiously.

"I only see the names of two adults on your registration," Letkemann said.

"Yes," said Johan. "This is my mother, Anna Funk. She and I were away when the list was drawn up. My son, Franz, got our passports. Her name must have been omitted by mistake."

Letkemann looked at Franz. "Oh yes, I remember you," he said. He smiled at Franz. Turning back to Johan he said, "Nevertheless, your mother must have her own passport."

"Listen brother," Johan replied. "Does it really matter to you whether or not my mother has a passport? It is we who are taking the risk traveling without proper documentation. She is an elderly woman who has just buried her husband, my father." When Letkemann didn't respond, Johan continued. "Do you really think the GPU, if they happen to check our documents along the way, will care about her? Quite frankly, I don't think they care about any of us. Something has happened. You've noticed there are no members of the militia or secret police here today. Where are they?"

"Yes, I had noticed. It is odd, I agree," said Letkemann. "I guess my main concern is whether there is enough room on the train for all those who have signed up. I suppose if, in the end, there is room your mother is welcome to travel with you. Otherwise…" Letkemann shrugged.

As it turned out, the train had plenty of room. Some families who had signed up for the transport to Leningrad did not make an appearance before it was time to leave. Perhaps, while waiting through the long days in the cold, they had decided to find warmer shelter and were unaware of the train's arrival. Or, they may have wanted to make a last minute trip to Moscow to purchase some essentials, or even a souvenir. They may have been waiting for an absent family member, or for money to pay for their passports. Whatever the reason, they missed their chance and Anna was given hers.

In response to the tangibly physical desire of the passengers who had boarded and sat restlessly waiting and willing the train into forward motion, the transport carrying 291 hopeful emigrants finally gave a lurch and began to move out of Perlovka Station.

The mood on the transport train was festive. Some passengers sang hymns of praise, thanking God for their imminent deliverance. Others talked loudly together, thrilled to finally have begun their journey to emigration. A few were more subdued, reflecting on their good fortune. The more thoughtful wondered at the wisdom of the choices made by those whose names had been on the list, but who had missed the train. Children chattered and stared out of windows, taking in the countryside slowly sliding by them—the train was not a fast one—and pointing at interesting sights.

With a few moments to themselves while the children were

TAKE A
NOTE
IT WILL LAST LONGER

Josée LaBelle
C 647.822.2774
O 905.845.4267

occupied, Johan, Elizabeth, and Anna talked quietly together, catching up on the events of their lives that had occurred during their weeks of separation. It was a somber conversation, for much of it at first revolved around Franz's last days, his death, and burial.

"As many people as could come were at the funeral," said Anna. "Some were afraid; the communists are making it difficult for us to meet together. There was a luncheon at the church. People said very nice things about my Franz." Her conversation was sentimental and banal, for she had yet to recover from the shock of her loss. "He was a good man."

Anna's eyes became unfocused as she sat with her hands folded in her lap, overcome by thoughts of her dear husband. She looked up, as if startled.

"Did you feel it?" she asked. "I thought for a moment he was here, right here, beside me! I could feel him."

Johan and Elizabeth watched Anna and knew that Franz was very near to them all. His presence was sensed like a melody hidden by the overpowering ambient noise of the day, but which is able to break through the babel just long enough so the listener is able to catch its drift and, with the help of memory, sing its tune.

For a while the trio was silent, caught by the tangle of their thoughts. Anna said, "I wonder how Ivan and Vera are doing. I left without a word to them. After all their years of serving our family, it seems such a shame. They were like friends." She paused a moment. "You know, without Ivan's intervention, who knows what might have happened to Franz, that time he was jailed. They were shooting the prisoners, did you know that?" And so the memories, both happy and sad, created threads of connection between the present and the past, alternately bringing feelings of gratitude, relief, sorrow, and anger.

"There is a lot we must try to forgive," reflected Anna.

Abe broke into the conversation. "The train is slowing down."

Everyone looked outside. Indeed, the train was slowing.

"It's probably nothing," said Johan. "Perhaps there is something on the track up ahead. There certainly isn't any station here."

"Yes," Franz agreed, the side of his face touching the window so he could see as far ahead as possible.

"I'd say we're about three kilometers north of the city," said

Johan. He remembered the terrain from his numerous trips to Moscow.

The train stopped.

Franz ran to the end of the car, opened the door, and stood on the outside platform. Leaning out he had a clear view to the front of the train. He saw a man on the ground next to the track pull a lever to activate a switch. Slowly the train began to move forward again, traveling from the mainline onto a siding. Franz watched as the train neared the man standing next to the switch. The man looked up at Franz as he went by. Franz continued to watch the man until the last car had passed him. The man pulled the lever again, resetting the switch to allow the next train to continue along the main line. He walked behind the train and was lost to view.

The train stopped.

Franz looked to the front of the train. He saw another man working another switch on the main line. He saw the engine of his train had been disconnected. It was picking up speed as it rolled away, onto the main line.

Franz hurried back to where his family was looking out of the window and wondering what was happening.

"We've been moved onto a siding," said Franz, perplexed. "Our engine has been disconnected. I watched it leave; it's gone! We're sitting here without an engine!"

Others had also seen what Franz reported. There was a burst of conversation as passengers speculated as to the reason for their delay. No official boarded the train to provide an explanation. In the absence of facts, the passengers' imaginations began to spin stories, both wild and logical. As the hours passed with no information and no movement, the speculations gave way to a gathering silence.

Eventually, the routines and necessities of daily living took the adults' attention away from their unanswered questions. Children were growing tired and cranky. Hunger began to dictate events. Mothers poked around in bags for food they had brought for the journey to Leningrad. Snow was gathered and melted in cold teapots to provide drinking water. A line formed at the door of the cubby serving as a toilet, where a hole in the floor served as a sewer. With no way to heat their carriage, as night fell the temperature in the car grew colder. Blankets and coats were tucked around shivering children. Parents and their young ones snuggled closer together to gain all the benefit of the warmth their bodies created.

In the darkness, some began to pray. The excitement of the day was forgotten. Uncertainty and worry crept among the passengers like thieves among the sleeping. And as sleep took the tired refugees one by one, the railcars grew quiet.

Johan slept fitfully. He dreamed of trains without engines, trains stuck in snowbanks, and of trains in danger of falling off of cliffs. A crying baby woke him in the night. Looking at his family, he was grateful they had not been roused.

Johan gazed through the passenger car's window. By the glow of the moon through gaps in low-hanging clouds, he saw the lonely, leafless aspens he had observed during the day still stood motionless among the tall evergreens along the shore of a frozen pond beside their train. The trees' shadows crept faintly over the ice and snow. Johan thought how beautifully desolate the scene was. He closed his eyes, and as he waited for sleep to come, noticed the familiar burning in his stomach had returned.

Chapter 25

November 3, 1929

It began to snow the morning after the second transport to Leningrad was left on a siding three kilometers north of Moscow. Lazy, unhurried flakes drifted downward, blown about this way and that by gentle breezes. In passing, they idly brushed the train's windows through which the stranded refugees strained for any sign of coming help, until the flakes finally settled into gathering sheets of white. The daily traffic of north and southbound trains rushing by on the mainline scattered the snow on the tracks, creating wild, swirling clouds that eventually found their rest in the trains' wakes. The softness of the new-fallen snow worked to subdue all sound and even the rattle of the passing trains was captured in the flakes' crystalline webs.

The peaceful, hushed stillness of the snow-covered world outside was in sharp contrast to the emotions of the perplexed refugees imprisoned in their idle railcars. Through their windows, they watched the flakes fall and wondered and worried. No one had come to explain their situation. No one came to offer assistance. As the days passed, their anxiety increased and their questions grew louder. "Why have we been left here? Who is responsible for leaving us here? What will happen to us?" With no answers, the questions became more mundane and more critical. "Our food is running out; who should go and buy some? Where might food be found? What if the train leaves while someone is gone looking for food?" The cries of the hungry, bored children became shrill; the remonstrations of their frustrated, concerned parents more stern.

It was on the third day that the snow-covered cars sitting idle on the siding were finally noticed by two men who appeared, seemingly, out of nowhere. Dusting the snow off of their shoulders, they stepped into the carriage in which the Funks and other passengers greeted them with a mixture of suspicion and anxious relief.

"What are you doin' here?" asked one of the men. "What are you all waitin' for?" He was shorter than the other man, but made up for the difference in height with his attitude of puffed up self-importance. His tall companion stood by his side, glowering at the refugees.

"We are on our way to Leningrad," said several voices at once. "We've been left here for three days! It's intolerable." And so on. Finally able to address their pent-up frustration and anxiety to someone who might be able to help, everyone spoke at once with the result no one could be clearly understood.

Johan stood and put his hands in the air in a gesture meant to calm the deluge of emotion rocking the car. "May I ask who you are? Are you from the government?"

Instead of answering Johan's question, the man said, "Ya can't stay here. Ya gotta get off this train."

There were a few subdued cries of alarm. Johan again raised his hands and calmed his fellow passengers.

"I'm sorry, Comrade, but we cannot do that." Johan said, turning back to the men who stood by the railcar's front-end doorway. "We are Mennonite refugees who have been given permission to emigrate. You can check our papers if you like. This train is to transport us to Leningrad. From there we will travel to Germany. We left Perlovka on October 31st—well, actually, it was in the early hours of November 1st— but for some reason, our engine was disconnected and we were left on this siding. We have been stranded here for three days."

The Russian snickered. "Germany, eh! I don't know nothin' about any a' that. But, be that as it may, ya all have gotta get off a' this train. Ya can't stay here."

"Are you a representative of the government?" repeated Johan.

The man looked annoyed by Johan's persistence.

Johan continued. "What gives you the authority to tell us to leave? And where would you have us go?"

"That's no concern a' mine," replied the Russian. He stroked his salt and pepper beard and, for a moment, looked uncertainly at his comrade. He pulled out a pocket watch. "It's eleven o'clock. I'll give ya until three this afternoon ta get yerselves off this train."

The two men turned and left.

The ultimatum was quickly passed from car to car. A furious

uproar followed in its path until all of the distressed passengers were involved in the same apprehensive debate. "We must not leave the train; we have permission to travel to Leningrad," said some. "The Soviets have abandoned us; we have no alternative," others countered. "We have women and children, babies and the elderly amongst us; we cannot undertake a forced march through the snow to only God knows where," still others argued. The truth of this reality was recognized by all. In the end, it was agreed the ultimatum would be ignored.

When the two Russians returned they were disgusted the train was still occupied. "You have no business still bein' on this train. We told ya ta leave!" the bearded one remonstrated loudly.

"Nevertheless," insisted Johan, "we will not leave it." He had been joined by representatives from the other passenger cars who came quickly when the men were espied coming toward the train. They nodded in agreement with Johan.

"You can't just decide ta live on a train," said the Russian, exasperated. "This ain't yer property." He wasn't sure what to make of the situation. After a moment's hesitation he said, "If ya insist on stayin' on the train, ya are goin' ta have ta pay."

"What do you mean?" Johan expressed the bewilderment shared by everyone in the railway car.

"One hundred rubles per car," announced the beard. "That's what it'll cost ya if ya refuse to leave."

His announcement caused an angry response from the determined refugees.

"No!" cried one. "We refuse!" others said firmly in contrapuntal chorus. "We have already paid for the use of these cars! Two-hundred and twenty rubles each!" shouted another. "Four hundred rubles!" came the cry from those still smarting from the fact they had been gouged for their last-minute passports.

The Russians cursed and shouted abuses. But they soon realized they were not about to win this argument and, muttering threats, stomped out of the carriage and off in the snow.

The next day, in the early evening, the two Russians were back. "We have good news for you," they smiled. "Tomorrow morning, at ten o'clock, this train is scheduled ta make a trip ta Riga, Latvia."

"Riga?" The refugees were baffled.

"If you want ta travel ta Riga, it'll cost ya seventeen rubles each. Otherwise, if you don' wanna go ta Riga, ya'll have to get off the train. If ya refuse, we'll be forced ta remove ya from the train and leave ya here. You can pay in the mornin'." The two Russians left without another word.

In subdued voices, the refugees debated this new development. Representatives from each car again came to Johan's carriage to participate.

"Perhaps we should pay," said some. "We don't need to go to Leningrad. Actually, Riga is better than Leningrad. If we're in Leningrad, we're still in the Soviet Union. Who knows what troubles could still meet us there. If we go to Riga, we're free."

"Yes," said one grandmother. "My son and his family emigrated through Riga in 1926. They made it to Canada. I have a letter from him here in my bag." She rummaged around in her bag and came out with a tattered piece of paper. She waved it in the air as evidence of the wisdom of her advice. "We should go to Riga."

There were many cautious nods and it seemed agreement was being reached.

Thinking about the issue of crossing the border into Latvia, Johan opened his passport and examined it. He quickly realized they had a problem. "I'm not sure they would let us into Latvia," he said loudly. "Look at your passports."

The car was silent as passports were being retrieved and inspected.

"These are not regular passports," continued Johan after a few moments. "These papers only give us permission to leave Russia. They don't even list us as Russian citizens. The Latvians won't recognize them. They'll refuse us entry. And then what? We'd be fools to pay for tickets that will only bring us more trouble than we already have."

The dawning realization of their predicament left the refugees feeling breathless with uncertainty.

"That's it then," they decided. "We stay. And we refuse to pay."

Apprehensive about what the next morning would bring, and exhausted by the emotion of the day, the refugees in the second transport to Leningrad sank into a tired lethargy. Their decision to continue their defiance left them wondering whether the secret police or the militia would finally make an appearance and force their hand. Mothers shushed their hungry children and tried to prepare them for sleep. Fathers ruminated over their plight, wondering at the brazen recklessness that had brought them to this. Some wondered if it might not have been better to have never left their homes in the first place. The bright hope that had lit their faces on the day of their departure from Perlovka was replaced by dark shadows and lines of worry.

Pulling her cranky daughter away from the window, a tired mother noticed a new figure coming out of the evening darkness, walking briskly toward the stranded train. "What now?" she groaned as many faces turned to look where she pointed.

In contrast to the two rough-looking men who had previously harassed them, this man was wearing a fine wool coat and a black astrakhan hat. He climbed the steps and opened the door to enter Johan's railway car. For a moment he looked about at all the women, children and men huddled together in the carriage. Through the vapor of their breath in the chilly air he saw the pitiful defiance in their eyes. Both he and they knew if the hammer came down, they were done.

The stranger grimaced. "This train will be leaving for Leningrad immediately."

The passengers sat up, unsure if they had heard correctly, unsure if they should believe what had been said.

"It is true," he said as if they quarreled with him. "The train will take you to Leningrad. When you get there, you can jump into the Neva River, for all I or anyone else care. Don't you know? You are wasting your time. Canada doesn't want you. Germany doesn't want you."

The passengers refused to believe his words.

He paused. "If you want my advice, you should take the first train back to your homes—wherever that may be. But, whatever you decide, we are finished with you."

True to his word, it wasn't long before an engine was connected to the passenger train. With no light in the car, Johan easily could make out the ghosts of the trees that had assured him, during their days on the siding, the natural world continued to exist as it should. As he watched, the trees began to drift away and disappear behind him.

"Is it true?" asked Elizabeth. She was sitting on the hard bench beside her husband. "Do you think something has happened and Canada doesn't want us?"

Johan shrugged but said nothing.

"Surely Germany will take us," Elizabeth said. After a moment she added in a softer voice, "Do you think there will be trouble in Leningrad when we get there? What did he mean, 'We're finished with you?'"

Johan didn't respond. He looked at his family trying to find comfortable positions in which to sleep and found hope in their comforting presence. Maria and Katrina were tucked up against their Oma. Anna looked content just to be with her beloved granddaughters—the grandsons had always been her husband's favorites while she favored her granddaughters. Franz, Abe and Wilhelm sat on bags on the floor and leaned anywhere they could find a backrest. Johan thought about how surprised he always was at a child's ability to sleep anywhere. He pulled Elizabeth closer to him.

"We'll be okay," he said hopefully.

Johan gazed out of the window, looking for lights, for some sign people could live a normal life. But he must have slept, for he missed the lights of Moscow and of the Leningradsky Railway Station, across the Kalanchyovskaya Square from Yaroslavsky Station—the place with which he had become so familiar since arriving in Moscow in August—where the train was switched onto the Moscow to Leningrad track.

All the next day, while the train was pulled steadily along, Johan was silent. And he was not the only one who looked forward with trepidation to their arrival in Leningrad. Aside from the children whose innocence and naivety largely protected them from the tensions of the journey, the messenger's words had unnerved the adults among the refugees. Where one might have expected joviality at finally being on their way after all the days of delay, Johan's car was filled with an uncomfortable air of unease and disquietude. The children, sensing the mood of the adults, were unusually reserved and compliant.

"Do you think the GPU will be waiting for us when we get there?" Franz asked his father at one point.

Johan thought of the refugees he had discovered in the boxcars in Chelyabinsk. They were being forcibly transported to Siberia. Could it happen to them? He tried to give Franz a reassuring look, but did not attempt to answer his question for he had no answer to give.

Another night passed before, looking ahead, Johan could see the lights of Leningrad shining though the trees in the distance. It wasn't long before the train rumbled into Oktyabrsky Station, the station named in honor of the 1917 October Bolshevik revolution, the western terminus of the Moscow to Leningrad railway line. Johan nudged Elizabeth. Franz noticed and followed their gaze. As the train came to a stop, they saw, stepping out of the shadows, armed men wearing the military uniform of the GPU coming toward them.

Chapter 26

November 6, 1929

"Hurry! Everybody off of the train! Quickly!" shouted an officer of the secret police who stood on the station platform.

Discombobulated passengers with sleep still in their eyes, tried to comply. Children were rushed down the steps of the train cars, followed by their parents loaded down with luggage until all the cars were empty and the refugees stood on the platform warily wondering what would come next. Johan noticed some of the GPU agents had lent a steadying hand to those for whom the last step was a large and dangerous one. He felt a tiny leap of hope in his heart.

"There are streetcars waiting for you in Vosstaniya Square in front of the station," shouted the officer. "They will take you to your next destination. Follow me!"

The refugees soon formed a ragged column. They marched after the officer who led them through the vaulted waiting room of the station, under the arched doorway and out onto the cobblestoned square. To the surprise of some—they had been suspicious of everything the officer had said—they found electric streetcars there, waiting for them. Once each car was loaded with passengers, secret policemen took up positions by the front and rear doors.

Johan wondered, "Is this a precaution or a courtesy? Are they worried we will try to escape?"

As his trolley began to move, Johan looked back and, in the dawning light of the day, he saw the beautiful Italian Renaissance façade of the station, and marveled at its Corinthian columns and two-story clock tower. He could not help but admire such functional works of art. Nor were these the last of the wonders of Leningrad for as the streetcar rattled along Nevsky Prospekt, he was awed by the architectural wonders of centuries—palaces, cathedrals, department stores, shopping malls, and the Russian National Library. It seemed every other building was a proclamation of the wealth and glory of ages gone by.

"What beauty!" Johan said. He nudged Elizabeth. "It would be wonderful to spend a few days exploring this amazing city."

"As if we would be allowed," she snorted. After a moment Elizabeth added, "What I want to know is, where are we being taken?"

Just then, Johan and Elizabeth noticed they were crossing over the Fontanka River on the Anichkov Bridge. They stared at the large, bronze statues of trainers with their horses mounted on pedestals at each end of the bridge. It was hard to take in so much extravagance; their senses became overloaded. The streetcar made a right turn, leaving Nevsky Prospekt. As they peered out of the windows, Elizabeth and Johan saw a vast square in front of the most ornate building they had ever seen.

"That must be the Tsar's Winter Palace," said Johan. "Father once talked to me about his trip here."

Too soon, the palace disappeared from sight. The streetcar crossed the Neva River and after a short while stopped in front of a large, three-storey building. Johan noticed a sign chipped into the stone frontispiece above the doorway, SOVTORGFLOTT, in bold capital letters. It was the Soviet Merchant Marine Building, the headquarters for the Soviet merchant fleet of overseas shipping and trade. It also served, he was to discover, as a guesthouse for foreign travelers.

The officer in charge of the detachment of secret police guarding the refugees had followed the parade of streetcars in his own automobile. Johan saw him enter the Merchant Marine Building. It wasn't long before he returned. On his signal, the GPU men began unloading the cars. When they were all standing on the street, Johan quickly distributed his family's luggage so everyone had something to carry. Eventually, all the families were organized. Directions were given. The column of refugees entered the building and began to climb up three long flights of stairs.

"Will you be able to manage?" Johan asked his mother after they had climbed the first flight. She seemed a little breathless.

"Don't worry about me," she insisted. "You look after your little ones."

By the time they arrived at the top floor, everyone was breathing heavily, their energy compromised by the lack of food and taxed by the weight of the many burdens they carried. But, there was no stopping, for they continued down a long hallway where families were brought into a large dormitory. The high ceiling was painted with faded images of ships on stormy seas and protecting angels hovering over them. Two walls had tall windows through which they could see the city. Wooden frames with straw ticks on them lined the walls. Rows of beds were also laid out in the center of the dormitory. Gratefully the refugee families chose resting places and laid down their loads.

However, there was no rest to be taken, for there was further business to be attended to. With no time to dally, the weary refugees were led to a large room where they found long rows of tables and chairs.

"Must be the dining room," Johan commented to Elizabeth. It was a large room with windows at one end. Looking at the high ceiling, he could make out an ornate scene of laughing figures participating in bacchanalian feast. Like the mural in the dormitory, the artwork on this ceiling was flaking and faded from years of dirt and smoke.

A tall man, with a large, flat, red nose beneath which grew a long, black moustache, stood before the refugees. He waited while everyone found a seat. The GPU officer stood beside him. His hands were on his hips; he was smaller than his comrade, and perhaps he wanted to make himself look bigger and more imposing.

"Welcome to Leningrad," the moustache began in a surprisingly friendly voice. "My name is Evgeny Lebedev. I will be your host during your stay here. Please consider this your home in the beautiful city of Leningrad. It is our pleasure to have you as our guests." Lebedev spread his arms wide. "This room will serve as your dining room. I'm sure you are hungry, so, once we have gone through a small formality, you will be served a warm meal."

Everyone was encouraged by Lebedev's words and smiled at this welcome news. Indeed, after days on the train with little food, everyone was famished!

"First, and I apologize this is necessary, but I'm afraid we cannot feed and house you for free..." Lebedev hesitated. "First, we will need to collect all of the money remaining in your possession. We will use it to buy groceries and other necessities you will use while you are here."

These words had hardly been spoken before the secret police

began moving through the crowded room, collecting money the refugees dutifully pulled out of their pockets and bags.

Johan's heart sank. He had hoped he would be able to take the remainder of their money out of the country with him, though he half-suspected it would not be allowed. Now, his family would be beginning their new life penniless. He thought of the teakettle in the bag with the rest of their belongings in the dormitory. The American ten-dollar bill was safely hidden in its hollow handle. "They will not be getting that," he thought.

It took quite some time before all the refugees' money was collected. When it had finally been handed over to the GPU officer, horizontal doors on the wall at the front of the room were opened, revealing a large buffet of steaming food ready to be served. Lebedev instructed the women to take their children to be served first. To his surprise—for he knew these refugees' story, and that they had not eaten properly in almost a week—the whole gathering stood to their feet and began to sing a prayer, "Praise God from whom all blessings flow, praise him all creatures here below."

Lebedev's state-nurtured atheism was shaken as he listened to the fervor, the sincerity of gratitude, and the complete harmony with which the throng thanked their God for the food he and his helpers had prepared. When the song was finished, the men in the dining room sat down. A long line formed as mothers helped their children fill their plates. Bellies began to growl as the savory scents tantalized those still seated and many diners' patience was tested as they waited for their turn to fill a plate.

To the refugees' surprise, the food was delicious!

When the meal was done, Lebedev again stood in front of the now contented, well-fed refugees and said, "Cleanliness is of utmost importance in a large facility such as this. We will now ask you to return to your room. You will be called out in turn, and be required to take a shower. There are separate shower rooms for the men and the women. The younger children will shower with their mothers."

Again the refugees seated at the tables smiled their gratitude at their host. It had been a very long time since most of them had been able to properly clean themselves. Johan had had the opportunity to take a proper bath when he had returned to Lyubimovka. But, he realized, his family hadn't had a bath since the middle of August! There had been no means to bathe in their Perlovka dacha. A shower sounded wonderful.

Lebedev was speaking. "While you are showering, your clothing and any bedding you brought with you will be collected and disinfected. Make sure you have nothing of value in your pockets. Everything will be heated to a very high temperature in our ovens. You understand."

There were nods everywhere in the dining room, though some, who against all odds had somehow escaped the cursed insects, were insulted. However, the majority of the refugees had been providing homes on their bodies for lice and fleas for so long they hardly noticed them anymore—or, at least, tried not to. They had found the best way to deal with infestations that could not be made rid of was to ignore them. The thought of finally having clean bodies and clothing was very welcome.

"It will take a few hours to kill any vermin that might be living in your clothing," continued Lebedev. "In the meantime, you will be given something to wear until your clothing is returned to you."

Everyone was dismissed and sent back to the dormitory to wait to be called for their turn in the showers. Lebedev stood by the doorway, chest out and hands behind his back like a little tsar, as the refugees filed by him on their way to their rooms. Many thanked him, and by the time the last ones passed by, he was beaming.

Showering proved to be an unwelcome ordeal. Several families were called out at a time. For those uncomfortable with their nakedness, being forced to shower with strangers present was embarrassing. Anna took it upon herself to provide a modicum of privacy for her granddaughters while Elizabeth did her best to soap them down with a bar they quickly found to be extremely unpleasant. The foul, chemical odor of the bar refused to be washed off—nor would the smell wear off of their skin until days later. By the time they were done, everyone was clean and free of vermin, but also quite annoyed.

After drying themselves, Elizabeth took up the gowns provided for them to wear until their clothes were returned. She grumbled at their condition for the gowns had simply been thrown into a large basket. Of course, they were wrinkled and shabby.

"Do these people not own irons?" Elizabeth asked no one in particular.

The gowns were made of coarse cotton, and were gray from many washings. Elizabeth handed one to Maria and another to Katrina. As everyone began to put on their gowns, they quickly discovered they were all the same size. Elizabeth was disgusted as she tried to pull her gown down to cover her ankles. Her legs had never been put on public display before! It was outrageous! She saw Anna was having the same difficulty. At the same time, her girls giggled at the enormity of their gowns. There was enough room in one gown for the two of them. Their hems dragged on the floor and their sleeves, before they were rolled up, were long enough to step on!

When Elizabeth, Anna, and the girls returned to their room, they discovered Johan and the boys were already there. They were wearing the exact same gowns! Elizabeth tried to protect her modesty, but it was no use. The girls were still giggling at their own gowns, and when they saw their brothers wearing theirs, they completely lost control. Elizabeth's frowns turned to chuckles as she looked at her husband in his absurd apparel. Before they knew it, everyone was laughing until their sides hurt. Perhaps it was the emotional letdown they were all feeling after so many days of tension. But Franz had never seen his father and mother laugh as hard as they did at the sight of them all wearing those silly gowns. He laughed, too, seeing his father's hairy legs below his garment's hem. It was ridiculous!

But, the refugees of the second transport to Leningrad were clean.

Unfortunately, it was not long before it was discovered that while they and their clothing had been cleaned and disinfected, neither the dormitory in which the refugees were staying, nor the straw-filled bedding provided for them to sleep on, were. The morning after they arrived, bedbug bites were found on many. Within days, lice were discovered and there was a new hatch of fleas. They hopped everywhere on the floor and found their way into anything lying upon it. To put a good face on it, Johan joked with his family about the Lithuanian and Latvian lice. The fleas were Flemish, Finnish, or French. The bedbugs were christened Bulgarian.

"After all," he said, "with the cleaning we went through, the critters we carried could not have survived. No, these are not Moscow bred. Sailors and people from countries all over Europe have probably stayed in this very dormitory. This is a hotel of sorts, after all. They probably brought the visiting vermin with them!"

And though Elizabeth didn't always appreciate his humor, she occasionally smiled at his attempts to make light of the situation. It certainly made it easier for the children.

Chapter 27

November 13, 1929

It was during this time Johan met another 'guest' of the Sovtorgflott who was not trying to leave the Soviet Union, but was actually immigrating to it. Isaiah Liebermann was a teacher from Dresden. A died-in-the-wool communist, he was bringing his family to live in what he enthusiastically called, "The Great Workers' Paradise." Liebermann, his wife, daughter, and son were staying in their own room in another part of the Sovtorgflott until the paperwork allowing them to enter the Soviet Union was complete.

Johan was never so surprised as when Liebermann told him that since the Bolshevik Revolution of October 1917, it had been his dream to live in the communist state. Thinking to dissuade him, Johan told him of some of his experiences as a resident of the "Workers' Paradise." Naturally, the idealist refused to believe the reality of compulsory 'voluntary' taxation, of grain requisitions that left farmers destitute, of the systematic elimination of successful farmers as a class, of religious persecution, and arbitrary arrest and torture.

"It may be a paradise for the workers, but believe me when I tell you it has been hell for us farmers!" Johan concluded.

Liebermann countered with the usual communist thinking. Grain must be requisitioned in order to feed the workers who live in the cities, surplus grain must be exported to raise capital to build the industrial infrastructure needed to modernize the state, laws must be implemented to compel recalcitrant and dishonest farmers to obey, the greedy kulak class must be eliminated for the good of the country, religion is the opiate of the people. Johan was nauseated by Liebermann's pompous decrees.

Afterward Johan laughed bitterly at the naiveté of the man. "He is a teacher, but his education is yet to begin," he said to Elizabeth. "The man is a fool. Worse, he is endangering the lives of his wife and children."

It was not only Isaiah Liebermann who was about to receive an education.

Liebermann had a son, Vladimir—"I named him after Vladimir Ilyich," he proudly told Johan—who was a year younger than Johan's son, Abe. The boys got on very well. Being confined inside for days on end left them bored and restless. Together they explored the many rooms on the third floor of the Sovtorgflott, some empty, others inhabited. When they tired of this, they sat by the Marine Building's large windows and dreamed of wandering the streets below. It did not matter that it was cold out. Anything would be better than this forced idleness.

One morning Vladimir—Vlad, as he liked to be called—suggested to Abe that they go out and explore the market they had seen through the window of a room on the north side of the building.

"I want to buy something for my mother. It's her birthday soon," Vlad said. "And you know Russian. You can help me."

As bored as he was, Abe eagerly agreed to the adventure.

"But what about the guards?" he wondered aloud. All the exits were blocked by stone-faced policemen.

"I'm sure you can talk the guy at the back door into letting us go," Vlad said.

The boys had gotten to know the guard during their explorations of the Sovtorgflott. He seemed a gentle soul, and, with his rifle slung over his back, he was not the least bit threatening to them. In fact, he had been happy to talk with the boys—Abe doing the translating—for he was as bored as they were.

Thinking nothing of it, Abe neglected to tell his parents where he was going.

The guard was hesitant, but finally agreed to allow the boys their excursion. He warned them to return before his shift ended. There would be trouble for him and them if they were tardy.

Abe and Vlad joyfully ran down the street until they found the market. Once there, the strangeness of the place took hold of Vlad. He could not read any of the little notes showing the prices of things, nor could he understand anything being said. The boys wandered and looked at the merchandise until something caught Vlad's eye. It wasn't perfect, but in the absence of anything better, he bought it.

"The stores in Germany have much better selection than this," he grumbled.

Abe had no money to spend, so he tired of their adventure sooner than Vlad. He was also hungry, and judging from the position of the sun, he thought it might be getting close to lunchtime. The boys decided to return to the Sovtorgflott.

When Abe and Vlad arrived at the rear door of the Marine Building and knocked on the door, they were surprised to see it was opened by a different guard. He held his rifle across his chest, at the ready.

"What do you want?" he growled.

"We are staying here," said Abe nervously. "The other guard allowed us to go out to the market so Vlad could buy a birthday present for his mother." He pointed to the parcel as evidence of his truthfulness.

The guard immediately became angry. "You are not allowed out of this building! How did ya get passed the guard?" Abe's explanation only further incensed him. "I could have ya arrested, d'ya know that?" The boys shook their heads. "How would ya like ta spend a night in prison?" The guard grinned malevolently. "That'd be an outing fer ya. There's men in there that could use a little present, if ya catches my meanin'." He leered at the boys.

The threat of prison frightened Abe and Vlad to their bones, but what the guard was implying totally escaped them. They had no idea what he was getting at. Fortunately for both of them, their childish innocence in this regard was still intact. They were, however, very uncomfortable with the way he was looking at them.

The trio was standing just inside the door, in the entryway leading to the stairs up to the third floor. They heard someone coming down the steps. It was Johan and Franz.

"Abe," his father said loudly. "We've been looking for you. Where have you been?"

Before the guard could react, Abe and Vlad ran to where Johan and Franz stood. The fear on their faces was enough to tell Johan they were in trouble.

"Yer boy took a little trip with his friend here," said the guard. "I was jist givin' them a lesson on what happens when little boys get outta hand."

"I see," said Johan, though he didn't. "May I take them with me back upstairs?"

The guard grinned maliciously. He fingered the trigger on his rifle.

"Sure, get outta here!" he said after a long minute. His eyes followed the boys as they climbed the stairs until they were out of sight.

Abe had one last view of the guard as he turned to begin the climb up the second flight. From the landing he saw the man at the bottom of the steps staring after him. Abe quickly looked away.

"What was that about?" Johan asked Abe as they arrived at the third floor.

Abe told his father what he and Vlad had done, and what the guard had said. Johan's face grew dark with anger. Abe did not ask what the man meant, but knew it must have been something bad.

"It was a foolish mistake to leave our building. You are lucky he let you come with me," Johan said as they entered the dining hall for lunch. The thought of punishing his son did not enter his mind. Abe had received enough punishment. Johan was sure a lesson had been learned.

To say the least, the thought of leaving the Sovtorgflott for a daytime adventure completely lost its appeal for Abe. The fright he had experienced in his altercation with the guard was something he would remember for the rest of his life. Thereafter he avoided any contact with Vlad Liebermann.

For six days the Mennonite refugees housed in the Sovtorgflott were served three hearty meals a day. With little else to do, they looked forward to each serving and were called to the dining room for breakfast, lunch, and dinner with clockwork precision.

"I wonder if the kitchen is being run by a German," laughed Johan contentedly after enjoying a steaming bowl of delicious borscht. "I've never known a Russian to be so prompt or to make such good food!"

During these days of waiting, Johan was in conversation with other men about the fact that, while they were being well cared for in

Leningrad, Leningrad was not where they wanted to be. When they approached Lebedev and asked about a reason for the delay, he shrugged his shoulders.

"I know nothing about any of that," he said. "I'm not the right person to ask."

When they enquired as to whom they could speak with who might know, he again said he could not help.

Johan verbalized the questions on everyone's mind. "Why has no ship been provided to bring us to Germany? Why are we still here in Leningrad?"

Also of concern was the fact the refugees were being kept in the building, almost as prisoners. Lebedev steadfastly refused all requests for day passes. Some of the refugees pleaded to be allowed out of the Marine Building. They wished to roam the streets of the city and do some sightseeing. From their third floor windows, the magnificent architecture of the Winter Palace could be seen on the opposite bank of the Neva River. Further south, the golden dome of St Isaac's Cathedral rose above the buildings surrounding it. Through the windows on the east side of the Sovtorgflott, the spire of Saints Peter and Paul Cathedral could be seen poking into the sky above the Peter and Paul Fortress. None of the refugees had ever been to the beautiful city before. Without exception, their requests for day passes were denied.

Had they given it any serious thought, the refugees would have realized leaving the building was foolishly dangerous. Without any sort of personal identification papers, they risked immediate arrest by any police or militiaman who happened to ask to see them.

On the seventh day after their arrival, no food was served. The refugees were perplexed but waited patiently until evening when the crying and complaining of the hungry toddlers could no longer be ignored. Johan and a few other men went to talk to Lebedev. Lebedev called the cook in charge of the kitchen.

"Why have these people not been fed today?" asked Lebedev.

"I'm sorry, Comrade Lebedev," answered the cook, "but the money provided by our guests to pay for their food is all gone." The cook shrugged his shoulders. "The larders are empty."

Johan and the others were shocked at this news. "But, you can't just stop providing meals for us."

"If you could give us some more money," suggested the cook. "We would be happy to supply more meals."

"But, you've already taken all our funds," said one of the men with Johan. His name was Andreas Loewen. He had been a banker in Omsk. "We have no more."

Lebedev had an idea. "Perhaps you could write to your relatives and have them send money to you?"

"That's ridiculous!" muttered Johan. Then, to Lebedev he said, "That would take weeks. We'd have starved to death by then!"

"True," admitted Lebedev. "Regrettably then, we cannot help you." He sounded truly sorry.

The conversation continued until Lebedev finally agreed to allow five men to leave the building the next morning.

"See what you can do," he said hopefully. "There must be a solution to your problem."

The solution, the refugees quickly realized, was to take any valuables they had to the bazaar and pawn them in exchange for food. Providing enough food to feed 291 people would be no easy task. While they waited, rings, necklaces, some bedding, even articles of clothing were collected.

The refugees' diet was reduced to bread and the occasional salted meats. Fortunately, there was plenty of tea to drink. The volume of liquid helped dull the hunger pangs, especially for the adults.

The day came when Johan scanned his family's possessions and found little of worth to take to the bazaar. All the family's jewelry had been pawned. Most of their spare clothing was gone. Any bedding left could not be spared except if it came to a crisis.

"You cannot take our blankets," said Elizabeth. "We're already sleeping without pillows!"

Johan knew he could not take the American ten-dollar bill from the teakettle. There was risk involved with using foreign money. It could only be obtained on the black market and now, as close as they were to leaving the Soviet Union, he was not about to do anything that could get him arrested. Besides, the bill symbolized the promise of a brighter future for the family.

Johan's eyes fell on the beautiful guitar Franz was quietly strumming as he sat cross-legged on the floor. It was such an unusual instrument, obviously made by a skilled craftsman. Johan had resisted taking it until now, for it was his gift to his eldest. He had not wanted to ask Franz, who obviously loved it, to make that sacrifice. But, he decided, he had no choice.

"Franz," said Johan apologetically. "I'm sorry. If we want to eat…" his voice trailed off.

Franz saw what his father was looking at and understood his meaning. He glanced at his younger siblings. They were listless and irritable from lack of food. Katrina had taken to sitting on her straw bedding and imagining elaborate meals with a straw doll Johan had made for her. Abe and Wilhelm were argumentative; Elizabeth frequently lost patience with them.

"Take it, Father," Franz said. He handed his guitar to Johan. "There are more important things we need right now."

Chapter 28

November 24, 1929

Breakfast was tea and the remnants of a loaf of black bread brought back from the bazaar the day before. Each member of the family received one slice, though Johan and Elizabeth made certain their slices were thinner than those given to their children. Johan surreptitiously slipped his slice into his pocket. Later he would give it to Elizabeth despite her protestations for, as he reminded her, she was eating for two—on his return from Lyubimovka, Elizabeth had finally told him of her pregnancy. Anna insisted she was not hungry, so her slice was divided equally between her youngest grandchildren who, nevertheless, complained, when they were finished. They were still hungry.

"That is all we have," said Elizabeth matter-of-factly. "Drink more tea." She was mortified that it had come to this. She hated seeing her children so hungry and hated that she could do nothing about it.

"We will be allowed to go to the bazaar tomorrow," Johan explained. "There will be more food when we return."

His words only served to heighten everyone's awareness of their hunger. The thought of having to wait that long for their next meal was not comforting.

All around the dining room, the same ritual was being played out in the other refugee families. What little food they had was shared equally by everyone. None had enough to satisfy their hungry appetites. Since the kitchen was no longer supplying food, there was no staff about. The refugees boiled their own water for tea, found their own plates and cups in the kitchen's cupboards, and washed up after themselves when they were done.

Johan was taking a sip of his tea when he noticed Lebedev enter the dining room. Lebedev looked around until he found one of the refugees' leaders with whom he'd had meetings. Johan saw it was Abraham Siemens. Siemens was from the Crimea. He had been a minister until his church's doors were nailed shut by the communists and his family put out into the street. Somehow he had scraped together the funds for train tickets; his family had arrived in Perlovka shortly before Johan's. He was a tall, thin man. His face was clean-shaven, at least it had been until his shaving kit was bartered away at the bazaar. Now his face was covered with the stubble of a grey beard. Even so, with his straight nose and strong chin, Siemens had an aristocratic look about him. In their time together on the train and in the Sovtorgflott, Johan had gotten to know him well. He quite liked him.

Johan watched as Siemens nodded at something Lebedev said. Lebedev turned and left. Siemens made eye contact with Johan and gestured for him to come to him. As Johan got up from the table, he saw Siemens was beckoning two other men as well.

When they were together, Siemens said, "We're being called to a meeting with a government official downstairs. A colonel of the GPU."

"Perhaps it's good news!" suggested a man standing beside Johan. His name was Heidebrecht. Heidebrecht had been a primary school teacher in Slavgorod, east of Omsk. He was short and quite rotund, though less so than he had been a few weeks before. Heidebrecht had a habit of folding his hands over his protruding belly because the one shirt left for him to wear had lost a strategic button and gaped quite shamelessly. With no needles or thread—they had all been bartered—he was forced to make do. However what Heidebrecht lacked in dress or stature he made up for in attitude; he seemed always to look at things from the bright side. "Could it be that a ship has finally been set aside for us?" he asked. "That must be it!"

"We'll see," said Johan noncommittally. He had an undefined, uneasy feeling. His stomach, which bothered him any time he was under too much stress, lately seemed to burn even before bad news was given. It was beginning to act as an early warning system. And his gut had been on a slow simmer for the past couple of days.

Andreas Loewen joined the group. He was a taciturn fellow of average build, whose face had the look of continuous surprise. However, his cautious manner indicated experience had taught him to be surprised at nothing.

When the four men arrived in the office on the main floor of the Sovtorgflott, the GPU officer who had accompanied them on the day of their arrival was sitting behind a small grey metal desk. They did not know his name, for he had never introduced himself. Nor did he introduce himself now.

Four metal chairs were found. When everyone was seated, the officer began.

"I will get straight to the point."

He did not address them as gentlemen, for that was bourgeois, nor did he call them comrades, for their very presence and the circumstances bringing them before him proved to him beyond a shadow of doubt they were anything but comrades. No, he considered them to be traitors to the cause of the great socialist state. It was all he could do to simply treat them civilly.

"This is how it is for you," the GPU officer continued. "Canada, the country you have set your hearts on going to, has made it clear in a cable to my government it is unwilling to accept any of you. Germany is refusing to have anything to do with you. They have informed us they will take none of you, even on a temporary basis." He paused. "It is clear no one wants you."

Johan and his friends were rocked by his words. They had been told these things before, but in this place—now—they could portend nothing but more hard news to come.

"For these reasons," the officer said, "my government has begun repatriating those of your co-religionists who are still in Moscow and its environs. As of one week ago, they are being loaded onto trains. Everyone without proper paperwork is being sent to Siberia."

Johan knew what the officer said was not entirely true. Repatriations, a kind word for forced resettlement, had been occurring since the middle of October. He had seen its horrible reality with his own eyes in Chelyabinsk. It sounded though, from what the officer said, that the trickle had been turned into a flood. Johan thought of his sister and her family, and of his stepbrothers' families. It hardly seemed possible that in such a short time they would have been able to complete their paperwork.

"Lord have mercy," Johan whispered under his breath.

The colonel was speaking. "So, here you sit, unable to provide for yourselves the necessities of life. No one wants you. You cannot stay here; you have no money." He paused as if to heighten the impossibility of their situation. "My government has no alternative but to transport you back to where you came from. Arrangements for your repatriation will begin to be made tomorrow morning."

The four refugees sitting in front of the officer of the secret police seemed to physically grow smaller before his eyes. Each one felt as if their life's-breath had been sucked away. Here was the moment of their defeat, the loss of everything they had gambled upon. It was the end of their quest and the beginning of their end. And as this realization sank in, they began to be afraid, not with the fear coming from an imagination run wild in the dark, but with the terror that comes from facing ones executioner. For that was what the officer's pronouncement meant. Forced transport, if they survived the journey in the frigid winter conditions, would mean exile or homelessness, and for the men, imprisonment or worse. Death would follow them wherever they went, and in one way or another, death would have them all.

Johan returned to his family in a daze. So great was his shock and distress at what he had been told that it would have made little difference if the officer had informed him that on the morrow he would be put before a firing squad. As the terrifying news spread throughout the dormitory, it was not long before soft weeping could be heard. So great was the distraught parents' alarm at their impending fate that many could not contain their emotions in front of their children. Children looked at their crying parents with large, frightened eyes and sobbed along with them without fully comprehending the reason for their shared sorrow.

Eventually the room quieted.

Groups of refugees huddled together in prayer. Others stood and stared out of the windows of their prison. They saw the world continuing on its daily routines. The sun was struggling to shine through a light skiff of falling snow. People walked to and fro on the sidewalks, taxis clattered down the cobblestone roads, shopkeepers sold their wares. While the refugees' world inside the Sovtorgflott had collapsed, nothing outside had changed.

From across the room where he had sought to comfort his family, Abraham Siemens called the group of leaders to him.

"This must not be," declared Johan as soon as they were together.

"God help us," said Heidebrecht, "but there must be something we can do to forestall this catastrophe, for catastrophic it will be for all of us if we are sent back." Heidebrecht was searching madly for the silver lining, but none was to be found.

"I agree," said Siemens, "and I have a plan."

Siemens had the group's full attention as he explained what he had in mind.

"We already have permission to go out for the day, tomorrow in the morning, to barter for food at the bazaar. The food will have to wait. What we must do is find the German Consulate and plead our case with them." His companions were slowly nodding as they understood his idea. "Does anyone have any paper? A pen? Ink?"

"I have some paper and a pencil," said Heidebrecht.

Everyone else shook their heads.

"That will have to do then," said Siemens. "Go and get it. We are going to write a letter to the German Consul-General explaining that 291 German colonists are about to be sent to their deaths." Siemens knew his words were hardly dramatic, for each of them felt the truth of what he said. He was stating a fact.

"Surely, they won't deny us entry when we're so close!" murmured Heidebrecht hopefully.

After asking for directions, the group of four determined men found the German Consulate-General on Vorovsky, or St. Isaac's, Square. It was directly across the Square from St. Isaac's Cathedral and barely a fifteen-minute walk from the Sovtorgflott. Approaching the building Johan saw its three-storey façade was of red granite. A row of fourteen plain columns standing from sidewalk to roofline separated large rectangular windows. The words 'stark' and 'strength' came to his mind as he thought about the façade's effect. A large bronze sculpture high up at the center of the roof portrayed Castor and Pollux. It symbolized a strong, unified Germany.

Fortunately, the Consul-General was in his office when Siemens asked for an audience with him. After reading their appeal and listening to their explanations he was surprised and profoundly moved.

"Two hundred and ninety-one Germans, old and young, children, women, and men, here, in Leningrad! And they're going to… Well, we know what they're going to do. We know what is going on in this country."

"Yes, and this very day the Soviets have started the process to transport us by force to Siberia," repeated Johan.

"It will happen within days," added Loewen.

The Consul-General asked his petitioners to wait in the anteroom. When they left his office, he called an aide.

"Wire this letter to Berlin. Mark it urgent. We must have a reply immediately."

Two hours later Johan and his friends were summoned.

"I have had a response from Berlin," announced the Consul-General. His face broke into a smile. "Berlin says, 'Let them come!'" He paused a moment as he saw the effect his words had on the group seated before him.

Johan felt his heart would leap from his chest. His eyes immediately filled with tears; his joy overflowed and ran down his cheeks. He could hardly contain himself as his mind and body absorbed the knowledge their salvation was at hand.

The Consul-General continued. "In the last weeks, a campaign called "Brüder in Not," Brothers in Need, has been launched in Germany. It is a drive to raise funds to help the German refugees trapped in Moscow to reach Germany and to care for them there until such a time as a country can be found that will accept them. The German public is being told in no uncertain terms that for you, the alternative to emigration from the Soviet Union is starvation in Siberia. The motto of the campaign is "The fate of a German is the concern of every German." Times are hard and the German government cannot manage such a commitment alone. President Hindenburg has himself committed 200,000 Reichsmarks of his own money for this cause and the private charities are raising millions."

Johan was barely taking in what the Consul-General was saying. He found he was trembling.

"My government will cable Moscow immediately. We will arrange for your transportation to Germany at the earliest opportunity.

Take heart, gentlemen, it will not be long now!"

When the group returned to the third floor of the Sovtorgflott and told the anxious refugees their good news, a cautious pandemonium broke out. Laughter and tears were mixed with enthusiastic, impromptu singing. The four parts of their harmonic hymns of praise to God conspired to nullify the force of gravity and, for a little while, raised the high ceiling even higher. Inasmuch as it might be called dancing—for German Mennonites did not dance—some refugees became quite animated.

But lurking beneath all of their celebration was a hard-learned skepticism and the unspoken question growing more insistent as their initial excitement wore off. "Are the promises to be believed?" Disappointment and betrayal had closely followed every step of their journey. Only time would tell whether the politicians would finally make good their word.

Chapter 29

November 27, 1929

The 291 refugees of the second transport to Leningrad stood in a long queue tucked up close to the wall of an abandoned warehouse on a quay by the banks of the Neva River. Looking west where the last grey of night was being chased away by the oblique light of the new day, they could see the shallow bay where the Neva's waters emptied into the eastern end of the Gulf of Finland. It promised to be a bright day, made brighter by the fact that, aside from the few exceptions, this was the refugees' first trip out of doors in three weeks.

Rays from the low-hung morning sun burst off of wind-whipped ripples and the splash from passing boats on the otherwise calm harbor waters. A few wispy white clouds meandered across the cerulean sky. The chill temperature of the breeze picking at caps and coat collars was the only evidence winter would soon set its steel clamp on the city.

The refugees were waiting, as patiently as might be expected, while members of the Leningrad militia picked through their meager belongings. They snickered in their sleeves at all the wasted effort. The authorities were looking for valuables but they would find none. Everything of value had been bartered at the bazaar in exchange for food. Some refugees shivered as they waited; in the past week, they had traded their coats, hats, and gloves for bread.

"I don't know why they're bothering," grumbled Johan. "They know we have nothing. I mean, look at us. We are a sorry looking lot."

Elizabeth and Anna, who were on his right, paid no attention to Johan's muttering. Their eyes were set on the large Russian steamship tied to the pier. It was the Alexei Rykov, named after a prominent Bolshevik who, until May of that year, had been the Premier of the Soviet Union. It did not matter that the Alexei Rykov's hull was rust-stained and its super-structure rather dilapidated. Nor did it matter that it was also carrying a cargo of freight being loaded as they watched. They looked at the ship with the eyes of those who saw in it the fulfillment of all of their hopes, for they had been told the Alexei Rykov would carry them to Germany.

Johan felt Katrina lean against his left leg. Looking down at his daughter, his mood softened. He saw she was scratching herself.

"I guess we'll be bringing our Leningrad lice with us," he said with a chuckle. "I have a feeling the Germans will not be impressed!"

Katrina looked at her father but did not share his laughter. She was fed up with the pests that had been bothering her since they had arrived in the Sovtorgflott. Something was always squirming on her or itching her or biting her and no amount of combing, picking, washing or disinfecting had made any permanent difference. She hoped with all the might of her ten-year-old heart the Germans were better at pest control than were the Russians.

Johan saw Katrina had a firm grip on the family's teakettle. It was old and blackened. Elizabeth had suggested she carry it.

"They won't look at a child carrying a teapot," she had said.

Johan agreed. "They'll not be interested in her," he thought to himself. "Our American ten-dollar bill will be safe."

A guard nearby said, "Hand in all valuables, rubles, jewelry. It is forbidden to take these items out of the country. Also, no diaries are to leave with you. Leave them at the table with your other valuables."

"No diaries!" murmured Johan. He didn't want the guard overhearing him but could not contain his indignation. "Why do they want us to leave our diaries?"

"They don't want us to remember," said Anna. "They want us to forget the injustices and the hurts and the torment they have caused."

"I suppose so," said Johan. "The communists are afraid the world will learn the truth about them. They don't want our story to be told."

Anna looked toward the Neva Bay. "They will burn our memories and throw the ashes into the Neva where they will be swept into the sea. I wonder if the sea is large enough to carry so much pain."

"We will never forget!" Johan averred.

An hour before dawn that morning Lebedev had appeared at the door to the dormitory where Johan and his family were rousing themselves from another restless night. The bedbugs, as usual, had fed mercilessly. In addition to the insects, the anticipation of another day in which their deliverance might arrive had kept their minds active. Sleep had come only in fits and starts.

Ever his polite self, Lebedev first apologized for the brief notice, then announced streetcars were assembled on the roadway in front of the Sovtorgflott. The refugees were expected to board them within minutes. He stood and watched with impatient amusement as parents corralled their children and bundled whatever belongings they had left. Some parents insisted on taking their children to the toilets, which had frustrated him. Others asked where they were to be taken, and he had been unable to tell them, which pleased him. He was happy to be rid of the troublesome refugees.

It did not matter to some among the refugees that Lebedev could not name their destination, for they no longer trusted anything they were told by a Russian. For all they knew, the streetcars could be taking them to a train and forced repatriation. As it was, the streetcars took them through dark streets—the darkness keeping them hidden from the curious eyes of onlookers—to the waterfront, on the pier, where they were again lined up, this time for inspection.

When it was his family's turn to have their possessions turned inside out, Johan refused to look at the man who fingered the hems of his coat and pants. The militiaman found no hidden money or jewelry. Johan smoldered with resentment knowing his wife and mother were being subjected to the same indignity. Another militiaman scattered on a table the few belongings they had left. There was nothing that interested him, so he turned away. Without a word, Elizabeth gathered them back up. A member of the GPU took from Johan the travel documents Franz had paid for, and any other miscellaneous identification papers Johan still had in his possession. And then it was over.

No one had to point the way, for other refugees were already boarding the Alexei Rykov. As his family walked from the pier onto the gangway leading to the ship, Johan looked down and saw the oily water separating the ship from the land. Stepping onto the steamer's steel deck, he felt as though he were in a dream, so surreal did it seem to him that he and his family should actually, at long last, be leaving Russia.

It was not until six days later, on December 2, that the Alexei Rykov steamed into the harbor of Swinemünde, in Prussia, on the northeast corner of Germany. The voyage had been difficult.

Two hours after leaving port in Leningrad, the steamer had run aground in the shallow waters of the Neva Bay. It had taken several days to work her free and even then there was trouble. The tugs pulling the steamer free had pulled her backward. The anchor, which was lowered, had been forgotten and the cable became tangled in one of the ship's screws. The Alexei Rykov had had to be towed back to harbor where the problem was discovered and corrected by deep-sea divers. Some refugees aboard the steamer had panicked when they saw they were returning to Leningrad. They thought they were the victims of a devious practical joke, and they were now being taken back to Leningrad to be loaded onto a transport for repatriation. They cheered with relief when the ship resumed its voyage out into the open waters.

Sailing over the Baltic Sea was a nightmare for the Alexei Rykov's passengers. The rocking ship was pounded by gigantic waves and fierce winds in a storm that had lasted for what seemed to them like days. The battered refugees in the hold had suffered terrible seasickness while fearing that at any moment the ship would fail and the sea envelop them. It had seemed to Johan the wind and waves were presenting one last violent, natural barrier meant to keep them from their journey's end.

Eventually the wind died, the waves settled, the clouds parted, and the sun returned. The refugees recovered their equilibrium and with it, their legs. They visited the mess where they were well fed. They strolled the decks, relaxed, and enjoyed the calm.

Johan and his family were among the many refugees on deck as the shores of Germany and the harbor at Swinemünde slowly took shape upon the horizon. None wanted to miss this momentous occasion by remaining within the steel walls of their bunker. As the breeze licked their hair and the blue waves of the Baltic Sea sparkled, the shore gradually grew in size. The air was chill—it was December after all—but no one minded. The shivering felt by many was not merely from the cold, but from a deeply felt excitement. All doubt was finally being removed from their minds that what lay before them was the fulfillment of their dream. They knew they had at last reached the land of their forefathers, the land from which their ancestors had emigrated in order to go to Russia. The historic journey of their people had come full circle.

Beside Johan stood Abraham Siemens. In anticipation of their arrival in a matter of a couple of hours, they were waiting for a service of thanksgiving to be organized. Leaning on the steamer's railing, they strained to look at the distant shore.

While gazing toward where their future lay, Johan was thinking about the past. He was remembering the transport he had stumbled upon in Chelyabinsk. The voices of the people trapped in the freight car and what they had told him haunted him. The thought that, while he and his family were hours away from walking upon a land of freedom, the Soviet government was at this very moment forcibly transporting thousands of his fellow refugees to unknown destinations in Siberia was unbearable. He prayed his sister's family and his half-brothers' families would be spared that fate.

"Tell me, Brother Siemens." Johan addressed his friend with the familiar language of their church tradition. "Is it right that we praise God and attribute to him our deliverance while our brothers and sisters in the Soviet Union are being transported from Moscow to the hell Stalin and his henchmen have prepared for them? Has God chosen us for deliverance and not them? Would God do such a thing—save us, but condemn them?" He paused, shook his head. "Tell me, how are we to understand what has happened to us, to our people?"

Siemens looked at Johan. Johan could see deep hurt in his eyes.

A man approached them and stood, hesitantly, seeing that Johan and Siemens were deep in conversation. It was Heidebrecht.

"We're ready to begin the service," he said apologetically.

Siemens looked a moment longer into Johan's eyes before he turned and walked away. He had no answer to give.

Swinemünde was a small town of around 19,000 people. When told by their government to expect a shipload of Russian Mennonite refugees, they embraced their assigned role with dedicated resolve. Because of the national "Brothers in Need" campaign, they were aware these were people for whom the alternatives were emigration or death.

Despite the expected language difficulties, they would make these refugees welcome. Great was their surprise when, as the first families to step onto their shore were met with warm handshakes and words of welcome, the refugees answered back flawlessly in their own language.

"You speak German!" was their amazed response.

The puzzled refugees thought it an absurd question. What other language should they have spoken? It would take more than one hundred and fifty years on Russian soil to wrest the German from their blood.

The refugees were overwhelmed by the generosity of the people of Swinemünde. The townsfolk had set up kitchens and prepared tables. After the refugees were all seated, a simple, nourishing meal that felt like a lavish banquet to them was served. Gifts of toys, and sweets were presented to the children. When the grateful refugees stood and sang their table grace, Johan wept with the sheer joy of it.

As they ate, Elizabeth became thoughtful and observed, "No other trains brought refugees to the Sovtorgflott while we were there. We were the last train to Leningrad."

"Yes," replied Johan. "But now that the German people have opened their hearts to us and Stalin has opened Moscow's gates, more trains will come. They will probably travel through Riga, the route taken by those who emigrated in the earlier years."

Johan chuckled. "The Consul General in Leningrad told us when the German Ambassador, von Dirksen, asked Stalin to give all German-speaking refugees permission to leave the Soviet Union, Stalin refused. Von Dirksen said, 'Fine, then Germany will have nothing more to do with your country.' Stalin quickly changed his tune and gave permission."

"But why?" asked Elizabeth.

"Because Germany is providing the skilled labor and the knowledge that is building the Soviet Union. It was the Germans who built the railway on which we traveled to Perlovka from Moscow. The Germans are helping the Russians build the Dnieper dam and an oil pipeline from the Caspian Sea to the Black Sea. Without Germany's help, Stalin's plan to industrialize the Soviet Union would take an extra fifty years."

"And yet," said Elizabeth, "at the same time as we were allowed to leave, they are still sending our people back to Siberia."

"Yes. While the right hand is sending us west, the left hand is sending us east."

Elizabeth was quiet. "What will become of us?"

Johan thought for a moment. "Now that Germany has welcomed us, we will be well cared for until Canada opens its borders. Our relatives in Manitoba will sponsor us." He looked fondly at Elizabeth, then at his children and his mother. For the first time in years he felt completely contented and at peace. "In the meantime, Germany will provide housing for us. Perhaps some of us will be able to work."

Elizabeth sighed happily, "We will need to establish routines and schools for the children. They must renew their studies. We want them to be prepared when it is our time to go to Canada."

"Yes," said Johan. "In the meantime, I will need something to do. Did you hear them when we sang? There are many good voices here among us. When we are settled in our refugee camp, I think I will start a choir."

An impromptu song of thanksgiving began among those seated at the table. It swelled unhindered from the refugee's hearts. All about Johan, people smiled and added their voices to the song. Johan's rich tenor and Elizabeth's soft alto blended into the beautiful four-part harmony.

Epilogue

April 10, 1930

Frank Brown was down on his luck. He sat with his back against the cold stone wall of Windsor Station in Montreal, Quebec, legs hunched up against his chest. A cardboard sign reading, "Hungry. Please Help," lay on the ground by his feet. He had placed his upside-down hat beside it, hoping someone would drop in a few coins.

Frank had been recruited in England, in the summer of 1929, by the Canadian Pacific Railroad and Steamship Company, to farm in Canada—Canada needed farmers, he was told. The problem was, Frank didn't know the first thing about farming, not that his ignorance stopped him from confessing that he did. When he arrived in Canada aboard the S.S. Metagama, Frank decided to do what he considered to be the only sensible thing. At Toronto, he left the train meant to carry him to a farm in Saskatchewan and looked for other work.

Jobs were easy to find, and Frank had plenty of work until what everyone was calling "The Crash" happened in late October. He didn't understand what the failure of the Stock Markets meant, but within a couple of weeks he was laid off. Unable to pay his rent, he was soon homeless. Since then he had wandered here and there, keeping his body and soul together by visiting soup kitchens. He had also found one could get a good meal by waiting outside the back door of a restaurant after hours. It didn't matter what appeared on his plate, as long as it filled his belly.

Somehow Frank ended up in Montreal. If asked, he wouldn't have been able to tell how he had gotten there. The lack of work and the begging had taken their toll on his spirit. He was depressed. The future looked bleak.

In the early morning hour, Johan Funk and his family got off of the Canadian Pacific train at Windsor Station. It was two days since they had landed in Canada at Saint John, New Brunswick. The voyage on the S.S. Metagama from Antwerp, Belgium, had been uneventful. The Funks were transferring to a train that would carry them across Canada, to Naco, Alberta. The Canadian Pacific Railway and Steamship Company had kindly extended credit for their entire trip from Germany to Naco.

Johan had tried to say the word, when he first learned where the farm they were being offered was located. At the refugee camp in Mölln, the man working for the Canadian Pacific Railway and Steamship Company had told him about the farming opportunity when the family's sponsorship had finally come through. The name sounded as foreign as the country in which it lay.

Walking along the station platform, the Funk family saw the man huddled on the floor. Johan was shocked.

"What?" he exclaimed to Elizabeth. "They have such poverty in Canada?" He was astounded. He had always been under the impression Canada was a land of great wealth.

His head in his hands, Frank Brown didn't look up when he heard a family approaching. They were speaking German. He knew this from his time in the trenches during the war. He could recognize German when he heard it, though he could not understand it.

Johan stopped in front of the man leaning against the wall. Images, remembered and imagined, danced through his mind like light on water. He thought of his family scattered to the four winds: his father buried in the frozen Siberian soil; his mother, whose medical condition disqualified her from immigration, now living in Germany with her daughter-in-law, Helena, whose husband, George Willms, disappeared in the chaos of the last days in Moscow; of Anna's other daughter-in-law, Rose Willms, mentally shattered after being forced to repatriate with her husband, Cornelius, to Isylkul where he was immediately arrested and fed into the maw of the criminal Communist prison system; of his brother Peter Funk and his family escaping in the darkness of night across the frozen Amur River into China; his sister, Sara, and her family waiting in Mölln for final permission to come to Canada. He thought of the dispossessed farmer in the forest at Lyubimovka whose last choice had been to die on a tree, and of the untold multitudes being turned out onto the street by a government working diligently toward their extermination. He remembered his infant daughter, Sara, who had lived only long enough to steal away with a portion of his heart, and of the child Elizabeth was now carrying, soon ready to be born.

Looking at the man on the floor, Johan felt the weight of the gift he and his family had been given, the inestimable gift of welcome in a new land and the freedom to make a fresh start. His heart swelled with the wonder of it.

Johan considered the man sitting on the railway platform with his back to the wall. Reaching into his pocket, he pulled out the precious ten-dollar American bill. Johan had retrieved it from its hiding place in the handle of the family's teakettle during their trans-Atlantic voyage. He and Elizabeth had rejoiced in how fortunate they were to have been able to save it. Stooping, he put the bill inside of the hat resting on the ground between the man's legs.

"Johan!" exclaimed Elizabeth. She was aghast her husband should give away their precious ten-dollar bill. It was enough to buy food for the family for a month. "What are you doing? We need that money."

"Yes," said Johan. "But I think he needs it more." He smiled. "Anyway, we are free now. We will work hard and we will earn many more Canadian ten dollar bills."

Without waiting for a response from the man, Johan and his family continued walking toward the station platform to which they had been directed, where they would board the train that would carry them to their new home.

Frank Brown looked up in amazement when he saw the gift he had been given. The family was already walking away. A young girl holding her mother's hand looked back at him and smiled.

Historical Notes

    This is a work of fiction based on the life experiences of my great-grandfather and great-grandmother, Peter and Elizabeth (Penner Willms) Funk, my grandfather and grandmother, Jacob and Maria (Friesen) Funk, and their children, one of whom is my father, Abraham Jacob Funk. In the novel, the first names of adult family members have been changed, as well as the number and names of children within the families, with the exception of my father's name.

    The novel tells the story of families desperate to escape the Soviet Union in the summer and fall of 1929. Specifically, it recounts the story of the transport of 291 German Mennonite colonists to Germany in early December 1929, via Leningrad and Swinemünde. Theirs was the second, and last, train of refugees sent to Leningrad. Dates and times used in the book are as historically accurate as can be determined, given that the memories of those who lived through the events sometimes provide conflicting evidence.

    The spontaneous migration to Moscow in the summer and fall of 1929, of people who had given up all hope of being able to survive under Stalin's repressive regime happened much as it was described in the story. Government policies designed to eliminate successful farmers (kulaks) as a class made life impossible for them. Mennonite farmers were singled out disproportionately because the government realized they would be very difficult to assimilate into the new Soviet society. As a people they were very independent in their thinking and had a strong sense of group identity centered on their faith and culture. As a result, Mennonites were by far the largest group who fled to Moscow in hopes of being given permission to leave. Estimates of the number of refugees range between 15,000 and 16,000.

    I have also tried to accurately reflect the political and economic conditions that delayed the eventual emigration of those fortunate enough to leave the Soviet Union and that, in the end, spelled disaster for those who did not. Canada was not willing to accept any refugees until the spring of 1930, due in large part to a vocal English population weary of German-speaking immigrants. The economic collapse at the end of October 1929, spelled disaster for Germany. Germany was still struggling to rebuild after its losses resulting from the First World War. The "Brüder in Not" campaign, spearheaded by many charities, including the Mennonite Central Committee, and President Hindenburg's personal intervention, made it possible for Germany to accept those refugees who eventually were able to come.

After a few days at the Merchant Marine Building in Leningrad—St. Petersburg, as the city is again called—the first transport of refugees sailed to Kiel, Germany. The Funk family was on the second and last transport train to Leningrad. They were first delayed for almost a week on a siding north of Moscow as a result of Canada's official refusal to accept ethnic German refugees from the Soviet Union until the spring of 1930. The events of the three week delay in Leningrad transpired much as they have been recounted in the novel.

When the agreement to transport refugees to Germany was finally reached, trains carrying them arrived in Germany daily from December 2 to 9. The last group arrived in Hammerstein, Germany on December 13. In total, 5671 refugees escaped to Germany. Of those, 3885 were German Mennonites, 1260 were German Lutherans, 468 were German Catholics, 51 were German Baptists, and seven were German Adventists. Another 323 people escaped to Germany by other means.

Approximately 10,000 refugees were forcibly repatriated, mainly to Siberia, though some were also sent back to the Ukraine and Crimea. Stories of their journey and resettlement are the stuff of nightmares and horrific examples can be found in the sources cited below.

Jacob and Maria Funk's transport of refugees was housed at Hammerstein for a time and then spent the remainder of its stay in Germany at a refugee barracks in Mölln. Jacob's mother, Elizabeth Funk, remained in Germany because an eye condition prevented her from coming to Canada. One of her daughters by her first marriage who also emigrated from Russia stayed with her. Elizabeth Funk died in Königsberg, Prussia, in 1935.

Family lore tells that one of Elizabeth's sons from her first marriage, who had lived with his family at Lyubimovka, also went to Moscow, but indecision caused them to miss the opportunity to emigrate. He was repatriated to Siberia with his wife and child where he was quickly arrested, never to be seen again. Distraught, his wife suffered a complete mental breakdown.

All of Peter and Elizabeth Funk's adult children and their families were able to settle in North America, some in Canada, others in the United States. My grandfather, Jacob Funk, and his family arrived in Canada on April 8, 1930. Relatives living in Canada sponsored them. And, yes, he gave away the precious $10 American bill to the first homeless man he encountered at the train station in Montreal.

Of the refugees who escaped to Germany, 1344 came to Canada, 2529 went to Brazil, 1572 to Paraguay, six to Argentina, four to Mexico, four to United States, and 458 stayed in Europe.

When talking about the estate he grew up on, my father always referred to it as Lyubimovka, Village of Love. He did not recall how the name was given. It is likely that the locals would have called the estate "Funke Khutor," Funk's Village. In the novel, the name Lyubimovka is given by Prince Dmitry Alexandrovitch Khilkov, the estate's first owner. I based this fictional character's profile on the life of Prince Dmitry Alexandrovitch Khilchenko, a Russian aristocrat whose search for justice in his country led him through military service to Tolstoyan pacifism, to Socialist Revolutionary, and ultimately to exile in a foreign country.

Material for my family's story came from a lifetime of conversations with my father, Abe Funk. More recent conversations with his sister, Aunt Annie Funk, added vital details. A video diary of memories spoken by Uncle Peter Funk as well as recollections of their father's tales about his childhood told by his daughters Ingrid, Alice and Judy were also helpful.

My biggest regret is that I never spoke with my grandparents about their experience. I can only imagine how difficult it must have been for them to uproot themselves in a mad gamble for a better future.

Sources I consulted for historical information include the Jacob Funk family's Canadian Mennonite Board of Colonization document; "At the Gates of Moscow," edited by H. J. Willms and translated by George G. Thielman; "Mennonite Exodus," by Frank H. Epp; "Design of My Journey: An Autobiography," by Hans Kasdorf; Erwin Warkentin's paper entitled, "The Mennonites before Moscow: The Notes of Dr. Otto Auhagen;" and Henry Paetkau's paper, "Russian Mennonite Immigrants of the 1920's: A Reappraisal."

David Funk
Abbotsford, April 2015

Glossary

Apparatchik	- a member of the Communist party and an unquestioningly loyal subordinate within the organization, a minor bureaucrat
GPU	- Joint State Political Directorate, the Secret Police.
Izba	- a peasant's small wooden cabin
Komsomol	- All-Union Leninist Young Communist League. The youth organization of the Communist party formed in 1918.
Kremlin	- a fortress
Kulak	- literally, "tight-fisted," term referring to affluent or successful farmers
Kuznetsky Most	- Blacksmiths' Bridge
Oblast	- political administrative district
Pereszelenzy	- resettlers, people being moved from one region to another within the Soviet Union
Plumi moos	- stewed plums, typically served cold
Prospekt	- Avenue
RUSKAPA	- Russia Canada Passenger Agency, a cooperative venture between the two governments to facilitate emigration from the Soviet Union to Canada
SOVTORGFLOTT	- Soviet Merchant Marine Building in Leningrad
Staraya Square	- Old Square in central Moscow
Trakt	- road completed in the mid 19th century connecting European Russia to Siberia
Troika	- three, as in three horses pulling side-by-side
Zwieback	- double-decker buns

Made in the USA
San Bernardino, CA
22 May 2015